Praise for DOUGLAS
and *AME*

"No matter your party ... going to get your atten... stands the forces shaping ... ...te— and he tells a heck of a goo...

—Dee Dee Myers,
Former Press Secretary to President Bill Clinton;
NBC News Commentator

"A great and scary read. Sure to cause waves."
—James Pinkerton, Fox News Commentator

"*America's Last Days* makes you sit up and pay attention. It's only fiction, but…"
—Tony Blankley, *The McLaughlin Group*

"A political thriller that makes you think."
—James Carville

"This is a very well done 'Seven Days in May' type of novel of government takeover. It is a fast-paced read that says a lot about our country and shows how the American people have very little say."
—*Midwest Book Review*

WELCOME TO THE INNER CIRCLE

The president acknowledged the noise of the helicopter as he said, "The general and I are taking a quick trip to Camp David for the afternoon. But come tomorrow, Wayne and I are going to leave to inspect this completed masterpiece. I'd like you to be with us, Ian."

Everything was coming at him way too fast. "I'd be honored, Mr. President. But why me?"

The president stood and started to walk toward his desk. Out of respect and protocol, the second he stood, Campbell and the general joined him.

Once the president reached his desk, he threw some folders into a briefcase, then looked up at Campbell and smiled with his perfectly capped teeth. "Why you, Ian? Well, when we get there, why I asked you to come on this little field trip will become blindingly obvious."

With that, he turned on his heel and headed to the door that led out to the Rose Garden. As the president walked, General Mitchell leaned close to Campbell and grabbed his arm. "We are leaving from the South Lawn at 0500 sharp, Navy. Don't breathe a word of this to anyone. There are forces larger than you can imagine at work here, and if you betray this president or his mission, your punishment will be eternal."

As the general flashed out the door to catch up with the president and his Secret Service in tow, Campbell was not even aware that his mouth was hanging open or that a cold sweat had just broken out down his back.

Other *Leisure* books by Douglas MacKinnon:

AMERICA'S LAST DAYS

Douglas MacKinnon

The
Apocalypse
Directive

LEISURE BOOKS NEW YORK CITY

To my niece, Chrissy (Cissy) MacKinnon
and my nephew, Chris MacKinnon.
You both mean the world to me.
If you are very good,
I'll let you split a Happy Meal.

A LEISURE BOOK®

August 2008

Published by

Dorchester Publishing Co., Inc.
200 Madison Avenue
New York, NY 10016

ISBN 10: 0-8439-6088-4
ISBN 13: 978-0-8439-6088-4

Visit us on the web at www.dorchesterpub.com.

ACKNOWLEDGMENTS

Thanks to Don D'Auria, Erin Galloway, Alissa Davis, and the entire team at Leisure Books. I am in your debt.

Thanks to my agent, Mel Berger, and Evan Goldfried at the William Morris Agency. Your assistance and friendship are invaluable.

A special thanks to my good friend, Mark Coyle. An author could not have a better publicist, nor a person a better friend.

To my brother, Jay MacKinnon, and my sister, Janice Ovide. Thanks for being there for me.

To Larry King, Bill Harlow and Chuck Nash. Thanks for your friendship and the honor of your blurbs.

Thanks again to those from our military, intelligence services, the Secret Service and the FBI, who were kind enough to review the manuscript, offer suggestions, and ask that I keep their names out of it. I have, and any mistakes are mine and mine alone.

The most special of thanks to Patrick Ryan Ovide (O-Vee-Dee) for being a daily inspiration, and as always, "My best friend in the whole wide universe!"

Finally, with my deepest love and gratitude, I thank my wife, Andrea. She is my rock.

THE
APOCALYPSE
DIRECTIVE

FACT:
There exists within the Pentagon, a mysterious and controversial religious organization that some believe represents a direct threat to the constitutional boundaries of our nation.

FACT:
This organization is growing in power and influence as it relentlessly focuses on adding to a membership already comprised of high-level officials from our military, the White House, other branches of government, and our diplomatic corps.

FACT:
An army general said President George W. Bush was "Appointed by God." An air force general—and one of the leaders of this religious organization—proudly stated in a widely criticized promotional video that he puts his God before his family, and . . . his nation.

FACT:
A supersecret program initiated in 1959 by President Dwight D. Eisenhower, designated with the code name, "Greek Island," was built under the world-famous Green Brier resort in West Virginia. Upon its completion, the 112,000-square-foot bunker was ready to house 1,000 people for up to 60 days.

"Greek Island" was to house all 535 members of Congress, essential White House personnel, and high-level staff in the event of an all-out nuclear war with the Soviet Union.

The facility remained top secret and ready for use until 1992, when a news organization revealed its location and purpose.

After its discovery, the man who headed operations at the supersecret bunker said it was entirely logical to assume that the U.S. would replace the compromised facility with something much larger and even more secret.

CHAPTER ONE

Sharks. All Tom Hiatt could think about were sharks. As he flailed about in the warm waters twenty miles east of Miami, he did not think about drowning, did not wonder what had just violently catapulted him and his best friend from their twenty-eight-foot Bayliner cruiser, was not curious about the incredibly loud ringing in his ears, and for the moment, did not care that his buddy seemed to be screaming and pointing up in the air.

Hiatt was not worried about things in the air. Things in the air weren't sharks. He was concerned only about the underwater prehistoric killing machines that were swimming around his boat just before he was ejected from it.

While, as a treasure hunter, he made his living on and in the water, the deep, dark secret that he tried and failed to keep from friends and family was that he had an almost pathological fear of sharks. Ever since he had first seen the movie *Jaws* as a nine-year-old boy, he instantly had an attraction to boats and the sea, and a hatred and loathing of sharks. A loathing that had only grown throughout his adult life.

As he had that thought, something hard brushed against his right foot, and Hiatt nearly levitated himself out of the water. When he splashed back down, his friend grabbed him and started to scream in his left ear.

"Tom! Calm down. It's me. Eric. I think we hit a mine."

Hiatt forced his eyes from wildly staring down into the blue-green water as he tried to confirm that his feet and legs were still attached, to look up at the darkly tanned face of his animated friend.

"What? We hit . . . what?"

As his friend tried to yell back at him, the water they were thrashing about in started to vibrate, splash, and whip around in a frenzy as the prop-wash of a Blackhawk helicopter began to descend upon them.

By instinct more than anything, Hiatt desperately reached for his cell phone clipped to his waist. While dripping wet, it still seemed okay. He looked down and saw one bar of signal. As salt water peppered and stung his face, he pushed a memory button on the phone and dialed a number in Washington, DC.

In the middle of the second ring, a static-shrouded voice answered, "Rachel Hiatt."

Just as Tom Hiatt was about to answer, the ocean around him went dark as it fell into the shadow of the Blackhawk. Hiatt looked up just in time to see what looked like a commando in the open door of the helicopter pointing something down at him and Eric.

Knowing he may have no time left, he screamed, "Rach, it's me! Off the coast of Florida. Looks like government is trying—"

Just then, the figure in the open door of the Blackhawk fired and the water all around Hiatt became electrified. As the electricity coursed through his body, Hiatt could barely think, could not breathe, and could not move.

As he slowly slipped beneath the surface, he watched in almost a dreamlike trance as his cell phone fell from his fingers and caught the filtered rays of the sun as it began its nine-hundred-foot tumble to the ocean floor below.

As water now filled his paralyzed and open mouth, Hiatt irrationally still wondered if he might become the victim of a shark attack.

CHAPTER TWO

One thousand miles to the north, President Shelby Robertson was sitting in his private study adjacent to the Oval Office. Before him on his small and simple desk lay the President's Daily Briefing. The PDB was the highly classified "eyes only" report compiled late each evening by the nation's various three-letter intelligence agencies, and delivered to the president by 6:00 A.M. the following morning.

Now in the third year of his second term, the conservative president from Alabama found himself remarkably at peace in a world gone mad. Twenty-three thousand Americans had been killed by escalating terrorist attacks on the homeland while he was in office, and the report he was now reading predicted with certainty that in the coming months more violent terrorist attacks would be visited upon the United States. Curiously, such hair-raising and mind-numbing predictions only confirmed his beliefs, and fueled the inner joy he felt during these darkest of times.

Though known to be a religious man by the American public, Robertson was careful to never wear his beliefs on his sleeve. Ever mindful that there was always someone out there—usually a reporter from the *New York Times* or the *Washington Post*—who would be more than happy to twist rational belief into something to be feared.

Robertson slowly closed the report and then tapped upon it a few times with his fingertips as he looked toward the ceiling and nodded his head in silent thought. He then stood and walked across the small study and knelt down before a one-foot-tall, ceramic statue of Jesus Christ that sat atop an end table. Prayer and meditation had been part of his lifestyle since his college years. Robertson was convinced that it sustained him, made him whole, and gave him the strength to make terrible decisions. Decisions that men who lacked unquestioned faith could never make because of the horrific consequences of such actions.

After one minute of meditation, Robertson stood and then said out loud to himself, "True belief . . . is everything."

As the president walked back into the Oval Office, one of the two phones on his desk quietly buzzed. Once seated in his bulletproof, high-back black chair, the president answered.

"Yes?"

"Mr. President," said his assistant from an office just outside of his. "General Mitchell is on the phone for you."

"Splendid. Thank you, Dorothy. Put him right through."

A millisecond later, the general was on the line. "Mr. President?"

"Wayne. How is the commander of the United States Strategic Command this fine day? And better yet, what is the status of our project?"

"I'm fine, Mr. President. As for our project, I'd rather update you about that in person."

The president tapped a pencil on the edge of his desk as he thought for a moment. "Agreed. Time, as you well know, Wayne, is of the essence."

"Yes, sir, Mr. President. I'll be there early tomorrow

morning, and I'm confident you will be quite happy with my report."

As the four-star air force general in charge of America's ground-based nuclear arsenal hung up the phone, he was mildly surprised at how calm and serene he was. A peace of mind bestowed upon him by God. His God. The one and only God in a world full of false idols and an evil soon to be confronted.

CHAPTER THREE

Rachel Hiatt started to tear up. She realized that as a Stanford grad with a law degree from Georgetown University, and a prestigious position as a newly minted political reporter for the online version of the *New York Times*, she was not supposed to cry. She knew that it was incumbent upon her to be a tough young professional woman advancing the cause of feminism in a still-male-dominated world.

Still, she cried. Her big, somewhat black sheep of the family brother had just called her in a panic, and her immediate reaction was to feel his pain.

"Where did he say he was?" she thought. "Florida?"

For the last twenty years, he had gone from one crazy job to the next, all the while trying to find himself and exorcise demons only he could see. Demons that tormented only him. And through all the job changes, through all the craziness, through all the pain, only one member of the family stood by him and supported him unconditionally. His baby sister.

Rachel tried to compose herself and think. She ran her fingers through her Audrey Hepburn-like short black hair and tried to remember. The last time she saw her only sibling was six months ago at a terminal at Ronald Reagan Washington National Airport. He was flying in from God knows where, heading to God knows where, and desperately needed to borrow five thousand dollars. Without telling her mom and dad, Rachel met him, hugged him, gave him the money and then watched him go through security, waving all the while until she could no longer see his lanky, six foot three inch frame.

"Government . . . did he say something about the government . . . what was that incredibly loud noise in the background . . . a train . . . a plane engine . . . maybe a helicopter . . ." As the thoughts and questions bounced around her head, she redialed his cell phone for the tenth time. And as the other nine before, it rang five times before his voice mail picked up. And as the other nine times before, she smiled through her tears as she heard his deep voice laughing and saying, "Hiatt. Tom Hiatt. The Jewish James Bond. Leave your number after the beep. And if you're a woman who's not my ex-spouse . . . or her flesh-eating attorney . . . please leave the directions to your heart."

Rachel loved that her brother was unashamedly corny and a hopeless romantic. Throughout his adult life, he would gaze across a room at a woman, lock eyes momentarily, instantly fall in love, and, just as quickly, have his heart broken. And always, after each and every failed relationship, he would seek out his little sister for a morale boost.

Over the course of the last ten years, the baby sister had morphed into the more mature of the two as her brother continued to take on a more childlike and irresponsible manner. As such, Rachel took it upon herself to be more protective of him as she monitored his unpredictable ways.

As she stared down at the black phone on her incredibly tidy desk, she took a deep breath, wiped the hint of tears from her eyes, and switched back mentally to the hard-nosed, cynical reporter she was becoming.

She then scrolled through her BlackBerry, found the

number she was looking for, picked up the phone and dialed a South Florida number for Tom's business partner, Eric Gonzalez. Surely Eric would know where Tom was and what he's up to, thought Rachel as the phone rang for the fourth time.

CHAPTER FOUR

Ian Campbell looked up at the digital clock on his computer, then yawned. Nine thirty-eight P.M. and he still had about an hour to go before he could clean his desk of the day's work. He paused for a moment to scratch his scalp through his thick, but very short, prematurely gray hair, and then went back to proofreading the memo he was about to send.

Many people would have gone home hours earlier, and truth be told, many of his co-workers had cleared out two or three hours before. Two things prevented Campbell from emulating them. The first was the very job he had. It was high profile, high pressure, and highly confidential. Mistakes could not be made and were never tolerated.

The second, and more important reason he found himself in his office long after his colleagues had called it a day was much more of a personal choice dictated by a work ethic honed by years of military training. Campbell was a graduate of the U.S. Naval Academy who subsequently served six years as a Navy SEAL. A Navy SEAL who, like the rest of the present-day military, had seen extensive combat in Iraq, Afghanistan, and parts of the world in which the United States denied it operated.

By the time he was twenty-eight years of age, Campbell had seen the absolute worst that humans could do to one another. Worse than what he witnessed, however, was what he had done in the name of self-defense and the defense of his comrades. As these life-altering events transpired and spilled out around him, he was somewhat shocked and more than a little grateful to notice that parts of his mind would shut down to compensate for the horror he had seen . . . and the lives he had taken.

Upon completion of his mandatory six-year term, he resigned his commission. Not because he held any animosity toward the navy or the military as a whole, but rather, because he could predict the future. He predicted in no uncertain terms that that the United States of America was going to be in the bull's-eye of varied and twisted terrorist organizations for years and decades to come. This promised only war and heartache for someone in his line of work.

As he killed on the battlefield, human life became more precious and sacred to him, not more anonymous and faceless, as it did for so many others. While he marveled at some of his team members' ability to treat battle and the killing of the enemy as nothing more than a three-dimensional video game, a larger part of him was sickened and saddened by their lack of emotion. Maybe he was in the minority in his profession, but he no longer had the stomach to carry out what would be demanded of him in the endless war.

Once out of the navy, Campbell had only a small idea of what he wanted to do next. As a child of poverty, he had always had a somewhat unnatural compulsion to give back to others, to work in a career that could at least marginally improve the life of a fellow human being. He thought the defense of his nation would fit the bill. Six years of harsh reality told him something else.

Campbell did not believe in spinning himself. He was well aware that he was fairly intelligent, had received a first-rate education, and had some rather unique skill sets.

But with all of that, he was also deeply and darkly aware of a greater truth. A truth that still woke him many a night drenched in a cold sweat.

At the end of the day, he was still a killer. Highly trained and polished, but still someone who took human life. He had taken uncounted lives in a number of theaters around the world, and in the six relatively short years he had served, had excelled at the task. This expertise exacted a very heavy price on his conscience and for all he knew, on his very soul.

As determined as the U.S. Government and the navy were to keep him, he was just as desperate to run from the graphic memories, to draw a clean breath of air, and just think for himself. After years of being told what to do, when to do it, and how to improve, by first, upperclassmen, and then commanding officers, he needed to escape that collective mind-set and revert back to a degree of individualism.

While nice in theory, the reality of such a transformation proved much tougher to pull off. Campbell knew he could instantly get a job with any one of the top-five private security firms in the world, each one extremely anxious to pay him fifteen hundred dollars per day or more, to protect CEOs, government staff, or convoys traveling to and from ultradangerous hot zones.

He did not give the firms nor their excessive pay a second thought. That part of his life was over. He had always told friends and family that even if one lived to be a hundred years old in perfect health, life was too short. He really believed that. As such, he was determined to vary his work experiences as much as possible so as to better enjoy the gift of life granted him.

Campbell did not pretend to be a Boy Scout. He knew his flaws far outweighed his positive attributes and good intentions. He liked women a bit too much, liked to drink a bit too much, and was more than a little arrogant.

Understanding that, however, did not sway him from an enduring belief that the strong had an obligation to help the weak.

Campbell was not an overly spiritual man and did not believe in organized religion. In fact, it was his experiences on the battlefield fighting and killing those who waged war in the name of their god that convinced him beyond a shadow of a doubt that organized religion could be more destructive than good. While he did believe in God, he did not believe there was a God who only loved and would only save those of his children who were loyal to one belief at the expense of other beliefs and untold millions of human beings.

While certain of that, he also knew that the human species was, for the most part, frail and fleeting. While a minority were very strong, incredibly self-assured, and in many cases, criminally corrupt, the vast majority were just trying to get by in life without being hurt or even noticed. After that select group came the weak, very good people who were either desperately poor, physically handicapped, or emotionally scarred through no fault of their own. People who for the most part had no voice in society. People who represented the world Campbell inhabited before his acceptance to the naval academy.

Many times when he lay awake daydreaming on the bunk of a nuclear-powered fast-attack submarine delivering him and his team to their next operation, he wondered what was in store for him after the military. While not knowing much about it, he had always been intrigued with politics. Politics, if done right, could help the weak and disenfranchised. And if one wanted to play in the major leagues of government, then that meant going to Washington, DC.

Without knowing anyone and without knowing better, Campbell decided he wanted to work for a United States senator. And only for a specific senator. While finishing his tour in the navy, he had read in the Pentagon news compilation called "The Early Bird" of a senator-elect from Virginia who had graduated from the naval academy and had gone on to serve his nation in combat in a prior war.

His own combat experience had taught Campbell to avoid extraneous effort at all cost. If there were a more direct way, even if that route could prove more dangerous, sometimes it was the better road taken. Rather than submit his resume to some chief of staff he didn't know and who most likely would not have a great deal of respect for his service, Campbell decided to cut out the middle man altogether. Toward that end, he decided to write a personal check for five hundred dollars to the newly elected senator's political action committee and get some face time with the senator at a small meet and greet.

Weeks later, opportunity presented itself. Within minutes of being served lukewarm coffee and a stale Danish at the government relations office of a well-known Virginia company, Senator Webster James walked up and introduced himself to Campbell.

"Do I know you, son?" asked the sixty-five-year-old senator.

The forty or so other people in the room were a bit surprised to see the senator walk up to the six foot one inch, athletic looking, well-dressed Campbell. Normally, it was the attendees who would be elbowing each other out of the way to get in a word with, or kiss the ass of, the senator. Not the other way around.

"No, sir. I've never had the honor."

The senator smiled as if confirming a guess. "Were you navy, son?"

"Yes, sir. I was just recently discharged."

A blowhard lobbyist for a pharmaceutical company tried to introduce himself to the senator while waving his business card, but Senator James ignored both him and the card.

"Officer?"

"Yes, sir."

"Academy?"

"Yes, sir."

"Assignment?"

"Naval Special Warfare."

The senator paused for a moment to take measure of the man before him, then nodded and smiled again. "SEAL?"

"Yes, sir. Six years."

The senator stepped closer to Campbell and blocked out the lobbyist. "And what are you doing here, son? Surely a donation to my PAC was not high on your list of things to do upon completion of your tour."

"No, sir. I didn't even know who you were until a couple of months ago."

That admission had several of the lobbyists rolling their eyes in amazement at such a stupid and naïve comment.

The senator smiled even wider as he asked a question to which he was quite certain he knew the response. "So, again. Why are you here?"

"I'd like a job, sir."

"Lots of good jobs in Washington, son."

This time it was Campbell's turn to smile. "No, sir. Only if you want to settle. I can't afford to waste my time settling. I need to learn from someone I would respect. I need to learn from you, sir."

Senator James burst out laughing and waved over a member of his staff. "Jenny. This is . . ." He looked Campbell in the eye.

"Ian Campbell, sir."

". . . Mr. Campbell. Can you please take his information and set up a time for him to meet with me next week."

"Thank you, sir," Campbell said.

James shook his head. "Don't thank me yet, Navy. Let's chat next week and see if we can find a fit."

Find a fit, they did. Over the course of the next five years, Campbell went from being military liaison for Senator James, to becoming his indispensable chief of staff.

As James had been an early and strong supporter of President Robertson, both as a private sector multimillionaire, and then as senator, the president was always mindful of the wishes of his good friend from Virginia. When Robertson lost one of his deputy chiefs of staff to an accident, Senator James quickly volunteered Campbell to fill the void.

His conversation with the president was short and sweet. "He's one of us, Mr. President. A true believer. He won't let you down."

While not quite "one" of them, Campbell had carefully conveyed that impression to James. Had he not let the senator think he was a strong evangelical, then James would not have pushed him on the president, nor would the president have ever hired him. A small price to pay, thought Campbell at the time, to get the job of a lifetime.

A year after that recommendation, Campbell found himself in his White House office with the time rapidly approaching 10:00 P.M. As he printed the memo he had been struggling with, he was already thinking about tomorrow's daily 7:00 A.M. senior staff meeting.

Sleep, as he had learned in Iraq, was an overrated luxury.

CHAPTER FIVE

Lt. General Arthur Ryan was a troubled and conflicted man. At forty-nine years of age, he felt he was wise beyond his years, understood the difference between good and evil, tried to vanquish evil during his almost three decades in the United States Army, and still maintained what many would consider a "normal" home life.

He was happily married with bookend children. One son who was attending the University of Virginia Law School, and a daughter who was getting ready to enter her senior year at Hayfield Secondary School in Alexandria, Virginia.

It was because he was so happily married that he now found himself speeding South on I-395 toward his town house in the Kingstowne section of Alexandria. Right before he was scheduled to give a briefing at the National War College at Fort McNair in Washington, DC, he had gotten a text message on his cell phone from his wife Nancy, telling him that she felt very ill, was on her way to the house, and hoped he could come home to take care of her.

As he pushed his Chrysler Sebring up over eighty mph, Ryan smiled with the thought of his wife using the word "hoped." As gentle and giving as she was, it was just like that woman to say "hoped." Since the day he first met her, she had always put herself last before all others. Today, even while sick, being no exception.

For Nancy to leave her teaching job at the Fairfax Baptist School could only mean she was really under the weather. Ryan knew that in the almost three years she had taught there, she had not missed a day, so for her to send him that message meant it had to be bad. While dedicated to his country and the army, his wife and children still came first.

It was exactly because his family came before all, that two days earlier Ryan had found himself in a fairly heated argument with not only his superior officer, but a friend and mentor of long standing.

While having a very civilized tea in the office of his boss located in the E ring of the Pentagon, Ryan volunteered that he had had a change of heart and not only felt that God should no longer come before family and country, but that upon deep reflection he felt he should resign from the all-but-secret organization his friend had sponsored him into just two years prior.

With that somewhat innocuous revelation, at least to Ryan's way of thinking, his friend of twenty years exploded into a very uncharacteristic rage. The four-star general across the table from him told Ryan that he was betraying the cause and the Lord at the worst possible moment. That there was no going back, that the mission was everything and that Ryan was making an unforgivable mistake that would produce consequences he could not fathom.

As Ryan watched spittle fly from his friend's mouth and land in his cooling tea, he decided that reason was the only course of action.

"Look, Peter," said the three-star general somewhat forcefully. "I can see that you are upset, but I think you are way out of line to blow this thing so far out of proportion. Just because I think my family comes first, and because of that decision, think I'm better off out of your organization, does not mean we cease being polite or stop being friends. I mean, come on. Get a grip."

The four-star general looked down at the table, noticed his spit, and used his napkin to wipe it up. As he did, he started to visibly calm down. The red was leaving his face and his breathing was returning to normal.

"Yes it does, Arthur," answered the general in the soft tone he was known for throughout the building. "That's exactly what it means. I trusted you and brought you into this organization. For you to do this to our Lord is unforgivable."

Ryan stood from his chair and now started to raise his voice. "Are you insane? I'm not doing anything to the Lord other than being a good husband and father. The last time I checked, that's how He wants me to lead my life."

The four-star general stayed seated and shook his head. "There is much more to life than our mortal families, Arthur. I'm very sorry you forgot that. Now please, leave my office."

Since that bizarre meeting two days earlier, Ryan had replayed the conversation over and over in his mind. And each time he did, he was more convinced than ever, that he did the right thing in confronting his friend and leaving the organization. He just should have done it all sooner.

Ryan pushed the thoughts from his mind as he pulled into his driveway, jumped out of the car and started to walk up to the steps that led to his front door.

As he did, more out of training than anything, he took a quick look around the neighborhood. While hot, it was a glorious afternoon without the hint of a cloud in the deep blue sky.

The streets were empty for the most part as the neighbors who did, were still at work. Toward the end of his street, he saw two middle-aged women with dogs, talking under the shade of an oak tree. Other than that, all was quiet.

Ryan put his key in the lock, opened the door and shouted, "Nancy. I'm home, sweetie."

Upon getting no answer, the general guessed his wife was upstairs in bed and most likely asleep. Thinking that, he closed the front door softly behind him, placed his briefcase on the front hall table, and started to walk toward the stairs leading to the master bedroom.

CHAPTER SIX

Rachel Hiatt walked out of the Aventura, Florida Police Department, shook her head and put on her sunglasses to protect her dark brown eyes from the still-intense glare of the late morning sun.

Without so much as a heads-up to her boss in the Washington bureau of the *New York Times,* upon getting the voice mail of Eric Gonzalez for the second time, Rachel decided that she had to fly to Florida. As it was already late in the afternoon, she grabbed her laptop and notebook and ran home to her small apartment on Massachusetts Avenue to pack. Seven A.M. the next day saw her jumping in a taxi to Reagan National Airport. Three hours later, she was getting blank stares from a detective and a uniformed officer at Aventura police headquarters.

"Look, Ms. Hiatt," the detective had just told her for the second time. "As near as I can tell, what you have here is a coast guard problem. If your brother was out on his boat 'somewhere off the coast of Florida'—which, by the way, encompasses millions of square miles—then you need to notify the coast guard. Until he's missing for more than forty-eight hours—and we don't even know if he *is* missing—we can't do a thing about it. So, if you don't find him by tomorrow this time, why don't you come on back and file a missing person report."

Rachel did not take the door off the hinges when she

stormed out of the building, but that was only because it was an exceptionally strong door.

She jumped back into her rental car and drove the two miles from the police station to "The Point," a high-end, luxury, condo complex that consisted of five fairly new, thirty-two-story, ivory white buildings. Inexplicably to her, it was where Tom lived. Seemed much too rich for his nomadic lifestyle. He once tried to explain to her that he was subletting the two-bedroom condo of a model from Argentina working in Europe, and then started to describe the relationship, but she stopped him before he could progress into details she was better off not knowing.

Two months after he moved in, he added Rachel's name to the "admit" list at the front gate, and had FedExed her a spare set of keys to his place. As he jokingly told her over the phone, "You never know. Maybe an angry husband will track me down and you will need to come rescue me."

Rachel pulled up to one of the guest parking spots in front of the North Tower of the complex, put the dark green Toyota Corolla in park, and tried to gather her thoughts.

As she did, three incredibly well-built Latin American women strolled by her car on the way to the health club inside the complex. All three were elegant, clearly came from money, and were not shy about showing off their assets in skintight jeans and low-cut tank tops or shirts that advertised breast implants done by the best plastic surgeon in Aventura.

At an athletic five foot, eight inches tall and weighing a healthy one hundred and forty pounds, Rachel considered herself a fairly attractive woman. But she also knew from conversations with her brother that Aventura was famous for having hundreds of women like the three who just passed by her vehicle. Better in her mind to get back to DC as quickly as possible where the competition was not nearly as intense.

Rachel walked through the front door of the building, nodded to the two security guards sitting behind a desk, and then used the plastic card with a memory chip that Tom had sent her to gain access to the opulent main lobby and the elevator banks beyond.

Once in the lobby, Rachel paused to let the air-conditioning of the building waft over her overheated and sweating skin. August in Washington, DC, was bad. But August in the Miami area was heat exaggerated to the point of being ridiculous.

Her day's attire was not helping with the heat. As a native of New York who had stayed in Washington after law school to take a job with the *Examiner*, Rachel was well aware of the reputation of DC women to not be as concerned with style as their counterparts in her hometown, Chicago, Los Angeles, or even Boston. Rachel thought the criticism a bit harsh once she started to live in the city, but nonetheless, never quite forgot it as she always tried to err on the side of being fashion conscious and feminine.

Today saw her wearing a navy blue DKNY pants suit with a simple white T-shirt, a gold necklace, and blue stiletto pumps. Upon picking up the rental car at the Fort Lauderdale International Airport, she immediately jettisoned her jacket into the backseat and wondered out loud why people voluntarily moved from cool to broil.

Once the sweat stopped rolling down the muscles of her back, she started walking again until she stepped into one of the waiting elevators. The building had thirty-two floors, and Tom lived on the thirty-first. As a reporter, Rachel knew that as people grew older they sometimes acquired fears, allergies, and phobias they did not have at a younger age. When she was a kid, she was fearless when it came to heights. Now, at the age of twenty-nine, she started to notice herself backing away from balcony railings on any floor higher than the tenth. As the elevator deposited her on the thirty-first floor, she was hoping there was no reason to set foot on Tom's balcony.

Tom lived in 3108. As she opened the door, her nose was greeted with the scent of dirty laundry, while her eyes were assaulted with a mess worthy of the *Animal House* fraternity. Beer bottles and Pepsi cans filled most flat surfaces, while clothes, clean and dirty, hung from the backs of chairs, or were draped over what looked to be a very expensive black leather sofa.

Since they were children, Tom had always been terminally messy and disorganized. Traits that Rachel knew led her to be excessively clean and anal in her adulthood. There was a happy medium somewhere, but neither one of them had found it.

Rachel wrinkled her nose at the smell, closed the door behind her, and took a quick tour of the rest of the apartment. Beautiful oil paintings and prints covered the eggshell white colored walls of the living room. All of the furniture, from the dining room set to the glass table in the breakfast nook, spoke of money. Clearly, Rachel thought, the class and decorations came with the model that Tom had been . . . seeing.

On either side of the central living room was a bedroom. The rather large master bedroom was off to the right, while a smaller, but still spacious guest room, was off to the left. Upon entering the master bedroom, Rachel got a true sense of the model's style. The room was pristine, beautiful, and untouched by her brother. Either Tom had orders to stay out of it, or out of respect for his friend, he had ostracized himself from that territory.

Tom's room, as she had suspected, looked like it had been searched by characters from a bad spy movie. Drawers were open, more clothes were everywhere, the nightstand was covered by trash, paperback books, and a red yarmulke. The bed was unmade, with the dark blue bed-spread and blanket lying in a heap on the tan wall-to-wall carpeting.

She had no idea what she was looking for, but hoped she would know it when she found it. Forty minutes into the search it dawned on her to push the "play" button on Tom's answering machine. To do that, she first had to find it.

After two minutes of looking around his bedroom, she saw the hint of a red blinking light flashing through a pair of Tom's underwear that was lying between the bed and the nightstand.

"Disgusting," she said out loud as she used a paper-back book to remove the offending undergarment from the answering machine. With the corner of the book, she pressed the "play" button and was immediately rewarded for her efforts.

"Tommy Boy. It's Eric. Rise and shine, mi amigo. Today we find some gold. We've got about forty miles of ocean to cover there and back so make sure that pig of a boat of yours is gassed up. I'll meet you at the Waterways marina at 7:30 . . . that's 7:30 this morning by the way. No more bullshit excuses from you. WAKE THE FUCK UP!"

That was the only message. Rachel took out her re-porter's notebook from her purse and played the message again as she made some notes. Once done, she looked over at the heavy sliding glass door that led from Tom's room to the large and sun-drenched balcony beyond. She took a deep breath, shook her hands, and forced herself to step out there.

As soon as her feet hit the polished white marble that covered the balcony, she was met with the sight of a large marina just across the street from the complex.

CHAPTER SEVEN

To most Americans, and indeed, to most of those on the planet who knew of its existence, the Pentagon had long since stopped being a building constructed of mere steel and concrete. Over the course of the last several decades, and most especially during the last number of years as terrorism progressively darkened more of the world, the building had morphed into an entity unto itself. A cauldron of mythology where the black arts of a nation under attack were practiced, perfected, and executed in anonymous and messy precision.

While the civilian population of the United States had settled, once again, into its dangerous cocoon of complacency with regard to the ever-escalating war against radicals bent on the nation's destruction, the same could not be said for those who worked in the five-sided repository of war on the Potomac. At least, not of those perched at the very top of the power pyramid.

Not only did these generals and admirals expect things to get worse, but two of them were actually counting on it. General Peter Breck of the United States Army and Admiral Frank Thomas of the United States Navy were both members of the Joint Chiefs of Staff, and together they wielded almost incalculable power.

At this particular moment, both gentlemen found themselves not at their desks planning a battle, but in the

Pentagon chapel, envisioning a new world. Aside from being flag officers in the United States military, both men also happened to be part of an evangelical organization called, "The Christian Ambassadors." An organization that virtually no one in the United States had ever heard of, and yet, it was a group in which its very select members hoped, dreamed, and prayed would soon alter the life of every human being now alive.

As the last of the attendees settled into the small but dignified chapel, General Breck rose from his front-row pew, straightened his dark green uniform, paused for a moment to adjust his simple, wire-rimmed glasses, and slowly walked up to the podium.

As Breck looked out at his fellow believers, he thought about the immense power he had earned. More than that, however, he thought about divine intervention and the boundless joy he felt at being an instrument for God.

Even with his rank and background as a combat soldier which saw him awarded the Silver Star, two Bronze Stars, and three Purple Hearts, Breck was a man of subtle mannerisms. He was the personification of "walk softly, but carry a big stick."

An instructor at West Point had once told him that the best way to be an effective speaker was not to talk loudly, but rather, to speak softly, with a voice just loud enough so those who were listening to you would have to strain a bit to catch all of your words. It was a style Breck had perfected in over thirty years of service to his nation.

The general quietly cleared his throat and then spoke to the fifty or so senior officers gathered before him.

"Ladies and Gentlemen. Before I begin, let us pause for a moment to silently pray for the soul of General Arthur Ryan. As most of you know, Arthur was senselessly killed at his home during a botched burglary. Such a shame."

After a moment of silence, the general continued. "That

vicious crime, as well as the evil that is growing in our nation and world, is all the more reason we need to push forward. At this moment, there are thousands of Department of Defense leaders working in the rings and corridors of this Pentagon. Through Bible study, discipleship, prayer breakfasts, and outreach events, our organization is mustering these good men and women into an intentional relationship with our Lord, Jesus Christ. We have done well, but we need to do much more as our time is running short. The Lord our God has asked us to help Him in the most historic and pious endeavor of our lifetimes. We cannot and will not fail Him.

"Like all of you in this holy chapel, my first priority in life, from the moment I wake until the moment I sleep, is my faith in Jesus Christ. After that, comes my family, and after that, comes my country. It is well that we don't forget that . . ." The four-star general then paused with a private thought that caused him to turn somber before continuing. ". . . bad things can befall *any* of us should we forget that order. While we can save our souls and the souls of our families, the fate of our nation and the world was determined when God created the universe. That He would now ask our help in carrying out such a divine plan is the ultimate blessing.

"Please bow your heads and join me in prayer that He shall continue to give us the strength to enforce His will."

CHAPTER EIGHT

Twenty minutes before the senior staff was set to convene in the Roosevelt Room of the West Wing of the White House, a still-elegant woman closing in on seventy years of age, with medium-length reddish-brown hair, almost-ivory white skin, and wearing a pastel yellow jacket and skirt combination, softly tapped on Ian Campbell's open door.

As Campbell had managed only two hours' sleep the night before, he barked out a loud "What?" before lifting his head to see who had disturbed his preparation for the meeting.

"Ian," said the woman with still-bright blue eyes. "May I have a minute of your time?"

Campbell looked up to see Eileen Dale standing in his doorway. As in a former cabinet member, former senator from Tennessee, and current vice president of the United States of America.

Campbell jumped up from his chair, sending it banging against the wall behind him, and almost saluted as he answered. "Madame Vice President. I apologize for my tone. I tend to be a bit cranky in the morning."

The vice president looked down at her silver Rolex watch and then back up at the deputy chief of staff. "It's six forty in the morning, Ian. I'd say that entitles all of us to be a little grouchy," she answered in a slow Southern drawl.

Campbell smiled as the vice president was kind enough to let him off the hook. "Yes, ma'am."

He then pointed to the small white Queen Anne sofa in his office. "Won't you please have a seat."

As the vice president walked into the office to sit on the proffered furniture, Campbell walked past her to close his office door behind her.

Once he reached the door, he looked quickly out at his assistant sitting at her desk and raised his eyebrows.

She instantly shook her head, rolled her eyes, and shrugged her shoulders. All in one seamless motion.

Campbell quietly clicked the paneled wooden door closed and turned to face the vice president. In the year he had worked in the White House for President Robertson, he had never had any conversations with the "Veep"— as she was called in the building—let alone have her pop up unannounced in his office sans staff and her Secret Service detail. While tired beyond any adequate definition of the word, he was still awake enough to be nervous and on guard.

"May I get you a cup of coffee, Madame Vice President?"

Eileen Dale shook her head. "I'd actually love a cup but I don't have the time for your assistant to go downstairs to the Mess to get me one."

"What Mess?" Campbell smiled. "They only serve Starbucks down in the most exclusive of all restaurants, and I hate Starbucks. Hence," he continued as he pointed next to his desk, "I have my very own coffeemaker that brews Dunkin' Donuts, nonbitter coffee, with no brainwashing additives."

The vice president laughed and nodded her head. "Great. Black. No sugar."

Campbell poured the vice president's coffee into a ceramic white mug adorned with the Seal of the President and placed it on the table before her. He then grabbed himself a Styrofoam cup sitting next to the machine, added some coffee, and then extra cream and sugar, and then sat in a blue wing-back chair to her right.

She picked up the mug and took a sip. "Very good." She smiled. "But I can drink from a Styrofoam cup as well, you know."

Campbell shook his head. "Not in this office you can't."

"Well, nonetheless, thank you, Ian."

Campbell squinted his eyes as he looked at the second most powerful person in the country. Eileen Dale had been a great choice as a running mate for then Governor Shelby Robertson. She was a tough, ethical, highly accomplished, Harvard educated conservative senator from a still-conservative Southern state, who brought just enough intangibles to the table to narrowly put her and Shelby Robertson over the top in their first election. Their second election was more of a cakewalk, and as Vice President Dale did not have any burning desire to run for president herself, she was actually given a chance by the chattering class to be one of the most effective vice presidents in recent memory. A chance that had long since gone by the wayside.

As brilliant, experienced, and dedicated as Eileen Dale was, she was still considered an outsider by most of the president's staff. Before he culled her from the political herd to be his running mate, she had no history with Robertson. In fact, she had only met him once before his anointing phone call, and that was when she had been a cabinet secretary in a previous administration, and he, the governor of Alabama.

In the minds of his dedicated and ultraloyal campaign operatives, she was less of a running mate, and more of a calculated gamble made to install their boss in the Oval Office. Once elected, they would have little or no use for her.

Fortunately for the newly elected vice president, President Robertson was wiser and less outwardly petty than his young staff. In his new vice president, Robertson saw public relations gains and victories that his staff overlooked from lack of real-world experience.

More than good sound bites, however, the president saw an insurance policy should he need to deflect attention or shift blame. Like a magician entertaining a crowd, Robertson had every intention of deftly and secretly transferring potential bad news and responsibility from him to her in the blink of an eye, with no one the wiser.

Now well into the third year of their second term, it didn't take a stroke of genius for the vice president to figure out that she was quickly being marginalized. For the first six-plus years, like clockwork, every Thursday at noon, she and the president would have a private lunch to discuss world events, the place of the United States, and the political opportunities that might be out there for the administration.

Two months ago, the lunches abruptly stopped. When the vice president tried to inquire as to why, she was rewarded with a fairly rude phone call from Kent Riley, the president's political guru and "strategic" advisor, who duly informed her, that for reasons of his own, "the president has decided that the lunches are no longer needed."

That was it. Other than some ceremonial events in the East Room and the State Dining Room, she had no further contact with President Robertson. She had been swiftly and completely frozen out and had absolutely no idea as to what sin by her prompted her exile.

As she sat before the deputy chief of staff, she gazed almost transfixed at the steam rising from her coffee and wondered how best to start the conversation. Fortunately, Campbell saved her the trouble.

"Madame Vice President. I have to say, that as much as I admire you, your being here right now is not making me feel very good."

Eileen Dale smiled over the rim of her mug as she took a small sip of coffee. "Why is that, Ian?" she asked when finished.

Campbell shook his head. "Why? Pardon my bluntness, but rumor has it that you are on the outs with the boss. And even though you and I haven't said five words to each other in the year or so I've been here, I now have the distinct honor of having you here, staring me down over a cup of fairly decent coffee."

"I can't imagine why there should be a problem with the vice president of the United States stopping by to visit with the deputy chief of staff to the president. We are, after all, paid to conduct the people's business."

Campbell had heard that even at sixty-six years of age the vice president was a health nut who insisted on working out two hours a day. Even when she was sitting just two feet from him, she still looked like a woman at least twenty years younger. Campbell, on the other hand, felt twenty years older as each second of the conversation progressed.

"Yeah," smirked Campbell. "That might be the way it is with you and your staff over in the Executive Office Building, but here in the West Wing, the people's business is usually defined by President Robertson and Kent Riley."

The vice president placed her mug down on the day's edition of the *Washington Times* and leaned in closer to Campbell. "Exactly my point, Ian," she said just above a whisper. "The power in this complex seems to be funneling down to just two men, and it's my thinking that you, more than most, may be able to express an opinion as to why that's so and what may be going on."

Instinctively, when the vice president leaned in, Campbell leaned back. "And why's that, Madame Vice President?"

"Because, Ian. For whatever reason, this president has

taken a real liking to you during the year you have been here. Don't take this personally, but I don't really understand why. You are not part of the Alabama mafia that has a death grip on this White House. You are an outsider. An outsider with a reputation as an independent thinker. For that reason, I suspect that you may not be totally accepted or trusted by Kent Riley and his collection of bootlickers."

Now it was Campbell's turn to look down at his watch. "Again, not to be rude, Madame Vice President, but I've got to conduct the senior staff meeting in about two minutes. Is there something you want of me?"

Campbell knew that he and Robertson had grown somewhat close during his tenure. While all of the reasons as to why may have escaped him, it was a relationship he did not want to trash by saying too much to the vice president.

"Yes," said the vice president as she stood and smoothed down her tailored, semi-tight skirt. "I'd like you to join me for dinner at my residence up at the naval observatory this evening. There is something important I would like to share with you. We can talk in private and get to know each other a little better."

Campbell stood up and shook his head. "Thank you for the invitation, Madame Vice President, but I'm not sure that's such a great idea."

The vice president turned her back on Campbell as she walked toward the door. Once she reached it, she placed her manicured left hand on the gold-colored doorknob and turned to face him.

"Do what you think best, Ian. That's, of course, entirely up to you. But being that this is the Robertson White House, two seconds after I walked into your office, Kent Riley was being informed of my presence. Information is power, Ian. Better for you that you gain as much as you can as fast as you can, before it's too late."

With that cryptic message, she opened the door, walked out, and disappeared down the hallway to the left. Amazingly, just as if she had scripted it, three seconds after the vice president was gone, Kent Riley was standing in the doorway with his arms folded across his chest.

CHAPTER NINE

At thirty-nine years of age, Gerald Donovan was on the young side to be a captain of an Ohio-Class Trident ballistic missile submarine.

He attained such a lofty goal at a relatively young age for three distinct, but intertwined reasons. The first being that he had graduated third in his class at Annapolis with an IQ hovering near 160. The second was that while an executive officer on his last submarine, he stepped in for his hesitant and overly cautious captain, and ordered two torpedoes fired into a People's Republic of China cargo ship.

Naval intelligence, Mossad, and the CIA had all determined that the ship was not carrying grain as listed in its manifest, but four disassembled Long March III missiles on their way to Iran. Missiles that had the range to reach Israel, and all of Europe.

Initially after the sinking, the Chinese went predictably berserk and threatened every diplomatic action under the sun. Later, when the United States showed, before a closed door session of the United Nations Security Council, a video of the contents of the cargo ship strewn across the ocean floor, the Chinese switched tactics and claimed that a renegade general had tried to send the missiles to Iran for a cash payoff. A general, they further claimed, who had just been executed for his crime. Months later, the

CIA determined that a general had indeed been executed. But one who was internally calling for greater cooperation with the West. The Chinese simply tried to kill two birds with one bullet.

The last and most important reason that Donovan found himself commanding his own boat was because, some time after he sunk the Chinese ship, he had been called in to meet with Admiral Frank Thomas. During the course of the conversation, Thomas discovered that like him, Donovan shared an unwavering belief and faith in Jesus Christ. A faith that transcended all other priorities. Soon thereafter, Admiral Thomas interceded to make sure that Donovan moved ahead of fourteen other highly qualified XOs to get his promotion to captain, as well as his own command.

Donovan was sitting in his small, but comfortable, captain's cabin, when there was a knock at his door. Donovan marked his place in the King James Bible he was reading and turned from the chair facing his fold-down desk to look at the door.

"Come in."

The narrow gray steel door opened and Donovan's XO, Rick Olsen, filled the opening.

"Good afternoon, Skipper. You told me to come see you when we were at periscope depth."

The balding, blond-haired commander nodded his head and pointed to his bunk. "Thanks, Rick. Why don't you close the door and then take a load off."

"Yes, sir," answered Olsen as he closed the door behind him and squeezed into the small cabin to plop himself down on the captain's rack.

"Anything out there?" asked Donovan as Olsen tried to maneuver his six foot four inch Ichabod Crane-like frame into a semi-comfortable sitting position.

"No, sir. It's clear for the moment. But being that we

are only twenty miles off the coast of Florida, it's not going to stay that way for long."

Donovan leaned down next to his left leg and opened the mini refrigerator underneath his desk. "Pepsi or water?" he asked as he grabbed a bottled water for himself.

"A Pepsi would be great, sir. Your little drill last night kept me up until about three. I could use a little caffeine to shake off the cobwebs."

The commander handed Olsen a can of Pepsi and watched as he opened it and took a long pull of the liquid inside. More than watching his second in command quench his thirst and jump-start the synapses in his brain, however, Donovan was looking for telltale signs of something out of the ordinary. He was looking for doubt, worry, suspicion, and most especially, rebellion.

Like Admiral Thomas carefully selecting him, Donovan had searched far and wide to find his executive officer. After speaking with the admiral and several high-level members of the Christian Ambassadors, Donovan was left with the files of eight exceptional, highly trustworthy, extremely spiritual executive officers. From that exalted and numerously decorated group, Donovan picked Olsen. That selection took place two months earlier.

For the last four weeks, Donovan, Olsen, and the other thirteen officers and 140 enlisted men who made up the crew of the USS *South Dakota* had been on station under the Atlantic Ocean off the East Coast of the United States.

Donovan considered himself a very tough, but fair, commander. He knew he had pushed his crew to the limit these last thirty days. Pushed them for a reason all but a few others on the boat would never know. One of those being the sleep-deprived XO before him sucking down the last drop of Pepsi from the can.

Donovan reached over and grabbed the empty container

from Olsen. "Another?" he asked as he placed the can in the small wastebasket next to the refrigerator.

"No, sir," answered Olsen as he rubbed one of his eyes. "One hit of caffeine a day is enough for me."

Donovan laughed. "Keep up that kind of talk, Rick, and I'll start to think you're a Mormon instead of a Baptist."

Olsen smiled in return. "No chance of that, sir. I'm not nearly good-looking enough to be a Mormon."

"Now that you mention it . . ."

After ten or so seconds of awkward silence, Donovan spoke in a much more serious tone.

"What do you think of the current state of the world today, Rick?"

Olsen pursed his lips and frowned just a bit as he answered his commanding officer.

"Kind of an odd question, sir. Is this conversation going to be off the record, so to speak, Captain?"

Donovan nodded in the affirmative but held his silence.

"In that case, sir, I would say that if things keep progressing the way they are, there is not much hope for mankind."

Donovan jumped on one word from the response. "You said 'mankind,' and not 'humankind' or 'the world's population.' Why is that?"

The XO lowered his voice almost to a whisper. "Again, speaking off the record between two friends, and with all due respect to my wife and two daughters, I believe the Lord our God created men as the superior gender. And quite frankly, if 'mankind' is good enough for our Founding Fathers, then it's certainly good enough for me."

Donovan offered up another all but imperceptible nod of his head. "As an answer, I'd have to say that yours was direct and offered no hint of political correctness."

Olsen's gray eyes suddenly went a shade darker.

"Political correctness is a major contributing factor to the collapse of Western civilization and the growing lack of spiritual faith that now plagues our very country, sir."

"Amen to that, Rick. And since you brought up religion and faith, how is yours?"

"Come again, sir?"

Donovan took a sip from his water bottle and then used the bottle to point at Olsen.

"We've never talked about it, Rick. But you seem to be a man of deep faith. Am I okay in saying that?"

"Yes, sir," answered Olsen with his voice now rising. "I happen to believe that Jesus Christ is our Lord and Savior, and all people must truly accept that if they hope to reach the promised land."

Donovan smiled with genuine warmth. "I'm very happy to hear you say that. It confirms my faith in you, and validates my search."

"Sir?"

The Captain shook his head. "Never mind, Rick. Above your pay grade. And mine, if truth be told." Donovan then lowered his voice as he asked the next question. "Have you ever heard of an elite and faith-based group called the Christian Ambassadors?"

Olsen nodded his head slowly. "Yes, sir. I have. Funny you should ask. Just by coincidence, when we finally docked at Jacksonville, I was going to try and figure out a way to join."

"No need to worry about that, Rick. Admiral Thomas sponsored me into that most holy and august of groups, and I'm about to sponsor you."

Olsen showed most of his teeth in a wide smile. "That would be the highest honor of my career and life, Skipper."

Donovan quickly shook his head, and then paused for effect. "No. No, it wouldn't, Rick. The highest honor of both of our lives will be to protect what is being built right now, eight hundred feet below us."

"Sir?" said Olsen again, fearful of asking too many questions or stemming the fountain of information.

"Quite simply, what is being built beneath this boat is being constructed by the very hands of God. As time progresses, and as you continue to prove yourself to me and the Ambassadors, I will tell you more. In the meantime, do you accept what I have just told you in faith and with no reservation whatsoever?"

Without really knowing anything, Olsen still suddenly felt an excitement he had not experienced in years, and a true spiritual purpose and calling he had never felt in his life.

"Yes, sir," snapped the XO as he stood. "Is that all?"

"No, Rick. That's far from all. There is still a great deal to tell you. But as I said, that will all come in time. You are the last piece of the puzzle for this boat. As of this moment, let me give you your standing orders which must be obeyed from this second on. Those being that if any vessel, and I mean *any*, foreign or domestic, cruise ship or fishing trawler, whatever, attempts to stop over this spot or makes any suspicious moves in this part of the ocean, I want you to immediately sink that ship. Do I make myself clear?"

"Yes, sir!" roared Olsen.

"Will I detect any hesitation or remorse should I give such an order?"

"No, sir."

Donovan stood and stepped even closer to Olsen in the already cramped cabin. "And if and when the time comes for us to launch our ballistic missiles, will you in fact insert your launch key and follow my orders to launch our birds . . . no matter what the target?"

"Yes, sir!" Olsen shouted. "You have my word."

Donovan extended his right hand. "Then welcome to the Christian Ambassadors, Rick. And may Christ our Lord watch over us and protect us as we shield that which He builds on the ocean floor."

CHAPTER TEN

After confirming with the harbormaster at the Waterways marina that Tom did indeed birth his cabin cruiser, the *Baby Black Pearl*, at the marina, Rachel walked over to the shops of the marina and grabbed an iced tea at the already crowded Café-Café delicatessen.

As she sipped her tea at a table just outside of the deli, she marveled at the long line of men and women waiting to be served. Most were in great shape, with all being from South America.

During her half-hour conversation with Vern the harbormaster, she learned that approximately 80 percent of the population of Aventura was from South America. All of whom before her seemed to live in a gym and favor designer labels and sunglasses. Many, like her, were also Jewish.

The more she learned about one of the wealthiest cities in the world that no one had ever heard of, the less likely it seemed that Tom would live in such a superficial setting. And yet, here she was.

"Should have named his boat the *Wandering Enigma*," Rachel whispered out loud as she moved her chair a foot to the left to catch up with the shadow cast by the table's green and white umbrella.

Considering the net worth of the town, and the clientele lined up outside the deli, she was not surprised to find that Café-Café also offered wireless Internet.

After breaking out her laptop, she proceeded to find the phone numbers for every Eric Gonzalez who lived within a ten-mile radius of her brother's apartment.

She found three and actually got lucky with the very first number she called.

"Alo," answered the voice of a young woman on the second ring.

"Hi. I'm sorry. But do you speak English?"

"Yes. Who is this?"

Rachel flipped open her reporter's notebook. "Is this the home of Eric Gonzalez?"

"Who wants to know?"

Rachel smiled to herself at the woman's protective and tough demeanor. "My name is Rachel Hiatt. I'm the sister of Tom Hiatt, and I was won—"

Before she could continue, the woman on the other end of the phone burst into tears.

"¿Donde está mi Eric? ¿Donde está mi vida?"

Rachel knew enough from her high school Spanish to understand that she was saying, "Where is my Eric? Where is my life?" over and over as she sobbed uncontrollably.

It took a full minute for the woman to compose herself. While she did, Rachel wiped away some fresh tears from her own eyes as she watched three young children play on a mini merry-go-round in front of an upscale ice-cream parlor directly across the walkway from Café-Café.

As she heard the woman's breathing return to normal, she tried once again. "Hello. I'm sorry. But I don't know your name."

"Lo siento. I mean, I'm sorry. It's Maria Gonzalez. The wife of Eric. My Eric and I are expecting our first child in two months, so I need him home right away." Upon

making the announcement, the woman quietly started weeping again.

"Maria. I know this is very hard on you. It's hard on me as well. Would it be possible for me to come see you now?"

"*Por supuesto*. Of course. I desperately need some company at the moment."

After getting the address for a condo building in Hallandale, a town less than five miles to the north of Aventura, Rachel drank the last of her iced tea and shook her head at the mindless collection of narcissists before her. She then stood, slung her laptop over her shoulder, and started her ten-minute walk back through the still-sun-drenched marina to get her car.

CHAPTER ELEVEN

After wrapping up the senior staff meeting, Ian walked out of the Roosevelt Room and took a left to cut through the West Wing lobby on the way back to his office.

He did this for two reasons. First, because he wanted to get a better look at the statuesque blonde that had started working there the day before. The second and more compelling reason to take a stroll through the West Wing lobby was because it was a great and easy way to gather intelligence. Many times, when someone was coming to visit the president, they were usually parked in the West Wing lobby before being escorted into the Oval Office.

As Campbell pushed open the dark wooden door leading into the lobby, he was more than a little surprised to see the four-star air force general who commanded the nation's land-based nuclear missiles, thumbing through a copy of the *Weekly Standard*.

"General Mitchell," said Campbell as he stood in front of the coffee table next to the general. "How nice to finally get to meet you."

The portly general looked up from his magazine, but made no attempt to rise from the small red sofa. "I'm sorry. But you seem to have me at a disadvantage."

Campbell extended his right hand. "Ian Campbell, sir. I'm the deputy chief of staff, and prior to my time here at the White House and in the Senate, served with Naval Special Warfare."

Upon hearing that last bit of the introduction, the general rose and shook Campbell's hand. "Nice to meet you, Navy. Where were you stationed when you served?"

"Pardon my language, sir, but pretty much anywhere there was a shit storm."

The general laughed. "Well, that outhouse has only gotten larger since you left, son."

"Yes, sir." Campbell then pointed at the open magazine. "Well, I'll leave you to your reading. Funny," he added as he started to walk away. "But I didn't see your name on the president's schedule for today. Had I known you were coming, I would have brought you some Navy football souvenirs."

The general smiled at Campbell's attempt at humor. "Yeah, well I'm just an old friend of the president's from back in our air force academy days. I guess we don't rate getting on the schedule. Since I was in town, I just decided to stop by to catch up. As for your generous offer, let's wait and see if Air Force doesn't actually beat Navy this year. If we do, I'll bring you some stuff instead."

"Deal. It was great meeting you, sir," Campbell said over his left shoulder as he walked toward the far door that led to the staff offices.

Once he walked through the door and it closed behind him, Campbell stopped and turned back to face the lobby and frowned. Every instinct he had was telling him something was not quite right about that last conversation. Had he been back in combat, he would have instantly started to dig a very deep foxhole and plant himself in the bottom. However, since he was now a civilian, the next best thing to digging a foxhole was to get on his phone and then fire up Yahoo.

Once back in his office with his door closed, Campbell dialed up the press secretary for the National Security

Council. It was a sign of desperation and curiosity that he would even call this woman. Her name was Tammy Han and Campbell had dated her for a month or so before he basically stopped calling her.

Han was a stunning, Princeton educated Korean American who had everything Campbell wanted from a woman. Like him, she was a former naval officer. Like him, she was a great all-around athlete. Like him, she was looking for a possible life mate. Unlike Campbell, however, she was looking for a much faster commitment. A pressure that scared Campbell away and made him commit the unpardonable sin of saying he would call her and then not following through. Campbell had taken the coward's way out, and Han was far from over the hurt.

As he heard her pick up the phone and say, "Tammy Han," Campbell actually closed his eyes out of embarrassment and anticipation.

"Hi, Tammy. It's Ian and—"

Click. Dial tone. She had slammed the phone down the second she heard his voice.

Campbell tried calling her three more times, but every call went into voice mail.

After the third call, he sent her an e-mail that read:

TAMMY. PLEASE CALL ME BACK RIGHT AWAY. THIS IS BUSINESS. DON'T MAKE ME WALK DOWN THE HALL TO THE NATIONAL SECURITY ADVISOR'S OFFICE AND TELL HIM WHAT A CHILD YOU ARE BEING.

Campbell then attached the red exclamation point and sent the e-mail. Fifteen seconds later, his phone rang.

"Ian Campbell," he answered with a false upbeat tone.

"What do you want, dickhead?"

Campbell laughed at the insult. "Well, I guess I want

to apologize first of all. I got a bit nervous that you were moving too fast and just stopped returning your calls. I was wrong and I'm sorry."

"Yeah, whatever, you spineless bastard. How you ever became a SEAL is beyond me. What the hell do you want?"

Now was not the time to try and flirt and be cute, but Campbell could not help himself as he remembered her incredible body that she kept in shape by working out one hour a day.

"What I want, Tammy, is to take the most complete woman I have ever known out to dinner to apologize in person."

"Spare me the bullshit. You and I are just strictly business from now on, buddy boy. So once again, what do you want that's so important?"

Campbell took a sip of now-cold coffee from the Styrofoam cup he had filled when the vice president stopped by. "Okay. I'm not going to argue. I just saw General Wayne Mitchell in the West Wing lobby. Is he supposed to be visiting with the president today or anytime in the near future?"

Campbell's question was rewarded with the sound of keystrokes as Han typed something into her computer.

"Nope," she finally answered. "He's not on the schedule for today or any day in the next month according to my calendar."

Campbell shook his head. "Okay. Thanks, Tammy. Sorry I bothered you."

As Campbell was getting ready to hang up, he heard her giggle and say, "Did he try to give you a Bible when he saw you in the West Wing?"

"What?" asked Campbell. "What's that supposed to mean?"

"Oooh," she answered. "You mean I know something that the all-powerful Ian Campbell is not aware of?"

"Apparently." Campbell's tone turned serious. "What do you know?"

"Word has it from reliable sources that General Mitchell is one of the those strict born-again Christians who interprets the Bible literally. A real freak. Part of the Christian Ambassadors that operate out of the Pentagon. Maybe he stopped by today to convert the non-believing heathens like me working in the White House."

That comment from Han caused Campbell to remember the tail end of a phone call the president had made to General Mitchell three weeks before. Campbell had assumed the president was in the Oval Office when he started to walk into the president's private study to retrieve a file he had forgotten in there from the morning's briefing. As he got to the partially open door, he heard the president's voice. A voice that had just said something nonsensical and somewhat ominous. Campbell stopped short of going in, and instead stood there for about twenty more seconds before retreating to his office. Han's comments about the general trigged the memory of that snippet of conversation.

"Ian? Hello? Are you still there?"

Campbell closed his eyes more tightly as he answered. "Yeah, Tammy. I'm here. Thanks for the 411. I'll call you later."

"Hey, Ian. Are you ok—" Before she could complete the question, Campbell had softly and gently hung up the phone.

CHAPTER TWELVE

Rachel stretched out her long legs at a small table for two in the sunroom of the condo belonging to Eric and Maria Gonzalez. As Maria made some lemonade and laid out some cookies, Rachel took a look out the window.

Five floors below her was a spectacular view of a canal, numerous palm trees, and the intracoastal waterway beyond that. And just visible between two forty-story residential towers was a sliver of the Atlantic Ocean. It seemed that basically every window in South Florida had some kind of amazing water view.

Maria walked into the sunroom carrying a tray and Rachel stood to help her. Instead of seven months pregnant, Rachel thought she looked more like twelve. While she hadn't put on excessive weight, her stomach looked enormous to a woman who really did not know all that much about childbirth and was in no rush to be educated.

Rachel grabbed the tray from Maria's hands and marveled at how elegant she looked being so pregnant. As she was quickly learning, Latin American women—especially those from Maria's home country of Venezuela—really did take a great deal of pride in their appearance. No matter what their social standing.

As Rachel placed the tray on the table, she took note that Maria had very thick, long, jet-black hair, dark eyes, an enviable olive complexion, and was wearing a short-sleeve, button-down yellow maternity shirt, with black slacks, and black high-heel pumps. All accented by a simple silver necklace with crucifix, and her wedding band and engagement ring.

Just looking at the rings almost caused Rachel to cry.

"Maria. Thank you for seeing me on such short notice."

Maria slowly sat in the other chair, and Rachel followed suit.

"Of course. I called the police just before you called, to report my Eric missing, but they said I needed to talk with the coast guard."

"Yeah. I got the same song and dance," said Rachel as she picked up her glass of lemonade.

Maria had her head bowed, but Rachel still saw the tear that she shed onto her lap.

"Maria. Did Eric tell you what he and Tom were up to?"

"Just something about finding the location where they thought some old ship went down in the 1700s," she answered with her head still down.

"Did he tell you where they were going?"

"No."

Rachel took a long look at the top of Maria's head, had a sip of her lemonade, put the glass down, and stood up.

"Well, thank you for your time and kindness. If I hear anything about Eric or Tom, I will call you right away."

With that, Rachel started to walk toward the door. As she did, Maria put her hand on Rachel's arm. "Eric did not tell me where he was going because he always left me a detailed map of where he was going . . . just in case. Would you like to see it?"

Rachel froze in place as her head spun a bit.

CHAPTER THIRTEEN

Ian Campbell pulled up his schedule on his computer and stared at it. It was jam-packed for the day and getting worse by the minute. As crazed as his day was becoming, he still had an urgent need to think and decompress for a few minutes. Too many thoughts were now bouncing around in his head, with one or two being so bizarre that he refused, for the moment, to entertain them.

He picked up his phone and dialed the extension for his assistant. "Janice," he said when she answered. "Can you please call Steve Phillips over in legislative affairs, and tell him I'm not going to be able to meet with his mayors at the moment."

"Ian. I don't think that's a good idea. He's got ten mayors in from all over the country, including one from Birmingham, Alabama. You remember Alabama, don't you, Ian? It's only the home state of the president."

Campbell had no patience at the moment to debate his assistant. "Yes, Janice. I'm well aware of the president's home state. But," he decided to lie, "as it turns out, I have to do something immediately for Alabama's favorite son."

"Okay," his assistant tsked. "I'll tell him. But then you have to buy me new earrings when Phillips melts mine off screaming at me over the phone."

"I promise. Just tell him to bring the mayors to the

Mess, buy them breakfast, and charge it to me. I'll try to get down there to join them for coffee."

Campbell hung up the phone and rested his head in his hands.

People make assumptions all the time and Campbell knew that two incredibly important people had made a conveniently wrong assumption about him. First, Senator Webster James assumed that Campbell was a strong, evangelical Christian. Then, because of the sales job given by James to the president, Shelby Robertson seemed to assume the same thing. Neither man had ever asked Campbell about his beliefs, and Campbell, in the interest of self-preservation and promotion, was more than willing to have them believe whatever they wanted.

Campbell knew that President Robertson had strong religious convictions. He also knew that the president went out of his way to hide those convictions from all but his trusted inner circle. Within the White House, that inner circle consisted of Kent Riley and the president's chief of staff, Julia Sessions.

Sessions had been with Robertson since before he became governor of Alabama. She was tough, politically ruthless, highly educated, and seemed to have only one mission in life: safeguarding Shelby Robertson.

Like a number of women in Washington, Julia Sessions found herself middle-aged and still single. It was an occupational hazard for those women who spot-welded themselves to powerful politicians to the exclusion of everything, including a personal life. Suddenly, the year or two they planned to work in Washington had become fifteen or twenty, and instead of being twenty-six with eligible men all around, they found themselves in their mid-forties, still without a husband or child. At that point, many of the women would pour themselves deeper into their careers believing that was all they had left.

Julia Sessions, while forty-four years of age and still

single, was anything but a handwringer. In her mind, she had just not met the man that could meet her high standards, and until such a time, was perfectly content to manage the life of the most powerful person on the planet.

Because Sessions was an extremely attractive blonde, the media had speculated for years that she and Robertson had something going on. Both while he was governor, and now as president. While such talk was hurtful to the First Lady, there was never one shred of evidence that anything of an immoral nature was happening.

Since Sessions, like Robertson, was an evangelical Christian, Campbell would have been surprised if they were up to something. That said, his time in Washington, and life in general, taught him that no one and no religion was beyond temptation or beyond hypocrisy.

Ultimately, Campbell couldn't care less if the president was engaged in extracurricular activity with Sessions. He was more concerned with the fact that she seemed to be going on more and more unexplained travel, and leaving him to do more and more of her work.

The one benefit in that unfair transfer of workload was that he got much more face time with the president. Almost every time they were alone, Robertson would ask him about his combat experiences and try to draw hidden details out of the reserved former warrior.

During those same conversations, the president would hint at bigger and better things for Campbell. "The biggest," the president said with a wink at a recent meeting.

The one time Campbell tried to draw him out on the subject, the president cryptically answered, "Just be thankful that you are a good Christian, Ian. Those who praise Him will reap their reward."

That was it. That conversation took place one month earlier and since then, nothing. The president's life had suddenly and somewhat mysteriously, thought Campbell, grown exponentially more busy.

While he had somehow earned the president's trust, Campbell decided that he was perfectly content not to be part of Robertson's White House inner circle. There was something very *Stepford Wives* about Sessions and Riley, and if becoming part of the president's clique meant you checked your mind and objectivity at the door, then much better to be an outsider who most still assumed was "one of them."

Just as Campbell started to let his mind refocus on the phone call he overheard the president making three weeks earlier, his own phone started to ring. Campbell looked at the extension in the window of the phone identifying the caller, and shook his head.

It was the president's private secretary.

"Ian Campbell," he answered.

"Good morning, Ian. The president would like to see you in the Oval."

Campbell let out a short sigh before asking the question to which he already knew the answer.

"When?"

"Only right this second," answered the always perky assistant.

CHAPTER FOURTEEN

Campbell grabbed a white legal pad from his desk, walked out of his office, out of the small suite that housed his office, took a right, and walked approximately forty feet down the beige-carpeted hallway until he reached the closed door of the Oval Office where two very large Presidential Protection Secret Service agents, silently and professionally, stood watch.

As he nodded at the agents and prepared to knock on the door, he thought about how prized and sought after his relatively small office really was. What most Americans did not know was that over 90 percent of the White House staff did not work in the West Wing of the White House. There was simply no room for them in a space that was designed for eighty or so people, and was now bursting at the seams with over three hundred.

Most of the staff worked in the gray, gothic Eisenhower Executive Office Building adjacent to the White House. It was in that building that "commissioned officers" of the White House, meaning people with the titles of *special assistant, deputy assistant,* or *assistant to the president*, could spoil themselves in massive offices literally the size of small apartments. Offices which were equipped with fireplaces, huge windows, refrigerators, sofas, and conference tables that would seat eight.

Campbell knew that his small office was at best one-fifth the size of those offices, and yet, had zero doubt that every high-level staffer in the Eisenhower Executive Office Building would practically kill to trade their ultra-luxurious office for a broom closet in the West Wing. A prime location that afforded them the chance to crow at dinner parties that their office was just steps from the "Throne" and the power it conveyed.

Campbell couldn't honestly care less about such superficial trappings. His childhood of poverty, punctuated by six years of military service that bore witness to the capriciousness and cruelty of life, separated him from most who trolled the hallways of the White House. In fact, as he rapped the knuckles of his right hand against the slightly curved door of the Oval Office, he fantasized about how nice it would be to have an office in the basement of the Eisenhower Executive Office Building. If not out of mind, at least he would be out of sight for a while and able to catch up on some work.

"Come in!" shouted the president through the heavy door.

Campbell opened the door and was not the least bit surprised to see General Mitchell sitting next to the president on one of the two white sofas that occupied the world-famous space.

The president was sitting in a yellow and white upholstered chair situated between the sofas. Both men were drinking orange juice from fine White House crystal, and neither man rose when Campbell entered the room.

"Good morning, Mr. President," said Campbell from just inside the entrance.

The president waved him over to the other sofa. "Ian. Close the door behind you and come grab a cup of joe or some juice," he said as he pointed to the silver tray on the table holding the coffeepot and carafe of orange juice.

As Campbell sat down on the plush sofa, the president pointed at General Mitchell. "Ian, this is Wayne

Mitchell, a good friend of mine from our air force academy days."

Before the general could answer, Campbell said, "Yes, sir. I had the honor of meeting the general in the West Wing lobby earlier this morning."

"Great. Then it's like old home week in here."

As Campbell poured himself a cup of coffee, the president looked over at General Mitchell and exchanged a knowing look. "So remind me, Ian. What kind of a security clearance do you have? Since I'm only the president, I don't know jack shit about those types of things. I'm guessing you have a high one or you wouldn't be my deputy chief of staff, or have done all that special ops stuff before."

Campbell took just a few seconds longer than needed to stir the cream and sugar he had added to his coffee. Before walking into the Oval Office he had surmised it was going to be an unusual meeting. But even at that, he was a bit taken aback by the president's question.

"Yes, Mr. President. I have a high security clearance. Mine is called SCI, for Sensitive Compartmentalized Information. It's one step above Top Secret. I am also authorized for the 'Q' clearance needed to see information pertaining to our nuclear assets."

The president nodded. "I knew it was something like that. Just wanted to make sure."

He then pointed at the general. "Before you walked in, Ian, I was regaling Wayne with some of your exploits on the battlefield in service to our nation."

"Very impressive. The Navy Cross. That's some serious metal," said the general as he stared at Campbell.

Like most who had seen the horror of combat up close and personal, Campbell did not like to talk about it, and especially did not like his service used as idle banter for unheard conversations.

"Thank you, sir," Campbell said to the still-staring four-star general.

"I know this wasn't on the schedule, Ian. But I wanted you to meet with General Mitchell so he can give you some background on a highly secret pet project we have been working on. I have been going back and forth on if and when to tell you about the project, but now, with Wayne here, seems an opportune moment for all of us to chat about it. Before the general briefs you, however, do I have your word that whatever information you hear will never leave this room?"

Campbell felt a nervous tic in his left eyelid start to jump. Something he always got when he was overtired or on edge. Before walking into the Oval, he was kicking around in his own mind how to surreptitiously try to solve the mystery of the president's overheard phone call of three weeks earlier. Now, it seemed, the president was about to fill in some of the blanks.

"Yes, Mr. President. You have my word," answered Campbell to a now-stern Robertson.

"Great," said the silver-haired, fifty-four-year-old president. "Wayne. Why don't you spin up our ex-Navy SEAL on our little baby."

"Yes, sir, Mr. President," said the general who had never taken his eyes off Campbell. "Before I begin, I'd like to stress again that this information is highly classified, and betrayal of it could irreparably harm the national security of our nation. Do I make myself clear, Navy?"

"Perfectly," answered Campbell as he looked into the somewhat-dancing eyes of the general.

"That's what I needed to hear. Thank you. Now let me begin by asking you a question. Have you ever heard of a project code-named 'Greek Island'?"

Campbell instantly recognized the name but could not

place it. "It rings a bell, sir. But that's about it at the moment."

"Well, let's stop the ringing. Greek Island was also a highly classified project. Only this one was initiated way back in 1959 by then President Dwight D. Eisenhower. In the midst of the Cold War with the Soviet Union, and under the constant threat at the time of nuclear annihilation, President Eisenhower wisely decided that we needed a supersecure bunker to house our government should the worst happen. Having made that decision, in 1959, he ordered the construction of this top secret facility to commence. The location, which years later was betrayed by those liberal bastards at the *Washington Post*, was hidden under the world-famous Green Brier resort in West Virginia."

"Okay," Campbell interrupted. "That's how I know about it. I think I saw the *Post* story, or something based on it, years ago."

"May I continue?" asked the slightly perturbed general.

"Yes, sir. Sorry."

"The facility was designed to protect every member of Congress, the president and vice president, and relevant congressional, White House, and military staff for up to sixty days. Once finished, Greek Island was capable of housing approximately one thousand people. As mentioned, and unfortunately for our country, some anti-American editors and reporters at the *Washington Post* deliberately revealed its location and purpose in a 1992 article. Once that betrayal happened, it obviously became necessary to abandon the facility."

The president leaned forward and held up his hand. "Sorry to interrupt, Wayne. But so I don't forget, tell Ian what the guy who ran Greek Island said after they had to admit it existed and then shut it down."

General Mitchell took a sip of his juice to wet his drying lips and continued. "Yes, Mr. President. Years later, the man who ran the then-compromised facility said it was only logical to assume that the United States would replace Greek Island with something much larger, much more technologically advanced, and much more secret."

Campbell saw where this was going but was still amused and somewhat troubled to see the president of the United States, and the man in charge of the nation's ground-based nuclear missiles, behaving like school-children.

The president then clapped his hands together so loudly that Campbell actually jumped from the noise.

"Sorry, Ian," the president said with a smirk. "I didn't mean to startle you. I'm a bit wound up this morning, and just wanted to confirm what you must now be thinking. Yes, we have replicated Greek Island. And I'm proud to say that it was done by my orders during my time in office. I'm told that the new facility is so amazing that it puts the science back in 'science fiction.' And I'm further told, that this supersecret national asset is now ready for my personal inspection."

"Just so you know, Navy," continued General Mitchell, "and so there are absolutely no misunderstandings, this program is blacker than black as far as our government is concerned. Other than two people up on the Hill, no one in Congress knows of its existence. It does not show up in any appropriations budget and for all intents and purposes, it does not exist. It is off the books totally. Sadly, neither Congress, nor most of our government, can be trusted to keep a secret as monumentally important as this. So, with the president bringing you into his confidence now, you should consider it the highest honor of your life."

Campbell nodded at the general, but did not speak. In his relatively young life he had experienced a number of singular moments, but nothing could top what he was now seeing and hearing. He had so many questions knocking around in his head that he didn't know which to ask first, or if he should ask any at all. Finally, his curiosity got the better of him.

"If I may ask, Mr. President. Where is this new bomb shelter?"

The president shook his head. "Ian, you insult the structure by defining it in such pedestrian and archaic terms. This particular project is truly unworldly in its design and mission. It is a city unto itself and was created to ensure the survival of that and those who are most needed to fulfill our destiny."

Campbell remained silent but wrinkled his forehead as he tried to comprehend the last part of the president's sentence.

"Amen to that, Mr. President," said General Mitchell.

Campbell swiveled his head to look at the general who, for the moment, only had eyes for his commander in chief.

"As for where this project is located, I'm afraid that I'm not quite at liberty to reveal that to you just yet," said the president.

"Understood, Mr. President."

Robertson leaned over and slapped Campbell on the knee. "Don't look so dejected, Ian. Just because I can't tell you where it is, does not mean I can't show it to you."

"I apologize, Mr. President. I did not get a great deal of sleep last night, so I'm not following you at the moment."

This time it was the general's turn to offer a wry smile. "You don't have to follow, Navy. You just have to obey orders and keep your mouth shut."

Campbell looked over Robertson's shoulder toward the thick, bullet- and bomb-proof glass of the window behind the president's desk, and watched as Marine One—the president's helicopter—magically and unexpectedly started its descent onto the South Lawn.

The president acknowledged the noise of the helicopter as he said, "The general and I are taking a quick trip to Camp David for the afternoon. But come tomorrow, Wayne and I are going to leave to inspect this completed masterpiece. I'd like you to be with us, Ian."

Everything was coming at him way too fast. "I'd be honored, Mr. President. But why me?"

The president stood and started to walk toward his desk. Out of respect and protocol, the second he stood, Campbell and the general joined him.

Once the president reached his desk, he threw some folders into a briefcase and then looked up at Campbell and smiled with his perfectly capped teeth. "Why you, Ian? Well, when we get there, why I asked you to come on this little field trip will become blindingly obvious."

With that, he turned on his heel and headed to the door that led out to the Rose Garden. As the president walked, General Mitchell leaned close to Campbell and grabbed his arm. "We are leaving from the South Lawn at 0500 sharp, Navy. Don't breath a word of this to anyone. There are forces larger than you can imagine at work here, and if you betray this president or his mission, your punishment will be eternal."

As the general flashed out the door to catch up with the president and his Secret Service in tow, Campbell was not even aware that his mouth was hanging open or that a cold sweat had just broken out down his back.

CHAPTER FIFTEEN

Forty-five minutes after lifting off from the South Lawn aboard Marine One, President Robertson and General Mitchell sat alone in the conference room of Laurel Lodge, an ultrasecure meeting room situated in one of the cabins of Camp David.

While most presidents loved the solitude and rustic nature of Camp David, Robertson could not stand it for a host of reasons. He appreciated the history of the facility and knew it was originally created by President Franklin Delano Roosevelt and named "Shangri-la," before President Eisenhower came along and renamed it after his grandson, David.

He also knew, as the White House historian had explained to him during his first month on the job, that a number of headline-grabbing events were either planned or discussed at Shangri-la–Camp David. Events such as the Normandy invasion, the Eisenhower-Khrushchev meetings, and the Bay of Pigs fiasco. It was exactly because of the sensitive nature of such talks that the presidents involved really appreciated the solitude of the 125-acre retreat located some sixty miles from the White House in Frederick County, Maryland.

Because it was over an hour's drive north of the White House was the second major reason that Robertson did not like the place. Because of the distance involved to travel there, and because of the increased security threats to the nation, the Secret Service always recommended that the best and most secure way to get to Camp David was to fly in by helicopter.

Robertson had never told anyone, not even his wife, Phyllis, that he was becoming more and more apprehensive about flying aboard Marine One. Years earlier, when he had been the governor of Alabama, the then head of his security detail, who himself was a former Presidential Protection Secret Service agent, had told him that, by far, the president was most vulnerable to attack when flying aboard Marine One. The agent had told him that even with all the countermeasures on board and the decoy helicopters, Marine One still presented a very inviting target for the thousands of Stinger shoulder-fired missiles that were unaccounted for around the world, and almost assuredly in the hands of various terrorist organizations.

More than being worried about being vaporized by a small warhead somewhere over the Washington ellipse, however, Robertson disliked going to Camp David because he saw it as a place where, in his mind, two weak-kneed liberal presidents had betrayed the State of Israel.

As an evangelical Christian, Robertson revered Israel for the symbolism it represented to his faith. Now, decades after the Camp David Accords of 1978, Robertson still believed that President Jimmy Carter forced Prime Minister Menachem Begin of Israel into an unfair agreement with President Anwar Sadat of Egypt. Two-plus decades after that giveaway, Robertson believed that then President Bill Clinton compounded the error when he forced Israeli Prime Minister Ehud Barak into what was clearly a suicidal agreement with the terrorist Yasser Arafat. Fortunately for Barak and Israel, and as Robertson and others had theorized at the time would happen, Arafat stabbed Clinton in the back and deprived him of the deal, and the Nobel Peace Prize that would have been his thirty pieces of silver for the betrayal.

As both treacherous acts had been orchestrated out of Camp David, Robertson was loath to walk its grounds. Given that, however, the president was still happy to admit to himself that as much as he disliked visiting the place, it did have one enduring advantage: it was out of the ear and camera range of the always prying media. And considering what was on his private agenda for today, that advantage outweighed all other objections for the moment.

The president leaned back in his large, tan leather chair and looked across the highly polished mahogany table at General Mitchell. "So, how do we really stand, Wayne?"

The general tapped the knuckles of his right hand against the top of the table very quickly. "Knock on wood, Mr. President. We seem to be in great shape. Some in our government have begun to ping us out of curiosity, but they really have no clue as to what we are doing. Even the liberals in the media only have a passing understanding of the Christian Ambassadors. They think they know it all, and as usual, only see what their biased and marginal intelligence allows them to see. They still think that the group only operates out of the Pentagon and is limited in membership to a few 'kook' flag officers and a couple hundred 'overzealous Christian' colonels, majors, and captains."

"And what's our real status?" asked the president as he stood to remove his suit coat in the slightly warm conference room.

"Could not be any better, Mr. President. We have our people inserted at the highest levels at Homeland Security, the FBI, the National Security Agency, the Justice Department, the Treasury Department, and even the Federal Reserve. While the media, our political enemies, and even those within our own intelligence agencies who have been trying to track us these last few months, may think we have but a few hundred members, when the time comes, we are going to shock them with our strength, our unrivaled ability, and our purpose of mission."

The president nodded but looked quickly toward the ceiling. "His mission."

"Of course, Mr. President. His mission. We are but His humble servants."

"Amen to that, Wayne. So," the president then continued with narrowed eyes, "how many people do we actually have in place around the country who are committed to His mission?"

"At last count, something over five thousand. And not just in the United States, Mr. President. We have ambassadors in our predetermined countries of interest who have volunteered to stay in place and carry out their essential duties when the time comes."

President Robertson bowed his head. "May the Lord our Savior bless them and take special note of their sacrifice."

"Yes, sir."

"Well," said the president as he stole a quick glance at the seven large LCD television screens attached to the wall at the far end of the conference room, and tuned to ABC, CBS, NBC, Fox News, CNN, MSNBC, and CNBC, "I had another vision last night in the body of a dream. As that is how the Lord our God speaks to us, I wrote down all I could remember when I woke."

"And what was the vision, Mr. President?"

The president pushed his chair back, stood, and started to pace the room. "It was truly beautiful. It was the angel Gabriel talking to me. And in my dream he reminded me that, 'As the Father raises the dead and gives life to them, even so the Son gives life to whom He will. For the Father judges no one, but has committed all judgment to the Son, that all should honor the Son just as they honor the Father. He who does not honor the Son does not honor the Father who sent Him.' "

The general watched the president as he was about to complete a lap around the conference table. "Do you think there was a message in that vision, Mr. President?"

The president stopped and turned to face Mitchell. "Oh, most assuredly. The angel Gabriel would not visit with me were there not a larger message."

"Yes, sir," said the general. "And what message did you derive from his divine words?"

Robertson crossed his arms and looked down at the cobalt blue 'presidential' cuff links that adorned his white, French-cuff shirt. "That Vice President Dale does not honor the Son. That, in fact, she may be conspiring against Him and against His most holy of missions."

"I've never had a good feeling about her," answered the general as he shook his head.

The president seemed truly sad as he looked back at his friend of over thirty years. "The time may be quickly approaching when we need to send her to sit in judgment before our Lord."

The general's eyes went wide with the scope of what the president had just uttered.

"I'm sure that can be arranged, Mr. President. We took care of General Ryan. But do you think it's really wise to up the ante so dramatically?"

The president again looked toward the ceiling. "It's not really my call, now is it, Wayne? And besides," he added with a slight grin, "as she really is not a true believer, then she's not one of us anyway, now is she? Much like the Muslims, the Jews, the Catholics, and the others, she was condemned at birth. We are but the instruments of her destiny."

CHAPTER SIXTEEN

Ian Campbell stifled a yawn as he walked up Massachusetts Avenue toward the visitors entrance of the United States Naval Observatory.

After his brief and unsettling meeting in the Oval Office with the president and General Mitchell, he was having a great deal of trouble organizing a rational thought. Part of the problem was an excessive workload, but most of it was his imagination. He wanted to think it was an overactive imagination, but his instinct was telling him it was most likely underactive by a factor of ten.

Something wicked this way comes, thought Campbell as he approached the Secret Service kiosk that framed part of the entrance to the expansive grounds of the observatory.

Campbell looked at the three Uniform Division agents behind the bulletproof glass as he pushed the call button on the intercom resting on the wrought-iron gate protecting the kiosk.

"Can I help you?" asked a metallic voice.

"Yes. I'm here to see Vice President Dale."

"Is the vice president expecting you?"

"Yes."

"What's your name?"

"Ian Campbell."

Campbell watched as the agent typed his name into the computer before him.

"Okay. Step through the gate when you hear the click and then place your driver's license in the open drawer."

Campbell did as instructed, was given a badge, screened, and then sent on his way to start his walk up the slight incline toward Number One Observatory Circle.

Since 1974, Number One Observatory Circle has been the permanent home for the vice president of the United States. Even at that, it wasn't until Walter Mondale moved in during January of 1977 that a vice president actually lived there full-time.

Before then, most vice presidents lived in their personal residences. A practice that became increasingly costly because of security and logistics, and one that was beyond impossible after September 11.

Prior to becoming the home to vice presidents, Number One Observatory Circle had been built in 1893 as the home for the superintendent of the United States Naval Observatory. Sadly for the superintendent, the chief of naval operations found the house so nice that he evicted the superintendent and claimed the home as his own.

As a former navy man, Campbell knew something of the history of the home, but couldn't really care less. He was more concerned with the fact that it was now 7:45 P.M., he was exhausted, had to get up at 3:00 A.M. the next morning, and was about to have dinner with an all-but-declared enemy of the president.

Five minutes later found him sitting in what looked like a small private dining room of the residence. As he waited, Campbell admired a couple of the paintings on the wall that were on loan from some of America's best museums. Nice to be American royalty, thought Campbell as the vice president strolled into the room.

"So good of you to come, Ian," said the vice president with a ready smile and her right hand extended.

Campbell stood and grasped the proffered hand. As he

did, he was surprised by the strength of her grip compared to the softness of her hand.

"My pleasure, Madame Vice President."

"Oh, I doubt that, Ian," answered the vice president as she motioned him to sit. "I suspect you'd rather be getting worked over by your dentist than be here with me now."

"Not at all," Campbell demurred as he sat.

While taking his chair, he took a quick glance at the vice president and noticed that she had changed from her yellow pastel skirt and jacket combination of the morning, to a rather formfitting Duke University warm-up suit.

As if tracking his eyes, the vice president said, "Sorry for my informal attire. I'm going straight from here to my gym upstairs and was just trying to save a bit of time."

Campbell nodded. "Saving time in our business is always a good thing."

The vice president smiled and rubbed her hands together. "Okay, Ian. Before we get started, what would you like for dinner?"

"Would it be possible to get a burger with no bread, some fries, and two Cokes?"

"Absolutely."

The vice president then picked up the phone in front of her. "Thomas. Could we get one hamburger with no bread . . ."—she then looked over at Campbell—"How would you like that cooked?"

"Medium-well if possible."

". . . medium-well with fries, and two Cokes, and I'll have a Caesar salad and a diet Pepsi."

As she hung up the phone, Campbell said, "Gee, Madame Vice President. You're making me look like a caveman."

"Don't be silly, Ian. Clearly you work out and have age on your side. I, on the other hand, need to watch what I eat."

"Not from where I'm sitting."

The vice president smiled at the response and kept silent for just a beat too long.

"Ian," she finally said, "do you consider yourself to be a religious man?"

Campbell took in a deep breath and let it out very slowly. "Can I answer by saying my mother always taught me it's best never to get into discussions about religion or politics?"

"Well," the vice president said with a smile, "if that's the case, you picked the wrong profession and the wrong president to work for."

Campbell took a few seconds to organize his thoughts. He was not surprised by the question. He just did not think she would hit him with it two minutes into the meeting.

"Am I religious? I consider myself to be a spiritual man. I don't know that I'm religious."

Just then, Thomas brought in the drinks and placed them before the vice president and Campbell; the vice president never took her penetrating gaze off of Campbell's eyes.

As the butler quietly walked out of the opulent room, the vice president asked, "What do you mean by that?"

Campbell shook his head and took a long sip of his Coke to get some caffeine flowing into his body. "Nothing really. I believe in God. I'm a Christian. But after what I've seen in my life—after what I've done—I don't believe there is a God in Heaven who favors one religion over another. I believe we are all God's children. As imperfect and ignorant as we may be."

The vice president nodded and continued to stare at Campbell until he broke the gaze by looking over her shoulder toward the spacious foyer.

"Okay," said Dale. "If that is the case, then why did the president hire you?"

Campbell refocused on the porcelain face of the vice president. "I'm sorry, Madame Vice President. I don't think I'm quite following you."

"It's rather simple, actually. You're now part of the president's inner circle. One of his most trusted aides. And he only hires true believers for his inner circle. So, if you're not a strict fundamentalist Christian, then how did you get in?"

"Funny you should ask. I've been kicking that around in my own head the last number of days."

"And has the question stopped rattling around in there long enough for you to answer it?"

"Somewhat," said Campbell as he offered a weak smile. "As we talked about this morning, Senator Webster James recommended me to the president. And as the senator is one of the president's oldest and closest friends, maybe . . ."

"Maybe the president just assumed you were one of them."

"Yeah. And for my own purposes, I've since worked it pretty hard to make them believe that's the case. The fact is, I like the president. We get along. That said, some of his people seem to work overtime to keep me at arm's length."

The vice president nodded. "I know. That's why I decided to invite you here tonight."

Campbell blinked his eyes a few times and frowned. "Yeah, well no offense, Madame Vice President, but I'm not sure my coming here was such a bright idea."

"So," said Dale as she traced tiny circles on the condensation collecting on her glass. "Why did you come then?"

Campbell shook his head, picked up his first Coke, drained it, placed it back down on the coaster with the Seal of the Vice President, and answered, "Curiosity. Instinct.

A chance to steal some silverware and sell it on eBay. I'm not quite sure."

The vice president continued with her line of thought. "If the president brought you in, he did so because he has no doubts that you are a like-minded religious zealot. Were it not to fill that special need, he could find a thousand people to do your job."

Campbell was a bit stung by the implications of her final sentence, but decided to let it go. "What do you mean by zealot? Are you stating that you believe the president of the United States to be a religious zealot?"

"Ian. I consider myself to be a good Christian. I'm a Baptist and evangelical who has a very good relationship with my congregation and the leadership of my church. That said, from what the president and Kent Riley have let slip, their collective thinking makes me look like an atheist by comparison."

Campbell was now wide awake. "And just what have they let slip?" he asked as his memory touched once again upon his own overheard troubling conversation between the president and General Mitchell.

Dale shook her head. "I'd rather not get into that just now. Suffice it to say that it was disturbing."

Before she could continue, Thomas quietly walked back into the room with their dinner, silverware, and condiments. As the servant went about placing things on the table, Campbell visualized his civilian career going up in flames.

When Thomas left, the vice president nodded at the food. "Please eat. Before it gets cold."

Protocol dictated that he not start before her. But since it seemed she was in no hurry to try her salad, and since his military training always stressed eating food when available as you never knew when the next opportunity would arise, Campbell speared several french fries with his fork and stuck them in his mouth.

As he chewed, the vice president verbalized what he feared. "Ian. You, better than almost anyone in this nation, know that all religions have their extremists. You fought Islamists on the battlefield and witnessed their literally suicidal devotion to their twisted version of their faith. As an evangelical, I have been taught to accept that it is possible for Christians to be wrong about important matters and that we should understand the need to be charitable toward others who serve Christ as best they can. That said, serving Christ can never mean killing people in His name as the Islamists do. Never."

Campbell's head snapped up from his plate with a slice of hamburger on his fork just shy of his mouth. He quietly put the fork back on the plate, wiped his mouth with the white linen napkin, and looked directly into the vice president's eyes.

"Madame Vice President. I have to say that I don't like the direction this conversation is taking."

The vice president looked down at her untouched salad, then back up at Campbell. "Ian. You are not required to stay here one second longer than you want. If what I say is making you uncomfortable, then you are free to go. But, as I told you this morning in your office, information is power. This discussion now, may bring you clarity later on. Shall I continue?"

"Yes," Campbell answered in a barely audible whisper.

"For far too many years now, Christians—and I'm including Catholics in that generic title—have been the punching bag of the Left and the Left-leaning media and entertainment industry. We are the only group left in this country that they feel they can attack, vilify, mock, and belittle, with complete impunity. They smear us on the news, in their movies, on their television shows, in various books, and in their newspapers. Hundreds of scientists who question Darwinism have been fired, had their grants taken away, and had their college websites shut down.

That is how the Left defends free speech in our country. As an academic in America, if you dare to speak of intelligent design, the liberals will crush you and end your career. They question our faith, they question our Lord, and they place their religion or atheism above us, as they openly declare themselves intellectually superior. Even though, in one way or another, Christians comprise over 75 percent of this nation . . ."

Dale paused to take a sip of her Pepsi before continuing. ". . . In the minds of the Left—because they do control the top one hundred newspapers in our nation, the major networks, most of the cable networks, the movie studios, the major book publishers, and the content on our television shows—they feel with absolute certitude that our defense of our faith, our defense of our morals, our defense of Jesus Christ, will fall on deaf ears. Because of their immense power, they believe they can censor the truth and squash the voices of Christians. And guess what. Up until this moment, they have been successful."

"What has changed?" asked Campbell as he felt the beat of his heart quicken.

The vice president shook her head. "Communications-wise, nothing. The Left still holds all the cards. They have made a mockery out of the First Amendment as they have worked to silence us while striving to drive God out of our nation. In their minds, things have changed for the better. Their soapbox gets bigger, their revulsion with Christians grows stronger, and their goal of making the United States a godless country seems within their grasp. But during their hedonistic advancement toward the goal line, the Left has failed to take two things into consideration."

Campbell was certain he knew one of them. "Those being?"

"They have forgotten that we are a nation at war. That

we are at war with an evil that means to exterminate us all. Most especially and ironically, those on the Far Left who produce the filth that so inflames the Islamists. But . . . and much more importantly . . . they are so fat, pampered, spoiled, and out of touch with the true realities of life, that they have forgotten that if you corner an extremely dangerous prey, it has but one option. It must attack to survive."

Campbell cleared his throat before asking the next question. "And who or what is the prey in this case, Madame Vice President?"

"Let's not fool ourselves, Ian. I believe that we have an obligation to the nation to be brutally honest with ourselves. And for us to do that, we need to admit that there are those in our own faith who have no problem twisting the word of the Gospel to fit their demented definitions. Men and women who are prepared to do anything in the name of God. In the name of defending *their* God."

"And I'm guessing you have some individuals in mind."

Dale shook her head. "Again, I'm not prepared to go into specifics at the moment. That said, have you heard of a group called the Christian Ambassadors?"

"Sure. Vaguely. A group of evangelical military officers operating out of the Pentagon."

"Partly correct. The Christian Ambassadors do operate out of the Pentagon. But, we also know them to be in the FBI, Department of Homeland Security, in our embassies, and in our very own White House. For some reason, they have yet to crack the CIA. I need to stress that I firmly believe that the vast majority of those who belong to the Christian Ambassadors are very good people. Their only desire is to spread the word of the Lord in a peaceful manner as they seek to coexist with all on our planet. They, like me, for instance, believe that 98 percent of all Muslims are good, hardworking people who want to harm no one and just seek to provide the best possible life for their families."

"But . . . ," Campbell said with a cold smile.

"But, like the Muslims or any group or faith, while their 98 percent are good law-abiding citizens just also trying to survive, 2 percent of the Christian Ambassadors have a starkly different and ominous interpretation of their mission. I believe this 2 percent manifests itself in the extremists that infect our faith and blasphemously presume to speak in the name of our Lord."

"And they represent the prey now cornered by the Left."

The vice president picked up her teaspoon to try and dispense some of her nervous energy. "Not just the Left. But also the Islamists who, in their minds, mean to wipe Christianity from the face of the earth. For the extremists in our faith, this moment in time represents an epiphany. A call to arms to literally be soldiers for Christ in the final earthly battle. They do not fear this time. They welcome it. They embrace it, and they give praise for it. For now is the time when things will be put . . . right."

Campbell closed his eyes again and slowly rubbed his face with both hands. With his face still in his hands and his eyes partially obscured by his fingers, he looked across the table at Dale for a full five seconds before speaking.

"Madame Vice President. Why are you telling me all this? What do you want of me?"

The vice president softly started tapping the teaspoon against the royal blue place mat beneath her plate. "Ian. I ask you again. Why do you think the president hired you?"

Campbell dropped his hands from his face and opened his eyes wide. "Madame Vice President. If you somehow think I'm some kind of soldier for Christ or one of these extremists you mentioned, then I most respectfully submit that you are full of it."

Dale smiled at the response. In all of her years in public life, colleagues and staff had treated her with such reverence as to want to make her scream. She was tough. She knew she was tough. She had clawed, kicked, fought and out-thought the competition to rise to the top of what was still primarily a man's world. She was not made of cotton candy or glass, and resented always being treated with kid gloves. Before her, she thought, was either a man who was supremely confident in himself, or a man who had grown so tired of his job that he was throwing caution to the wind. No matter the reason, she found it refreshing.

"Well," said Dale with the smile still on her face, "I may in fact be full of it, but not with regard to this subject. I'm not accusing you of being an extremist. Actually, just the opposite."

Campbell nodded once to himself as if coming to a conclusion about the person sitting opposite him. "Okay. All right. Then what can I do for you?"

The vice president shook her head. "I have absolutely no idea. Ian, the president is an extremely bright and capable man. He knows your background and he wants you for something more than pushing papers and giving mindless briefings."

"Like what?" asked Campbell as it became obvious to him that the vice president was not enamored with the duties of the deputy chief of staff.

"Again. I have no idea. But I suspect that you are going to find out soon. I have a feeling that things are coming to a head."

"Why?"

The vice president stood. A signal to Campbell that he was dismissed.

"Things said, and more importantly, not said. But Ian, when you do find out, it is my hope you will tell me immediately. These are dangerous times we live in. Sides are being chosen and we still don't understand the rules."

CHAPTER SEVENTEEN

After leaving the vice president's residence at about 9:30 P.M., Campbell decided he needed to walk a bit to clear his head. As he hiked toward the DuPont Circle metro station, he was certain that he was the only senior staffer for the president who—at least on his own time—traveled the local area primarily by public transportation. As a poor kid who grew up in the Dorchester section of Boston, Campbell was used to taking the subway and buses and saw no reason to change now just because he had a "power" title and was invited to all the DC A-list parties.

Ten minutes into the walk and Campbell was covered in sweat. This particular hot August night in the nation's capital saw the temperature at ninety-four degrees with over 80 percent humidity.

The more he sweated, the better he felt. After leaving the Veep's home, Campbell could feel the knots starting to form in his upper shoulders from the tension, as well as the telltale signs of a spasm from his chronically bad back. The heat was more than welcome as he navigated the eclectic residents, ubiquitous protest signs, and outstanding restaurants of the area.

Once down in the system, and as he prepared to board the incoming Red Line train, Campbell's past military training subconsciously kicked in. During the last two years, the subways of DC and New York had been rocked by three terrorist explosions. Two in New York and one in Washington that had killed a total of 270 and wounded more than 600. Despite the risk and now constant fear, the vast majority of New York and DC subway riders had answered the attacks with a resounding, "Screw you," directed at the terrorists. To stop riding the systems was to tell the killers that they had won, and these riders—Campbell included—were damned if they were going to send that signal.

That said, Campbell knew from training and subsequent briefings that the safest parts of the train would be in the first or last cars. When and if the terrorists were going to send in another suicide bomber, it was common knowledge in the intelligence community that they would try to target the middle cars to cause the most death and destruction. Without even giving it a thought, Campbell got in the tail end of the last car on his way, eventually, to downtown Rosslyn, Virginia, and his one-bedroom condo at River Place.

It was exactly because he was a creature of public transportation that Campbell had bought his condo in Rosslyn in the first place. It was just a fifteen-minute walk across the Key Bridge to Georgetown, and the subway station was just two stops away from either the White House or the Pentagon.

Once home, Campbell was greeted with six phone messages, which he refused to play. The phone messages prompted him to unclip his BlackBerry from his belt and take a quick look at that. Another six messages. Three from Tammy Han, one from his assistant at the White House, one from the president's secretary, and one, ominously, from Kent Riley, President Robertson's personal attack dog.

Campbell blew them all off as he went to his refrigerator and grabbed a beer. Aside from the convenience of its location, the best thing about his condo was its balcony and its spectacular view of the Potomac, the Kennedy Center, and Washington's monuments beyond that.

Campbell perched himself at his table for two outside and watched as a United Airlines airbus, framed by the dark blue sky of dusk, traced the river on its way to Ronald Reagan Washington National Airport. He next put the cold glass of the bottle to his lips and didn't take it away until half the beer was gone.

After putting the beer back on the table he looked at the Washington Monument, and then at the White House partially obscured behind it, for a full sixty seconds before yelling, "What the fuck!"

CHAPTER EIGHTEEN

After the president retired for the evening, General Mitchell remained in the conference room and contemplated the orders he had just been given. While those orders had been verbalized by a human being in the guise of President Robertson, Mitchell was absolutely certain that they had been sent by God.

For reasons known only to Himself, the good Lord had decided that Vice President Dale must be eliminated to further His mission here on earth. Mitchell required no more information and no rationalization. The fact that the Lord was entrusting him with this highly complicated and critically important task gave him an inner peace that confirmed to him that the end-time was near and a new beginning would soon dawn.

Mitchell walked to the end of the conference room and picked up the STU (secure telephone unit) phone, and dialed a number. When the call was answered, General Mitchell immediately said, "Go secure" to the other party.

At that point, both he and the other party inserted a crypto-ignition key into their respective phone terminals. After that, Mitchell pressed the "Secure" button on his phone and waited fifteen seconds before speaking.

"Do you know who this is?" asked Mitchell.

"Yes, sir," answered the male voice.

"Good. We were quite pleased with your work regarding General Ryan. *He* was quite pleased with your past assignment. So much so, He has asked that we carry out His next mission."

"Yes, sir."

General Mitchell knew the man on the other end of the phone quite well. He had been a Special Forces Green Beret for twenty years before retiring as a master sergeant and going to work for BlackOps, the private security firm now operating in much of the world as a proxy for the U.S. Government.

After tracking his career for years through various sources, Mitchell approached him two years ago and asked if he would be willing to leave BlackOps to join their elite and sacred group. Mitchell knew the answer to his question before he asked. In the name of the Lord, the gentleman jumped at the chance and now led a team of 200 of the most dangerous, gifted, and ruthless individuals on the planet.

"It seems that He has decided that Vice President Dale has outlived her usefulness here on earth and must begin her journey toward salvation."

The other party did not respond for a number of seconds. "Are you 100 percent sure about this one, sir? Aside from the extreme difficulty of the mission, there is a real risk of exposure even if we are successful."

"You know better than to ask a question like that. This is the wish of our Lord."

"Yes, sir. My apologies."

"No apologies necessary. You have proven yourself to Him time and time again. Your place by His side in Heaven is assured."

"Thank you, sir."

"The where and the when of this operation is up to you and your team. That said, I think it would be fortuitous if the Islamists could be blamed for the assassination. Such a result will go a long way toward justifying our ultimate mission."

"Yes, sir. Consider it done."

Mitchell hung up the phone, waited a few seconds, and then removed his key from the terminal. Time to go to sleep.

CHAPTER NINETEEN

Four A.M. the next morning found Campbell sitting in his office in the West Wing staring at a note he had just taken out of his office safe. It was the note he had written three weeks prior when he had overheard the snippet of conversation between the president and General Mitchell.

The note read:

> *Thought I just heard the boss tell General Mitchell that they had been blessed with being the instruments the Lord would use to protect the Holy Land and bring about the end-time. Crazy. What the hell is that all about?*

Campbell rocked back and forth in his chair as he looked at the words, "the end-time." Since first overhearing that conversation, he had Googled everything he could find on the end-time. From the insane to the serious, he had printed reams of material on the subject. All of it now resting in his safe and all of it making him want to escape to a private island in the South Pacific, dig a very deep hole, and start crying.

Before being privy to the vice president's troubling and bizarre thoughts earlier that evening, Campbell had mostly tried to pretend that he had not heard the conversation between Mitchell and the president. With the vice president's words, that strategy was right out the window.

Before beginning his research, Campbell was aware that the end-times, or "end of days," usually referred to eschatological writings in Christianity, Judaism, and Islam. He knew that end-times is often depicted as a time of tribulation that precedes the predicted Second Coming of the Messiah, a person who will usher in the Kingdom and bring an end to suffering and evil. The specific details of this, however, depend upon the particular faith that is being studied.

In this case, however, Campbell did not have to focus on the teachings of Islam or Judaism. He knew the president's faith and knew where to look. And what he found brought him no comfort.

Most evangelical Christians accept and promote specific ideas regarding the end of the world. Campbell had been told by fundamentalist friends in the past that certain events must happen prior to the return of Jesus, and that some of these events, as stated in Matthew 24—such as wars, famine, earthquakes, persecution, false prophets, lawlessness, and a hardening of hearts—were happening now.

Beyond that, the end-times would also be signaled by the Rapture. A time when born-again Christians will literally rise from their kitchen chairs, car seats, schools, aircraft, or anywhere else they happen to be at the moment, to meet Christ in the sky. The Rapture can only happen in conjunction with the Tribulation. The seven-year period before the Second Coming of Christ during which the Antichrist will be in power.

Campbell shook his head to try and focus on what he had read and was remembering. He knew a number of strict evangelicals and fundamentalists who took these teachings very seriously. In their minds, there was no doubt that these were the words of the Lord, and their interpretation of them was literal.

Away from the ugly stereotyping by the media that the vice president had mentioned at dinner, Campbell knew these people to be great neighbors and friends who believed in their country and who always tried to live by the Golden Rule. On his last SEAL team, he had served with a fundamentalist Christian who had willingly sacrificed his life to save the lives of three of his comrades. Uncommon valor combined with uncommon devotion was the hallmark of that man and many of his beliefs. Because of that knowledge, Campbell was loath to jump to any conclusions or to condemn an entire faith.

That sympathy aside, Campbell understood that his position in the White House and his responsibility to his nation dictated that every lead had to be followed to its natural and truthful conclusion. No matter who was involved.

The deputy chief of staff sat in his chair and massaged his forehead. Were the president and General Mitchell involved in something secret? Something dangerous? Were others in the government of the United States acting in concert with them? Was there really anything to be worried about or was all of this just a product of overthinking what would ultimately prove to be an innocuous situation?

While Campbell had no idea, he also knew that the vice president was a highly accomplished person who was not given to flights of fancy. Something was spooking her and that was a red flag that could not be ignored.

With that thought, Campbell's mini coffeemaker began to sputter and spit signaling that the brew was ready. He quickly poured himself a cup and, given his continued lack of sleep, decided to drink it black instead of adding his customary cream and sugar.

As he took his first sip, his phone rang.

Campbell looked at the caller ID box on his phone and

saw that it said, UNKNOWN CALLER. Given that, as he picked up the phone, Campbell was positive who was calling.

"Good morning, General Mitchell."

Campbell was greeted by several seconds of static. Thinking maybe he had guessed wrong after all, he said, "Hello. Someone there?"

This time, a quick laugh rang in Campbell's left ear. As if a minor bit of gamesmanship had just been won. "Thought you would be there, Navy. There's been a slight change of plans. When you are ready . . . which had better be in five minutes . . . there will be a town car waiting outside the ground-floor entrance of West Exec to take you to Andrews Air Force Base. Once you get there, you will be taken to an aircraft. All of this is close hold, so finish your cup of coffee and get your ass into that car."

Before Campbell could even answer, Mitchell's voice had been replaced by a click and then silence. General Mitchell may have had a number of positive attributes, thought Campbell, but warm and fuzzy were not two of them.

As Campbell threw the files back into his safe he smiled with the thought that Andrews Air Force Base was at least a forty-minute drive from the White House and that he could probably take a quick catnap in the back of the town car.

After going to the bathroom before starting his journey, Campbell hustled downstairs to the ground floor of the West Wing and was just walking past the desk manned by a Uniform Division member of the Secret Service, when Kent Riley came bursting through the double doors leading to West Executive Avenue—the most exclusive of streets located between the West Wing of the White House and the gothic Eisenhower Executive Office Building.

The beefy and balding Riley stopped dead in his tracks as he saw Campbell coming toward him.

Riley looked down at his watch and then up at Campbell with a sneer. "Here a little early for the senior staff meeting, aren't you, Ian?"

Since he had first met him, Campbell had nothing but contempt for Riley. He had quickly categorized him as one of many conservative "chicken-hawks" running around the nation's capital. Men who would never slow or "demean" their fast-rising academic or political careers to serve their nation in the military or one of its intelligence services, but who still thought nothing of sending the "lower classes" to fight and die on foreign battlefields.

Riley was well aware of Campbell's exemplary and heroic military service and had quickly surmised that Campbell had little use for him. While he would admit it to no one, Riley was intimidated by Campbell, knew the president was fond of him, and saw him as a threat to his career and to the imminent plans of his president. Because of that, Riley, like a school-yard bully, used rudeness and bluster to disguise his intimidation.

"You're here," answered Campbell with no expression on his face.

"I called you last night, Ian."

"I know."

Riley narrowed his eyes. "You're supposed to call me back."

"Why?"

"Because I'm the fuckin' strategic advisor and I outrank you."

Campbell shook his head as he looked Riley up and down. "You know, Kent, I guess it's a good thing you never tried to go into the military."

"Why's that?"

"Because if you did, you would have been fragged by your own men on your very first night patrol."

The Secret Service agent at the desk failed to suppress a laugh as he tried hard to focus on the computer screen in front of him.

Riley looked down at the agent and then back up at Campbell. "Whatever Mr. Big, Bad Navy SEAL. Where are you going?"

"Out," said Campbell as he purposely walked into Riley on his way out the door toward the waiting town car.

CHAPTER TWENTY

Eileen Dale lay in her bed staring at the ceiling before turning to look at the digital clock on her nightstand. It was now four twenty in the morning and she'd had no more than thirty minutes' sleep since walking Campbell out the door.

Instinctively, she moved her arm across the left side of the bed but found it empty. Her husband of thirty-eight years was, at this moment, up in New York City, presumably sleeping comfortably in preparation for a speech he was giving at 10:00 A.M. at the Waldorf Astoria.

Like her, he had once been a two-term United States senator. His home state of Oklahoma would have elected him forever, but after twelve years of partisan bickering, he tired of the hateful politics and decided to accept a highly lucrative seven-figure offer to become the CEO of a very powerful telecommunications association in Washington.

Over the course of their marriage, they had been blessed with two wonderful children and all the things benefiting one of Washington's best known "power couples." Her husband was loving, attentive, faithful (a rare trait for most male politicians), and totally devoted to her and the kids.

Sadly, she knew the empty left side of the bed had signaled an evolving change in him. Once she became vice president, he had grown more distant. His male ego still seemed to be having a difficult time accepting that his wife was now part of history as the first female vice president.

As the political and media spotlight sought her out, he just as quickly shrunk back into the shadows and threw himself more and more into his career. She understood it was just a defense mechanism, but that understanding did little to ease her loneliness or pain. She missed and needed her husband.

She reached over, switched on the light of her nightstand, and grabbed the phone. She then looked down at the number of the Waldorf that he had left her and dialed it.

"Good morning," answered an upbeat female voice. "The Waldorf Astoria. How may I help you?"

"I'd like the room of Richard Dale please."

After four rings and just before the hotel answering machine would have picked up, her husband answered.

"Hello."

"Hi, Richard. It's me."

She could hear him moving around and most likely trying to figure out what time it was.

"Eileen. Sweetheart. Is everything all right? It's past four in the morning."

"I know, dear. I'm sorry. I just wanted to call to say . . . I just wanted to say . . ."

"What's wrong, sweetheart?" he asked in a much stronger voice.

Eileen Dale's instinct and sixth sense was telling her that everything was wrong but she did not want to sound like a raving lunatic to the man she loved. She was not yet prepared to share the dark thoughts she harbored regarding the president and some of his minions.

That said, as much as she was the vice president of the United States, she was still a woman. Still a human being who was frightened and needed to be comforted.

"Nothing, Richard. It's silly, I guess. When you went out the door yesterday I forgot to tell you that I love you."

Her husband laughed warmly into the phone. "I love you too, sweetheart. I really do. Now why don't we both get back to sleep and I'll see you tonight."

Dale felt a tear run down her face as she took a deep breath. "Okay, dear. That's right. We'll see each other tonight . . . won't we?"

"Of course, Eileen. Geez, what's got you so shaken?"

Dale quickly wiped her eyes with the back of her right hand. "Just politics of the day. You remember that stuff. Good night, Richard. I love you."

CHAPTER TWENTY-ONE

Upon his arrival at Andrews Air Force Base, Campbell was escorted to a large hangar far from prying eyes. As deputy chief of staff to the president, he had been to the sprawling base a number of times but had never seen this particular building.

As the town car rolled to a stop, Campbell looked toward the east and saw the first hints of dawn breaking over the horizon. He then turned his head and looked toward the brightly lit and extremely well-guarded hangar. Aside from the expected assortment of Secret Service agents—Presidential Protection, Uniform Division, and Emergency Response Team—there was a large contingent of air force commandos. Everything about this hangar said "Go Away" and Campbell wished he could.

Before exiting the car, he saw General Mitchell quickly waddling toward him with a disapproving look upon his face. The general grabbed the door handle and yanked the back door open.

As soon as he did, Campbell felt the heat from the tarmac envelope his body. Another humid, blast-furnace day was about to assault Washington.

"Let's move it, Navy. POTUS is waiting."

Campbell thanked the driver for the ride and then stood next to the general. He smiled slightly as he looked at Mitchell. By the general saying "POTUS," he was trying to convey that he was hip to the shorthand some in the White House used for *President Of The United States*. Personally, Campbell always used "The President" or "The President of the United States," and thought that anyone who used POTUS was grandstanding and trying to impress someone else within earshot.

Campbell nodded. "So, are you going to tell me where we are off to this fine morning? I guess the new facility you mentioned yesterday in the Oval, but where exactly?"

As way of answering, Mitchell smartly did an about-face and started to walk toward the aircraft in the hangar.

Campbell shook his head and chuckled. "Games upon games," he said to himself as he shuffled behind the four-star general.

As he walked, he looked up at the blue, white, and silver air force aircraft. The common misperception among the public was that only the huge Boeing 747-200B that the president flew aboard (there were two such 747s) was called Air Force One. The fact of the matter was that *any* air force fixed-wing aircraft that the president flew in was designated by the radio call sign Air Force One.

All such aircraft were flown and maintained by the Presidential Airlift Group and were assigned to the Air Mobility Command's 89th Airlift Wing. That wing, in turn, being hosted by Andrews's 316th Wing.

The large aircraft looming before Campbell was not one of the 747s but a smaller Boeing 737-700 series. The air force called the aircraft a C-40B. While the body of the C-40B was identical to that of the commercial 737-700, much beyond that was different.

The C-40 had state-of-the-art avionics equipment, an integrated global positioning and flight management system, and a heads-up display. The aircraft also had the very latest in traffic collision avoidance and enhanced weather radar.

The cabin was equipped with a crew rest area, a distinguished visitor compartment with sleep accommodations, a small conference room, two galleys and business-class seating with work tables. The aircraft had been converted from the commercial version to an office in the sky for senior military and government leaders.

Because of who it flew, communications aboard the C-40B was of paramount importance. With that in mind, the aircraft provided broadband data/video transmit and receive capability as well as clear and secure voice and data communication. Such capability gave its VIP government and military guests the unique ability to conduct business or war anywhere around the world using on-board Internet and local area network connections, improved telephones, satellites, television monitors, and facsimile and copy machines.

When he first took the job at the White House, Campbell had made it a point to learn as much as possible about these aircraft. He did this for two reasons. First, because his military and intelligence training taught him the value of knowing everything about any ship, aircraft, or vehicle he was aboard. Second, while as a young boy growing up in poverty, Campbell had—for reasons he had never figured out—developed a serious interest in aircraft and spacecraft. Before life stomped on his early dreams, he had even fantasized about being an astronaut.

When things would get unbearably bad at home, or when his family had gotten evicted again for nonpayment of rent, Campbell would get on the "T" and take the train from Dorchester to Logan Airport. Once there, he would spend hours watching the planes take off and land, speaking with pilots, and on rare occasions, being allowed to walk inside a cockpit or plane by a kind flight attendant or pilot who sensed that all was not right in his world.

As Campbell walked up the stairs to board the C-40B, he remembered some of the background of the aircraft, but such details were best pushed far to the back of his mind. He was about to be center stage and knew he would have to be at the top of his game to remotely keep pace with the president and Mitchell.

As he walked into the aircraft, Campbell was met by an attractive female air force sergeant. "May I get you a coffee, Mr. Campbell?"

"That won't be necessary, Sergeant," said Mitchell as he walked up behind her. "There is already coffee and juice in the conference room where Mr. Campbell needs to be . . . now."

Campbell smiled at the steward as he stepped around her and followed Mitchell down the aisle. As expected, once inside the conference room for six, Campbell saw the president sitting at the head of the table looking at a copy of the *Washington Post*. Beside the *Post* were some other newspapers as well as the President's Daily Briefing.

Without looking up from the sports page, the president said, "Grab yourself a cup of coffee and park it. Word has it that you haven't been getting much sleep of late."

"Thank you, Mr. President."

After getting his coffee and a plain donut from a table at the far end of the room, Campbell sat two chairs from the president, took a quick sip of his coffee and yelped, "Ouch!"

The president finally looked up and laughed. "Sorry, Ian. I like really hot coffee. I think when they bring it in here, it's still boiling."

"No, worries, Mr. President. Taste buds are really overrated anyway."

At the conclusion of the sentence, Mitchell walked into the room and softly closed the door behind him.

As he did, Campbell looked around and made a gesture toward the front of the plane. "I'm a bit surprised that we are taking this aircraft. I thought when I got here, I'd be getting on one of the 747s."

While Campbell had directed the statement toward the president, he was not surprised, but still annoyed, when Mitchell answered.

"You should know better than that, Navy. That ride is way too conspicuous. Brings us attention we don't need this A.M."

"Besides," added the still-smiling president, "you've been on those 747s so much, I thought I'd mix it up for you. Kind of a present for you coming on this trip."

"Thank you, Mr. President. My pleasure."

As he answered, he felt the presence of Mitchell standing behind him. A presence that made him more than a little nervous. For that reason, and to lay down a marker, Campbell spun around in the high-backed black leather office chair and looked up at the four-star general.

"I'm sorry, sir. Is this your seat?"

Mitchell looked over at the president and smirked before looking down at Campbell. "Not at all, Navy. You sit right there. I'm just going to grab a juice and then I'll join you boys."

As Mitchell did that, Campbell took a quick glance at the president who had once again lowered his head to read. Ironically, as he focused on Robertson, Campbell had memories of being in the principal's office back in elementary school waiting to be disciplined for some prank.

How simple it was back then, thought Campbell as he waited to be told something.

Three hundred yards from the president's aircraft, a two-man sniper team finished going about their business.

If someone were standing five feet from them, they would have been hard-pressed to spot the two. Hiding on the edge of a tree line, both were covered head to toe in grass brush capes, had camouflaged faces, and seemed all but invisible to the naked eye.

Both men had been snipers in Iraq with most of their work having been done in Fallujah. Each man had recorded over one hundred confirmed kills. As they had been psychologically screened before beginning sniper training, neither man felt remorse over the killings. Nor did they feel elation. Their job was to find and kill the enemy before he found and killed their comrades and that is exactly what they did—better than almost anyone on earth. They took great pride in their skill, in their dedication to their country, and for the hundreds of American lives they saved. Beyond that, it was simply a job.

A sniper team consists of two people, the sniper and the spotter. In this case, both men hidden from the view of those protecting Air Force One were fully qualified snipers. The older of the two generally took on the responsibility of the sniper. But, as they had been together for years, it was not uncommon for them to rotate responsibilities. They did this first, to maintain proficiency, and second, to reduce eye fatigue during protracted missions.

While it was the sniper's job to take the one shot to get the one kill, it was the spotter's job to detect, observe, and assign the target. He also had to read the wind, make the calculations for distance, the angle of the shot, correct for atmospheric conditions, and gauge the lead for a moving target. Beyond that, he had the additional burden of being the security for the team. For that reason, he usually carried an assault rifle as well as his own sniper rifle.

This particular early morning in Maryland saw the team carrying two SIG SG 550-1 sniper rifles as well as one M-4 assault rifle. The 550 was manufactured in Switzerland and was a .223 Remington, semiautomatic detachable magazine weapon. While it was mostly the choice of police forces around the world, this battle-tested sniper team preferred it for its simplicity, reliability, and size.

As Air Force One started to roll from the hangar toward the runway, the younger of the two snipers whispered, "Did you get the shots?"

The older man laughed quietly. "Yeah, I got them. First time in my career I've used a long-range camera instead of a rifle, but orders are orders. Let's get back and report in."

With that, the two-man team broke down the $6,000 camera with the long-range lens, and quickly and quietly melted away from the area.

CHAPTER TWENTY-TWO

As Air Force One leveled off at 37,000 feet, the president finally put down his briefing papers and looked up at Campbell. He studied him for several seconds before speaking.

"Do you consider yourself to be a loyal man, Ian?"

Campbell focused quickly on the president, then looked at Mitchell who was smiling with the question, then looked out one of the windows just over Mitchell's shoulder at the cotton-white clouds bathed in sunshine and topped by the deep blue of the sky at altitude, then back at the president. As his eyes traveled from point to point to point and back, his mind tried to contemplate the traps hidden in such a question.

Campbell cleared his throat. "Yes, Mr. President."

"How so?" asked the commander in chief as he rose from the small conference table to get himself some juice.

"How so?" repeated Campbell.

The president was well-known for being a bit of a clothes-horse. He took great pride in his appearance, and Campbell guessed the black suit with white pinstripes the president was now wearing had to be worth over three thousand dollars. Beneath the suit was his usual, highly pressed white French-cuff shirt, centered by a soft-gold power tie. The whole ensemble being complemented by a matching soft-gold handkerchief in the front breast pocket of the suit.

"Yes, Ian," said the president with a smile. "How so? How do you consider yourself to be a loyal man?"

Campbell shrugged. "I guess the obvious answer is that I'm loyal to my country, loyal to my family, and loyal to my friends."

The president sat back down and placed his juice into a cup holder built into the conference table.

"Excellent, Ian. Very good answer. I'd expect nothing less from a man with such a highly decorated military background."

Campbell felt himself being steered toward a corner and was powerless to stop the momentum. "Thank you, sir."

"Understanding that, are you loyal to anything else, Ian?"

Campbell looked back at the president but did not answer.

The president rubbed his hands together to remove some of the moisture from his glass. "Let me make this a bit easier for you, Ian. Do you believe in God?"

"Yes, Mr. President. I do. I think you knew that before you hired me."

"Wonderful. Of course you do," said the president as he stole a quick glance at the general.

"And do you believe in Jesus Christ, Ian?"

Campbell nodded ever so slowly without speaking.

The president turned up the candlepower of his smile. "Great. And do you consider yourself to be a good Christian?"

Campbell permitted himself the luxury of a faint smile. "I have my flaws, Mr. President, but I try to be a good person."

The president let out a small laugh. "What is a human without flaws? My mistakes in life would most likely fill a phone book. Perfection is left to our Creator, Ian."

"Yes, Mr. President. I suppose that's true."

"There's no supposing involved, Navy," interrupted Mitchell with a raised voice and narrowed eyes. "Our Lord and Savior is perfect in every way."

The president tapped on the table to bring Ian's attention back to him. "The general makes a very good point, Ian. But I'm sure you are in complete agreement with his statement anyway. I'm guessing you just misspoke when you said 'I suppose.' "

Over the course of the last year, Campbell had had a number of real discussions with the president. Some of them personal, some innocuous, with most related to the business of the White House. In all of those discussions, none began as surreal as the dialogue now taking place in the rarified air of Air Force One.

"Yes, sir," said Campbell. "God is obviously perfect."

"Splendid," said the president. "And that brings me back to my question of loyalty. Are you loyal to God, Ian?"

Even though the air-conditioning was keeping the conference room at sixty-six degrees, Campbell started to feel uncomfortably warm. "Am I *loyal* to God?"

"Yes, Ian," answered the president as the smile dissolved from his face. "Are you loyal to God? Or more to the point for the purposes of this discussion, are you loyal to Jesus Christ?"

Campbell shook his head. "Well, I guess I've never thought of loyalty in quite that way, Mr. President."

The president leaned back in his chair. "Oh, but you should, Ian. You just said you are loyal to our country, loyal to your family, and loyal to your friends. Is that right?"

Again, Campbell nodded without speaking.

"And you said you believe in God and believe in our Lord and Savior, Jesus Christ."

"Yes, sir," said Campbell softly.

"So," said the president leaning back toward the table

and Campbell, "if you believe in God, then you have to believe that He created our nation, He created your family, and He created your friends. He is also responsible for this earth we are now flying over and for our universe. Isn't that the only conclusion one can draw if one truly believes in God?"

"Yes, Mr. President."

"Okay. So to try and complete the circle on this, where do you rank your loyalty to Jesus Christ?"

"Sir?" asked Campbell stalling for a moment of time that he knew would bring him no clairvoyance.

"On a list that would include our nation, your family, your friends, and Jesus Christ, to which or to whom would you be most loyal?"

Campbell could hear his heart pounding in his ears as he looked at the malevolent and possibly maniacal stares of the president and Mitchell.

After several seconds of awkward silence, he said, "I guess I've never really given that question any thought."

General Mitchell slammed his fist down so hard on the table that the president's glass flew from the cup holder and fell to the beige-carpeted floor.

"Well, you'd better give it some thought, Navy. And you'd better give it some thought right this fuckin' second."

CHAPTER TWENTY-THREE

Rachel Hiatt sat in the back of the forty-two-foot Sundancer cabin cruiser and tried as hard as she could not to throw up.

Under a cloudless early morning sky, the boat had only seconds earlier entered the intracoastal waterway on its journey to the Atlantic Ocean. As it softly pitched and yawed to all but invisible waves, she could already feel the coffee she had grabbed from the ostentatious clubhouse at the Point start to slosh around as it sought the nearest exit.

As she quickly leaned over the side of the boat and let her body violently deposit the coffee into the blue-green waves of the waterway, Maria Gonzalez and the owner of the cabin cruiser looked down at her from the cockpit and started laughing.

"I'm sorry to laugh, Ms. Hiatt," said the owner of the boat. "But if the almost-flat conditions of the intracoastal are going to make you sick, then I suspect you are going to hate the three-foot swells we are going to hit once we are in the ocean."

Pedro Gonzalez turned from looking at Rachel to stare back over the bow as he proceeded at ten knots toward the open ocean. As a first cousin to Eric, he had been as worried as the rest of the family with the news that Eric, Tom, and Tom's boat had gone missing. Until he had gotten the phone call from Maria and Rachel the night before, he was at a loss as to what to do. Like Rachel, the Aventura police had blown him off with bureaucratic language which translated to, "You are on your own, buddy."

Before the Miami real-estate market imploded, Gonzalez had managed to make himself a few million dollars flipping multiple high-priced condos. He got out just before the bubble burst and decided to reward himself for his opportune timing by buying the toy he was now piloting.

Since he was a child, Gonzalez had always had a love for boats, and decided, at forty-two years of age, and with a full bank account, he should indulge himself for at least a few years before figuring out the next chapter of his life. Looking for a missing relative was the last thing he expected to do with such a luxury item.

Rachel sat back up, wiped her mouth with a napkin she had picked up with her coffee, and slowly made her way to the head below to wash her face. Two minutes later, she was back out with her breath smelling of the Listerine she had found in the tiny cabinet under the sink.

"Sorry about that," she said as she smiled up at Pedro and Maria. "Normally, I handle the water a bit better. I'm not sure why it's bothering me now."

"Most likely a combination of lack of sleep and stress," answered Pedro in perfect, nonaccented English. Like Eric and Maria, he was a transplant from Venezuela. He had come to the United States to get an MBA from Stanford, and had never looked back. As much as he missed home, he would not go back until the murderous dictator now in power was forced out of office by the people who suffered under his totalitarian rule.

Rachel nodded at Pedro and winked at Maria. "I hope that's all. If not, you guys might have to throw me overboard to save yourselves from my convulsions."

Even in the midst of her great worry, Maria managed a full and natural laugh. Rachel reached over and touched her arm in response as she took a few seconds to ponder her two boat mates.

A combination of her discussions with Tom and her own research had told her that Venezuela was one of the most class-conscious countries on Earth. While the wealthy were loath to admit it, many of them did think of the poor and the middle-class as second-class citizens.

Like most Latin American countries, Venezuela's population was made up of about 5 to 10 percent elite, with the other 90 to 95 percent being at or below the poverty line.

During his first run for office, the thug who ran the country and now proudly aligned himself with Islamic terrorists, used the elitism of the wealthy to great effect to openly and honestly swing the vast majority of the country his way. Since that time, he stole a couple of elections, while making a mockery of the Constitution, Congress, and the Supreme Court, before finally ending the pretense and installing himself as dictator for life.

Next to Rachel were two distinct examples of that Venezuelan wealth paradigm. Pedro—as Maria had related his and her history on the drive to the marina—came from an upper-middle-class family from Caracas, while she came from one of the ranchos that ringed the capital city. As her only means of salvation, she had made her way to the United States as the maid for a former cabinet minister and his wife who fled the country to escape the retribution of the dictator.

While the cabinet minister and his wife were quite nice and refined, they still expected Maria to work at least ten hours a day, six days a week. It was during one of her days off that one of her friends, a fellow maid, had taken her down the street to window-shop at the exclusive Bal Harbor Shops of North Miami.

While seated at an Italian restaurant near the front of the shops, Maria's friend discreetly pointed out two men at the next table. One of the men, who was dressed in an elegant blue suit, kept looking at Maria, trying to catch her eye.

Clearly, he succeeded, thought Rachel as she looked at Maria's round belly.

Eric, like Pedro, had come from some money and was educated in the United States. After trying and failing at a few businesses, he somehow managed to hook up with Tom and his dreams to salvage treasure from the deep.

Pedro interrupted her thoughts as he held up the directions given to him by Maria. "With any luck, we'll be at this spot in about an hour and a half."

Maria looked at the paper as she reached for Rachel's hand.

"What do you think we find in this place?" she asked as her eyes started to tear up again.

"Trouble," answered Pedro as he increased their speed.

CHAPTER TWENTY-FOUR

Campbell knew what the expected answer was and decided then and there to tell the president and Mitchell anything they wanted to hear to try to further earn their trust. The last two days had been a blur of inconceivable information and innuendo and he was still not convinced that he was not having some kind of detailed and elaborate nightmare from which he would awake at any moment.

"Jesus Christ, Mr. President. I'm far from the perfect Christian, but I do believe in our Lord and I do believe that He created Heaven and Earth. And if one thinks that way, then clearly, our loyalty has to be to Him before all others."

The president folded his hands. "I suspected you thought that way, Ian, but to tell you the truth, I've also had my doubts. It's nice to have you finally confirm it."

As the president spoke, Mitchell walked around the table to pick up the president's glass from the now-damp carpet.

"No need to do that, Wayne. One of the stewards will get it when we are done here."

"No, sir, Mr. President. I made the mess and it's my responsibility to clean it up."

The president chuckled to himself as he ran his hand through his perfectly coifed white hair.

"There you go, Ian. What do you think of that? A

four-star general on his knee cleaning up a mess he made."

Campbell looked down at the blue-suited figure mopping up the juice with a handful of paper napkins, and then back up at the president.

"I'd say it's a good lesson for us all, Mr. President. That we need to clean up the messes we make."

The president sat up straight in his chair as if someone had just sent a jolt of electricity through his body. "Exactly, Ian. That's exactly the point."

The president then stood and pointed to a map of the world framed on the windowless side of the conference room. "And what about the world we live in, Ian? Isn't this the biggest mess of all?"

Campbell shifted his chair to keep the general in peripheral sight as he answered the president. "I'd say it's looking a bit more hopeless with each passing day."

"And why's that?"

"Uncertainty. Chaos. War."

The president laughed out loud as he tapped the far right-hand side of the map. "Oh, come on, Ian. No need for such a diplomatic bullshit answer. We are all men here. We are all sons of our Lord."

The president then turned his head and motioned at Mitchell. "Wayne, why don't you grab a chair and tell our former Navy SEAL why the world is such a mess."

The general stood, placed the fallen glass on a tray on the counter, wiped his hands with some dry napkins, and sat opposite Campbell. "Yes, sir, Mr. President. My pleasure."

He then bore his eyes into Campbell. "Navy, the world's a mess for numerous reasons. Reasons that continue to threaten traditional Christian values and the security of our people. First and foremost, it's the fuckin' Muslims and the collection of terrorists that speak for them around the globe. Next, it's the liberals. They have taken over our media, our schools, and our colleges. They hate Christianity and want it purged from our union. Next, these very same liberals, both ours and those in Europe and elsewhere, think it's their sworn duty to not only protect Islamist killers, but to give them safe haven into our countries. Wouldn't want to hurt the feelings of a future suicide bomber. In addition, the liberals think that borders should be banned as they seek ways to make the world one giant multicultural state. An idiotic idea that flies in the face of what the Islamists have in mind . . . which is to kill them all. Next, we have Mexico. The drug cartels have bought most of that government—along with a number of our own members of Congress—and Mexico is escalating the invasion of its army into the sovereign territory of the United States to kill and kidnap our citizens. As they do that, the corrupt in our very own Congress insist on sending Mexico billions in aid so they can continue the attacks. Further south, Venezuela, with the help of Iran, has gone nuclear while much of the rest of the continent is under Socialist rule and despises the United States . . ."

The general paused and looked over at the president.

"No, no," said the president with a wave. "Please continue, Wayne. I'll add my two cents in a minute."

"Yes, sir, Mr. President," said the general, who then launched back into his monologue.

"Speaking of Iran, try as we might, the world was unable to prevent that country from building its now-estimated ten nuclear weapons. Because they went nuclear, the Sunni Islamic countries of Egypt and Saudi Arabia have now done the same to counter the threat they feel from that Shiite majority country. Because Egypt and Saudi Arabia now have nuclear weapons, Israel is going bat-shit as it sits perched in the middle of total annihilation. Worst of all, and to complete the circle, the nut jobs that run Iran—"

"Please," interrupted the president, "allow me to finish the thought."

"Of course," answered the general as if he were responding to a cue he had heard a number of times in the past.

"Ian," said the president barely above a whisper, "what do you know about the 'Twelvers' who make up the majority of Shiite Muslims?"

Campbell shook his head. "Not too much, Mr. President. I suspect my SEAL team dealt with a few from time to time on the battlefield. Beyond that, I guess I don't know as much as I should."

The president nodded in response. "Yes, Ian. The fact that you have encountered these people up close and personal is one of the reasons you are now on this trip. But I'll get to that at a later point. As the general just started to mention, our main focus needs to be on the Islamic Republic of Iran and its demented leadership. That leadership is firmly in the Twelver camp. In a nutshell, Twelvers make up about 90 percent of the entire population of Iran. They are also the majority in Iraq and Azerbaijan, and represent substantial numbers in Afghanistan, Turkey, Pakistan, Lebanon, Syria, India, and Bahrain. Twelvers believe that the third son was the rightful ruler of Islam and get their name because they believe that there are twelve Imams. The Twelvers believe the last of these Imams is still alive and has been hiding in a cave for more than one thousand years. Most importantly, as we have seen in our intelligence briefings, and even on some of our news shows, those who run Iran have, with growing frequency, been asking 'God' to hasten the arrival of Imam Al-Mahdi—the last of the Imams now hiding in a cave."

"Is that something that can be hastened?"

"Oh yes, Ian. In their minds, most definitely. Of course, to hasten his return, they would have to create the right conditions. Unfortunately for all of us, those conditions are war, bloodshed, and worldwide chaos. They plan to bring this about with the destruction of Israel, the United States, and other countries that oppose their beliefs. Those who run Iran have called Israel a 'tumor' that must be 'wiped off the map.' Clearly, they plan to go after Israel and the West with nuclear weapons. Do not forget, Ian, that these people do not fear death. The fact is, they welcome it. For them, nuclear war is a small price to be paid to return the Mahdi and open the gates to Heaven. These Twelvers literally believe that we are the Antichrist and must be exterminated."

Campbell's head was swimming from the information and his own thoughts. His earlier conversation with the vice president was moving front and center. "And what is the endgame for having the Mahdi return? What happens then?"

General Mitchell let out a grunt with the question as the president answered. "It's all quite simple, really. The Imam Al-Mahdi will first come back to Mecca, and then go through Medina, with his final stop being Kufa, Iraq. At that point, he has taken over the world and has created an Islamic caliphate where, as had been said by the Twelvers, he will offer the religion of Islam to the Jews and the Christians still left alive. If they accept, they will be spared. If they refuse, they will be put to death."

"Mr. President. I guess with you telling me all of this, you believe these Twelvers to be in a position to carry out their plan."

The president was now walking laps around the conference table as he spoke. "That's right, Ian. Absolutely. This is a very dangerous sect. So dangerous, in fact, that back in 1979 the Ayatollah Khomeini not only banned them, but tried to kill the leadership as he felt they were too volatile and would hurt the cause of Islam. Well . . . that was then and this is now. Those that lead the Twelvers believe, without a doubt, that neither the United States, nor the rest of the world has, and I quote, 'the stomach for a long or even a short war. Victory will be ours.'"

The president paused as he stood opposite Campbell. "And you know what, Ian? They are absolutely right. Our Congress does not have the stomach for it. Our European allies don't have the stomach for it. Nobody does really except maybe Israel and . . ."

Campbell obediently bit on the dangling hook.

"And?"

The president resumed his seat at the head of the table. "And . . . those who truly place their loyalty to Jesus Christ before all others."

Campbell sat silent for a few moments as he felt the beginning of what promised to be a throbbing headache.

In those few seconds, he was transfixed with the thought that but for a few differences, what the president had just described with regard to hastening the return of the Imam Al-Mahdi, was basically the same formula pushed by fundamentalist Christians to hasten the return to Earth of Jesus Christ. Obviously the president and Mitchell understood that, and just as obviously to Campbell's way of thinking, both men would have violently squashed such a comparison because in their minds, Islam was a false religion with Christianity being the only true faith.

"But," said Mitchell to bring down the curtain on this act of insanity, "as you just stated that your loyalty is to Christ before all others, then such information must bring you great comfort."

Campbell nodded at Mitchell but then turned his head to face the president. "I'm sure, as I learn more about the situation, my comfort level will continue to grow."

President Robertson reached over and patted Campbell on the shoulder before standing.

"It will, Ian. It truly will. But as you work to digest all of this information, keep in mind the one absolute. That being, under no circumstances can we allow these fanatics to destroy the State of Israel. It's our solemn duty to protect the birthplace of our Savior."

"Amen to that, Mr. President," said Mitchell who stood with the president.

"Now if you don't mind, Ian," said the president to a now-standing Campbell, "I'm going to go to my room for a few moments to freshen up before we land in Florida."

CHAPTER TWENTY-FIVE

As Air Force One was crossing into Florida airspace, two homeless men were quietly rummaging through a trash container near the Mayflower Hotel on Connecticut Avenue.

The Mayflower was one of Washington's most prestigious hotels and had played host to the rich and famous for well over fifty years. As such, it did not look good to have homeless people loitering in front of the establishment. Tended to make the wealthy clientele uncomfortable as they headed to or from their highly priced rooms or suites.

With that thought in mind, the head of the security for the hotel sent a newly hired member of his detail out to encourage the men to move it on down the road. The hotel detective had spent twelve years as a DC cop and felt he had a pretty good way with the destitute and homeless. As he approached the two men, he widened his eyes and slowed his gait. Longtime law-enforcement personnel generally gained a sixth sense from the streets and his was now telling him that what was before him was not quite right. For some reason, the image did not fit the template that had been chiseled into his mind by his decade plus of work as a police officer.

One of the men was black while the other looked to be Hispanic. While that fit the pattern for many of the homeless in DC, that was one of the few things that did as the former cop walked up to them. His experience had taught him that, for the most part, the homeless—especially homeless men—tended to be lone wolves. They liked to operate on their own and tended to be fearful and untrusting of other homeless men.

The fact that these two men were acting in concert to rifle through a trash can was a bit unusual. The fact that it was August in Washington and they both had on long winter coats was also somewhat of a red flag.

As he came within about ten feet, both men stopped what they were doing and turned to face him. The black man was the taller of the two—about six foot two by the detective's estimate—with the Hispanic male being a bit wider. Both were wearing deeply soiled clothes and both were covered in dirt. Almost too much dirt.

As the hotel detective got within three feet of them he was hit with a powerful smell of alcohol and body odor.

"Hey, guys," said the detective with a big smile. "Aren't you up a bit early for breakfast?"

The tall black man staggered on his feet slightly as he faced his questioner. "Is there a problem, mister? We're not hurting no one. We're just looking for some food and a few stray smokes."

The detective noticed the stagger, but when he looked into the man's eyes he saw something much different. The eyes were anything but out of control. They were clear, sharp, and constantly surveying the area even as the question was asked. But, more than that, there was a strange lifeless quality about them. Much the same as looking into the dead, uncaring eyes of a circling shark.

The detective had seen eyes like that in the past. Rarely, but he had seen them. Eyes that had belonged to a select few gang members who had taken great pride in not only the number of murders they committed, but in the savage brutality of the crimes. Stone-cold killers.

The detective not only stopped his progression, but

instinctively backed up a step and assumed a defensive posture.

"No," he said as he continued to smile. "Nothing wrong with that at all. It's just that I'm new on the job and my bosses at the hotel asked me to move you guys away from the property. I'm just trying not to get fired. You know how it is."

"What's a matter," the black man slurred. "We givin' that place a bad name?"

As his buddy spoke, the Hispanic man slowly placed his hands into the outside pockets of his grimy black cloth coat. The detective caught the movement out of the corner of his eye and retreated another couple of feet.

"Hey, I'm not sure what they are thinking. I'm just do-ing what I'm told."

The black man stepped closer and offered a cool smile. "What's the problem, bro? You one of us. You doing the bidding of the man, now?"

"No. I'm not doing anyone's bidding. I'm just trying to earn a living so I can take care of my family."

The Hispanic man kept his hands firmly in his pockets as he spoke for the first time.

"Oh, you got a family. That's good. That's nice. Fami-ly's all important. Man should take care of his family. That's his duty . . . as a man. You agree?"

The detective nodded as his mouth started to go dry.

"Well," continued the Hispanic, "I hear this neighbor-hood ain't really safe no more. Crime is rising fast around here. If I had me a family and all, I might get me a job somewhere else. Fast like."

"Sounds like good advice to me, bro," agreed the black man. "Real good. In the meantime, to show you we're good guys—and so as not to get you in trouble or nothing—we're gonna leave now. Okay?" He then pointed around the corner. "ABC News has got much better trash anyway."

With that, both men started to walk toward him. The black man glided past, while the Hispanic man deliberately grazed his shoulder into the detective as he walked by.

To the detective, it felt as if he had just brushed up against a slab of steel. As the two men shuffled forward and took a right down DeSales Street, the detective knew that he had just been given a reprieve from a death sentence. He had no idea what he had just walked into, and he did not really care.

With absolutely nothing to go on but a feeling and his past training, he decided—then and there—that he was going to quit as soon as he walked back into the hotel. Beyond quitting, he also decided to move his family—that night—to his brother's house down in Raleigh, North Carolina.

Second chances were few in life, and he had just been given one.

As the flow of traffic on Connecticut Avenue increased with government and corporate workers driving to the office, none noticed the small electronic device disguised beneath the bottom of the trash can just visited by the homeless men. Nor would they notice its mirror opposite on the trash can across the street.

CHAPTER TWENTY-SIX

Fifteen miles to the east of Miami, and Rachel Hiatt was actually feeling better. A combination of the great weather, the warm ocean breeze, and the adrenaline seeping into her system made her seasickness but a bad memory.

Wearing a white tank top, beige khaki shorts, and leather sandals, she now lounged in the back of the boat with her eyes closed as she let the strong sun beat down on her pale skin. As she relaxed, her mind did the normal thing and wandered.

She thought about Maria, she thought about the police, but mostly, she thought about her brother lost somewhere in this great expanse of water. She smiled to herself as she remembered his infectious laugh and . . .

"Ms. Hiatt. You need to come up here immediately."

Rachel snapped open her eyes and tried to get them to focus on Pedro. The minutes under the sun had made things somewhat diffuse and hazy.

"What's wrong?" she asked as she centered her gaze on his deeply tanned face.

"Please come up here and take a look for yourself."

Rachel moved as fast as she could and joined Pedro in the cockpit. What she saw made her grip the railing all that much harder.

Fast approaching from the east were two Navy Mark

V Special Operations Craft. Each boat was eighty-two feet long, almost eighteen feet wide, was armored, and looked like the military equivalent of a souped-up, ultrasleek, very fast "cigarette" boat favored by certain drug runners.

Each vessel had a crew of five and was capable of carrying up to sixteen passengers. The passengers in this case were Navy SEALs. Each boat was equipped with 7.62mm Gatling guns, as well as twin 12.7mm and 25mm guns and Stinger missiles.

The two Mark Vs were closing on the cabin cruiser at well over fifty knots. Fearing a collision, Pedro brought his boat to a quick stop as he stared wide-eyed at the fast-attack boats coming his way with large American flags flapping wildly in the speed-induced wind.

"What's going on?" asked Rachel above the roar of the closing engines.

"Nothing good!" shouted Pedro above the noise as his boat started to rock violently from the massive wake produced by the navy boats. "Ms. Hiatt. I suggest that we don't admit we are out here looking for your brother or anyone else. Much better I think, to play the fool."

As he spoke, Maria popped her head out from the cabin below where she had gone to rest.

"Pedro. ¿Cual es el problema?"

"I have no idea what the problem is," he answered in English.

As the two Mark Vs came within one hundred feet, Rachel could not only see the very intimidating weapons on board, but could also see that they were manned and pointed directly at them.

She leaned in close to Pedro's ear and asked, "So, what should we say?"

"Just that I'm some rich idiot testing my new toy out in the open water. Simple as that."

"Do you think they will buy that?"

"I have no idea, but I do know it's better than the truth."

As he said that, one of the officers on the Mark V closest to the Sundancer said over a megaphone, "This is the United States Navy. Stand fast and prepare to be boarded. Please keep your hands where we can see them."

With that command, Rachel, Pedro, and Maria all reflexively raised their hands into the air.

"Is there anyone aboard the vessel other than you three?" asked the naval officer.

"No, sir!" yelled Pedro.

As the first Mark V began to tie up to his boat, Pedro noticed that the other kept a safe distance with all of its weapons trained on him and his passengers.

In quick order, the officer and four Navy SEALs boarded his boat. As the officer and two SEALs approached the three now in the cockpit, the two other SEALs immediately went below to search the rest of the cabin cruiser.

As he walked up, none of the three were pleased to see that the officer had his sidearm drawn.

"Good morning, Captain," he said as he addressed Pedro. "My name is Lt. William Smullen. May I ask what brings you out into these waters this fine day?"

As Pedro prepared to answer, he was stunned to see the two Navy SEALs also point their M4A1 assault weapons in his general direction.

"Nothing much, sir. Just wanted to take my two friends out on my boat and show off a little."

The officer, like his men, was wearing a helmet and goggles, but even at that, his blue eyes seemed to radiate a light of their own as they quickly surveyed Pedro's boat.

"Seems like an expensive vessel," said the officer when he turned back to face the three.

"I guess so," smiled Pedro. "I think it cost about three

hundred thousand dollars, but I'm not really sure. My dad bought it for me."

That statement produced the expected grunt from the officer who turned his attention to Maria.

"What are you doing out here, ma'am? I would think a woman in your condition would want to remain home and close to a delivery room."

Upon being addressed, Maria looked at Pedro in a panic, but did not answer.

"I'm sorry, sir. But her English is not very good. She still has about two more months to go and wanted to get some fresh air."

With that, the two commandos emerged from below deck. "All clear, sir," one reported as they took positions near the bow.

The officer nodded his head and smiled at Rachel. "And you. What's your story?"

"Nothing," answered Rachel in a strained voice. No matter how much you see it on television, at the movies, or imagine how you would handle it, she thought, the reality of having heavily armed men threatening your safety was more than a little intimidating. "I just wanted to join my friends for the ride."

"Is that right? Well, it is a nice day," said the officer as he looked toward the sky.

"Tell you what," he continued. "Why don't the three of you break out some ID and then place them on the captain's seat there. After you do that, I'd really appreciate it if you could all raise your hands again and keep them there."

The three did as ordered. Once they put their driver's licenses on the chair, the officer scooped them up, read them and then handed them to one of the commandos who took them back to the Mark V.

As they waited, Rachel let the reporter in her take over. "Lt. Smullen. What exactly is that boat you are on?"

Smullen admired her shape for a few seconds before looking into her sun-squinted brown eyes. "It's a Mark V, ma'am. Or a 'Swick' as we call it, which stands for Special Warfare Combatant Craft."

Rachel nodded her head as she looked at the Mark V. "Well, it looks very . . . lethal."

"It serves the navy and our nation well, ma'am."

Rachel pushed a bit further. "May I ask why you are stopping us, Lieutenant?"

The officer waved his left hand in the air to encompass the ocean while keeping his right hand, and the 9mm pistol it held, pointed in their general direction.

"Yes, ma'am. It seems there are a number of drug smugglers and even pirates operating in this area. In the past, they have interfered with naval operations. It's our job to make sure that doesn't happen again."

Rachel smiled at the blond-haired officer. "I'm guessing we don't fit the profile of pirates or drug smugglers."

"No, ma'am."

As the officer answered, one of his men came back with the IDs and whispered into his ear.

The officer slowly nodded his head before looking up at the three. "Well, everything seems to check out fine. That said, until further notice, these waters are off-limits to civilian watercraft. So, you are hereby directed to head back to your home port immediately."

Pedro was only too happy to comply. "Yes, sir. How much time do we have to leave the area?"

The officer looked down at this watch. "Oh, I'd say about two minutes from the second we get off your boat."

The anarchist in Rachel pushed a little harder. "And if we are still here in five minutes?"

The officer stepped closer to her with zero amusement showing in his lean face. "As we will fire on your vessel exactly two minutes and one second after we depart, I suspect that in five minutes, what's left of you will be scattered across the waves and quickly eaten by predators."

With no further prompting needed, Pedro had his boat heading at full speed back toward the coast fifteen seconds after the last commando had stepped off.

CHAPTER TWENTY-SEVEN

After a typical smooth landing at Homestead Air Reserve Base in South Miami Dade County, the president and his team were quickly escorted to four waiting Blackhawk helicopters.

Forty-five minutes later, Campbell watched in fascination as the president's helicopter cautiously touched down on the rolling deck of the USS *Ronald Reagan*. During his six years as a SEAL, Campbell had often landed on the deck of an aircraft carrier, and every time he did, he wished he was in a combat theater instead. Such was his fear of the mechanics involved in putting a gyrating, oscillating piece of flammable steel on top of a rolling, yawing larger piece of steel.

The president's helicopter attached itself just fine and soon it was his turn. As his Blackhawk swooped in toward the deck, the other two Blackhawks orbited the carrier and provided additional firepower until the president's party was secure.

As Campbell got off the helicopter, he was met by two armed Navy SEALs and an officer. He instantly recognized the officer as someone he had served with years earlier.

"Hey, Stan," said Campbell. "Great to see you. I guess you decided to make the navy a career after all."

The officer stuck out his right hand and warmly shook

Campbell's. "Ian. Had no idea you were on this bird. What a pleasant surprise. Yeah, with the whole world becoming more and more of a cluster-fuck, I decided that the best and safest place for me and my family was right where I was."

Campbell smiled in response as he started to walk with the officer and the two enlisted men who fell into line behind them. "So, what's the deal here?"

"Need to know, buddy. Need to know. But," laughed the officer, "I'm guessing the little field trip you are about to go on will clear up most of the questions you now have."

Campbell nodded but fell silent in thought. Based on the conversation he was privy to the day before in the Oval Office, he knew that the president was most likely taking him to see the new bunker that General Mitchell had described in some detail.

When he first left the White House, he thought that maybe the new facility was hidden somewhere at or below Andrews Air Force Base. After landing at Homestead Air Reserve Base, he wrongly guessed the same for that location. Since boarding the Blackhawk and landing on the deck of the aircraft carrier, he decided to give his mind a rest and see how the facts were about to play out. Anything and everything now seemed possible.

Campbell was taken directly to a wardroom where the president and Mitchell were waiting. Aside from the ubiquitous Secret Service detail, Campbell was surprised, but not shocked, to see Admiral Frank Thomas in a quiet but animated conversation with the president.

The admiral had always worn his religion on his sleeve and had been known as the "Bishop" by those under his command. Since Robertson had become president, Thomas had quickly and efficiently risen through the ranks to his present-day title of chief of naval operations. Meaning that, aside from serving on the Joint Chiefs of Staff, the four-star admiral was currently the highest ranking officer in the United States Navy. As such, he exerted considerable control over one of the most powerful war machines known to humankind.

The three men stopped what they were doing when Campbell entered the room. Upon seeing him, Admiral Thomas immediately walked over to introduce himself. With the admiral now standing before him, it was all Campbell could do to resist the urge to salute. While he knew that, except when on the bridge, saluting on a naval ship was not required, old habits still died hard.

While Thomas was only about five feet, ten inches tall, he was a man who wore his immense power and influence very comfortably. The minute he entered any room, the inhabitants knew that the voltage meter had just spiked. Saluting—required or not—seemed like the natural thing to do.

"Nice to meet you, Mr. Campbell," said the admiral. "Did you and I cross paths during your naval career?"

"No sir, Admiral. I did not have the honor and that was my loss."

The admiral smiled with the compliment but then got right to business. "Happy to hear that you are part of this team, Mr. Campbell. I have no doubts that you will be quite pleased with what the president has in mind for you."

The admiral's comment, instead of making him more curious, made Campbell that much more apprehensive. "Yes, sir. I am thrilled to be of service."

Thomas stepped closer, grabbed Campbell's arm, and lowered his voice. "We all serve a higher calling now, Mr. Campbell. We answer only to Him and our mission is everything."

Having little clue what the admiral was hinting at, Campbell neutrally answered, "Yes, sir."

Just as he answered the admiral, General Mitchell snapped his fingers and looked over at Campbell.

"Okay, Navy. It's showtime. I'd suggest you go hit the head and empty your bladder and bowels, because what we're about to show you might cause you to piss and shit in your diaper."

CHAPTER TWENTY-EIGHT

Vice President Dale left her residence at the naval observatory, entered her armored limousine, and prepared for her very swift ten-minute ride to the White House.

Since September 11, 2001, both the president's and vice president's motorcades had been beefed up considerably. Like many previous presidents and vice presidents, Eileen Dale was not very well-versed on the extraordinary means employed to keep her safe. While she was eternally grateful for the expertise and sacrifice of the United States Secret Service, she felt that the best way to honor them was to do her job to the best of her ability.

This morning's motorcade consisted of eight DC motorcycle cops, four marked DC police cars, a spare armored limo, the vice president's limo, an SUV with four Presidential Protection Agents from the Secret Service, a control car with staff personnel, another SUV with a Secret Service SWAT team, and an SUV with a Secret Service ID team.

In the limo with the vice president were two Secret Service agents up front, and the head of her detail in the back with her.

"I guess I don't have to worry about losing you in a crowd today," said the dapperly dressed gray-haired agent.

Dale looked down at her red pastel suit. "No, David. I guess you won't."

David Langworthy looked over at his charge and smiled. He had been with her for almost one year and was honestly shocked to find that there were still public servants who actually cared about the public, instead of every facet of their political careers.

Langworthy had been with the Secret Service for nineteen years. In that time he had protected a number of presidents and vice presidents. Most were polite but considered him and his fellow agents little more than accessories to the White House or the motorcade. One president treated him like family, two vice presidents invited him to dinner, but most kept their distance. In one famous incident within the Secret Service, Langworthy had managed to get himself screamed at by the then president, while his wife—the First Lady—actually threw a Bible at his head. All of this because he was doing his job by preventing them from leaving a church through an unsecured entrance.

"All set, Madame Vice President?"

"Yes, David. Thank you."

With that, Langworthy rapped on the partition and ten seconds later the motorcade started on its short journey.

Two minutes into the trip, the vice president placed the morning's intelligence briefings on the seat next to her and looked across the cabin at Langworthy.

Langworthy felt the weight of her gaze as he scanned the streets for anything out of the ordinary.

"Yes, Madame Vice President?" asked the agent as his head swiveled from side to side to take in both sides of the street.

"David. Could you look at me for a moment?"

Langworthy turned to look at her and immediately noticed that her face seemed lined with worry. "Is there something wrong, ma'am?"

Dale nodded slowly to herself for a few seconds. "Yes. Actually, I think there is something incredibly wrong."

Because of his position and duties, Langworthy was not prone to emotion or surprise.

"Do you want to tell me about it?" he asked in a very soft voice.

"Yes, I do. In the interest of our national security, I think that it's imperative that I speak with you. But before I tell you anything, I need to ask you a question."

"Of course," answered the agent with a smile that never reached his hazel eyes.

"Do you consider yourself to be a spiritual person?"

That question was not on the mental list Langworthy had just reviewed. "Do I consider myself to be spiritual?"

"Yes," answered the vice president. "Quite a simple question, really."

As the agent prepared to answer, the motorcade flashed past the front of the Mayflower Hotel on its way to the White House.

A passing that was not only noted, but recorded and timed.

CHAPTER TWENTY-NINE

Campbell, the president, General Mitchell, Admiral Thomas, and thirteen other people were now one hundred feet beneath the surface of the Atlantic Ocean and descending rapidly. The large submersible they occupied was attached to several cables and was being lowered by a crane on the USS *Ronald Reagan*.

Campbell found himself sitting next to a chief petty officer who seemed bored by the experience.

"I guess you've done this a few times before," said Campbell.

"Yes, sir. A few."

"What exactly are we in? Seems pretty big for a standard submersible."

The CPO became more animated with the question. "Oh, yes, sir. This here is called Simon. You know, like one of them chipmunks. The one she is based on was named Alvin, so your United States Navy decided that this one should be called Simon. I guess the successor to this one will be called Theodore."

"Nice to know someone still has a sense of humor."

"Yes, sir. Just so you can appreciate what we are in now, I'll give you a little history on that Alvin. That submersible was built in 1964 by the Applied Sciences Division of Litton Industries. She—even though it's named Alvin we still call our ships she . . ."

"Yes, I remember."

The CPO turned in his chair to face Campbell. "Oh, I'm sorry sir. Were you in the navy?"

"Six years," Campbell said.

"What was your MOS?"

"Naval Special Warfare."

"SEAL?"

Campbell nodded as he looked toward the front of the sub where the president, Mitchell, and Thomas were seated. He could see them talking, but their voices were drowned out by the noise of the dive.

"Wow," continued the CPO. "Tough duty. My brother tried to become a SEAL but he washed out of BUDS. He's still in the navy. Stationed in San Diego now."

"You were saying."

"Oh, yeah," laughed the CPO. "As you are former navy, you will appreciate this. We had Simon specially built for the facility you are about to see. While Alvin was designed for only three people, Simon can comfortably hold thirty. While Alvin was only twenty-three feet long, eight feet wide, and twelve feet tall, Simon is one hundred and fifty feet long, thirty feet wide, and twenty feet high. While Alvin's operating depth was 14,764 feet, Simon's is . . . well . . . it's classified, but suffice it to say that there ain't no part of the ocean floor she can't sit down on."

Campbell smiled at the now energetic chief petty officer. "Well, seeing as we are just off the coast of Florida, I'm guessing we are not going too much deeper."

The CPO looked up at an LCD above the pilot, which read 380 feet. "Oh, we still got a ways to go, sir. We've done some dredging out here to make it deeper."

CHAPTER THIRTY

Simon gently docked with something, and Campbell looked over at the LCD depth gauge. It read 924 feet. Campbell popped his ears for about the fourth time and stood to join the line of those exiting the submersible.

Campbell was still amazed to see that instead of climbing a ladder, the passengers were exiting the craft through a side door, much the same way one would get off a jet. When he got off of the submersible, he found himself standing with the others in what looked to be a twenty-by-twenty-foot airlock. As soon as the door that led to Simon was sealed, the door toward the front of the room opened.

What it opened to was well beyond anything Campbell had imagined. As he followed the herd into the next pen, he was amazed to be standing in what looked for all the world like a lobby of any five-star hotel—that is, if said lobby was protected by six commandos, had a state-of-the-art security monitoring system, and was equipped to pump a nerve agent into the room should it be breached.

The room looked to be about forty feet by fifty feet, had a ten-foot-high ceiling, was covered in a rich royal-blue wallpaper, had white crown molding, four dark-cream-colored upholstered chairs, two coffee tables, various oil paintings of U.S. landmarks, and a front desk manned by two very attractive women.

James Bond comes to the ocean floor, thought Campbell as the president, Mitchell, and Thomas walked up to face him.

"Welcome to Project Neptune, Ian," said the broadly smiling president. "What do you think so far?"

"I'm in shock, Mr. President."

"Well, keep your emotions in check because I'm told we haven't seen anything yet."

Campbell shook his head as he looked around the elegant room. "I just can't believe we are nine hundred feet beneath the surface."

"It gets much more amazing than that, Ian," said the president. "Frank, why don't you give Mr. Campbell the thumbnail description. That said, even when you do, he won't believe it until he sees it with his own eyes."

The admiral stepped up closer to Campbell. "Yes, sir, Mr. President. My pleasure. Mr. Campbell, as the president just said, this facility is named Protect Neptune. No facility in the world is more secret and no facility in the world is more secure. Neptune has been built into a huge natural cave in the side of a mountain on the ocean floor. The top of Neptune is covered by three hundred feet of solid rock. We've built a blast wall in front of the facility that is fifty feet thick. While it may sound the stuff of science fiction, in reality, what we've done is just build something the size of a large cruise ship, and place it underwater. Neptune has four docking ports, five levels, can house over five thousand inhabitants, has its own newspaper, television and radio stations, can distill over seven hundred thousand gallons of fresh water per day from the sea, make her own oxygen, is powered by four nuclear reactors that can operate for over twenty years without refueling, has enough food and supplies to operate for five years, and when fully operational, will be protected by two hundred commandos and one Virginia-Class nuclear-powered attack submarine. And, as an additional safety valve, we have built a backdoor that connects to a narrow, six-mile tunnel which leads to a small Bahamian island owed by one of our . . . benefactors. There is much more, but that is the thumbnail the president asked me to give you."

"Thank you, Admiral. I'm sure what I'm about to see will dwarf what you just told me, but your description still seems like something out of a science-fiction movie."

"Nothing science fiction about it, Navy," said General Mitchell. "This facility is as real as the multiplying threats that we now face from the Islamists and others. We built it because we had to build it." The general then paused for effect before continuing. "We built it because we were ordered to build it."

Campbell suddenly felt light-headed. "Who asked you to build it, sir?"

The president put his arm around Campbell's shoulders and answered. "Our Lord, Ian. Our Lord asked us to built this incredible place. Now, knowing that, I have a question for you."

"Yes, sir," said Campbell as his palms started to go moist.

"How would you like to be in charge of security for this sacred facility?"

In a morning of surprises, that question was the biggest for Campbell. Even at that, he knew there was only one proper answer to give at this place and time.

"Mr. President, I'm stunned by the question, but would be honored to serve you . . . and our Lord, in any way you deem fit."

"Thank you, Ian. We'll get the nickel tour of the place before you have to give us your final answer. Although, once you see it all, I suspect you'll be begging to reside at Neptune."

Campbell smiled at the response before turning serious. "Yes, sir. I'm sure. Now if I may, Mr. President. Do you mind if I ask an obvious question?"

"Why not, Ian. I'd be more than a little troubled if you didn't ask."

Campbell looked into the faces of the president, General Mitchell, and Admiral Thomas before speaking. "Thank you, sir. Well, I guess the obvious question is—why did the Lord order you to build Neptune?"

"Quite simple, Ian. The Lord ordered us to build this facility so we would have a home to ride out the end of the world."

CHAPTER THIRTY-ONE

Two days later, a mentally taxed and incredulous Campbell was back in his office, fixated on nothing, when he was buzzed by his assistant.

"Yes, Janice?"

"There is a Rachel Hiatt from the *New York Times* on the phone. Says you know her."

Campbell remembered that she had come over for a briefing with a few other reporters just after she had started at the newspaper. While he did not really talk with her at the time, she seemed professional, bright, and more than a little attractive. As much as Campbell's mind could use a respite, now was not the time.

"Tell her I'm busy, Janice. Maybe in a couple of weeks."

Ten seconds later, his assistant was back on the line. "She insists that you will want to talk with her. She says it's urgent."

Campbell looked at his television for a moment. The sound was turned down, but he still cringed at the sight of an anorexic blonde in a short skirt debating politics on Fox News. Someone needs to give that woman a sandwich, he thought as he spoke into the handset of his phone.

"Fine. If it's so urgent, then have her give you her date of birth and social security number, wave her into the building, and tell her to get her ass down here if she wants to speak with me."

Campbell hung up the phone and started to slowly massage his temples. Since coming back from Neptune, he had a constant, low-grade headache that he could not shake. The tour of the facility made the fictional sets from the *Star Trek* and *Star Wars* franchises look cheesy and outdated by comparison. It was, as President Robertson described it, "A futuristic Christian fortress under the sea built to usher in a pious new millennium."

Campbell's constant headache came from trying to read between the lines of the dark and disturbing messages hinted at by the president and Mitchell. Did they have intelligence to suggest that Islamic radicals were about to go nuclear in the United States? Did they fear that the now-nuclear-armed Iran was about to ignite a nuclear war with Israel? Was the fact that Pakistan had just been taken over by extremists playing into their menacing chatter? While Campbell was allowed to see much of the daily intelligence reports, there were still sections reserved solely for the president and others higher than him on the political and security food chain.

Upon completion of the surreal tour of Neptune, Campbell had reiterated his strong desire to run security for the facility. He knew it was what they wanted to hear and he hoped it would buy him some time. Time to learn something, time to wake up, or time to convert his bank account into gold coins and go into survivalist mode.

Rachel Hiatt now found herself sitting on the same sofa occupied by the vice president days earlier. She was wearing a black pants suit, a red T-shirt, and black Chanel high-heel shoes.

Campbell had just finished placing two ice-filled glasses of Coke on the coffee table as she settled in.

"I'm sorry," said Hiatt. "Do you mind if I take my

jacket off? Per your request, I just schlepped it over here from Eye Street, and now I'm melting."

"Be my guest," answered Campbell as he watched her stand and take off the jacket. As she maneuvered out of the garment, he tried to steal a look at her impressive figure without appearing obvious. Like most men, he thought he had perfected the tactic, and like most women, Hiatt knew what was coming.

She sat back down, took a welcome sip of her soda, and then smiled across at Campbell.

"Schlepped?" he said. "Now there's a word you don't hear everyday."

Rachel laughed. "Well you do if you go to visit my Jewish grandparents."

Campbell instantly held up both hands. "Hey. Whoa. I wasn't asking about your religion or anything. Just commenting on the word."

"Relax, Ian." She smiled. "Oh, can I call you Ian?"

"Sure."

"Great. Thanks. Call me Rachel. I'm not from the PC police, Ian. The fact of the matter is that I think we've all gotten way too sensitive about race, religion, and humor. Way too sensitive."

"Okay," said Campbell. "I guess it won't surprise you for me to say that I agree completely."

"Well . . . since this is the most conservative White House since Ronald Reagan . . . no, I'm not surprised."

Campbell now offered a sly smile. "And since you've proclaimed your freedom from the shackles of political correctness, am I allowed to say that your hairstyle looks great?"

Rachel instinctively touched her short black hair. "Only as many times as you'd like."

Campbell mentally downshifted his testosterone as he reminded himself that the person sitting across from him, while beautiful, was also a reporter for the *New York*

Times. A paper that had gone after this administration hammer and tongs for seven ink-stained years.

"So," said Campbell as he tried to regain the authoritative high ground, "what's so urgent?"

"Yes. Thank you again for seeing me. I'm not sure where to begin my story. You might find it a bit bizarre."

"Try me," said Campbell as he found himself warming to her dark brown eyes.

"To begin," said Rachel as she inched closer to Campbell, "this is personal. It has nothing to do with work, nothing to do with the *New York Times*, and nothing to do with politics. I'm here to talk about my brother."

"What about him?" asked Campbell as he took a quick look at his TV screen to see if any real news had made it on the air.

"He's disappeared."

Campbell looked back at her. "No offense, Rachel. But that sounds like a problem for the police."

"Offense taken," she answered as her lips drew thin.

"Are you serious? Why?"

"Yes, I'm serious. I don't mean to pick on you, but it's been one door slammed in my face after another."

"How so?"

"Well, first the police told me to take a hike. They said it wasn't their problem."

Campbell shook his head. "Hold up. I thought missing persons was one of the things they did."

"Normally. But they told me I had to go elsewhere."

"Where?"

"The coast guard."

Campbell took a quick sip of his soda and spilled a few drops on his light gray tie. "Shit . . . whoops . . . sorry about the language."

Rachel leaned over the coffee table and handed him a napkin. "That's okay. It's both human to spill things on ourselves and then hurl profanity about when the liquid collides with our hard-earned dollars masquerading as clothes."

Campbell took the napkin and tried to blot, rather than wipe, his tie. As he did, he said, "Why the coast guard? Your brother have a boat?"

"Yeah. He fashions himself to be a modern-day treasure hunter. He's always been the square peg in a world full of circles, if you know what I mean."

Campbell laughed. "Indeed I do. I feel four-sided on most days myself. So," Campbell continued, "I'm guessing he was out on his boat at the time he went missing."

"Exactly."

"And where was he when all of this happened?"

Rachel paused, closed her eyes as if fighting off the urge to cry, and then answered. "He and his friend Eric were about twenty miles to the east of Miami when their boat just seemed to disappear."

Campbell immediately felt a knot tighten in his stomach. He then stood, walked over to close his door, sat back down and faced her. "Why don't you tell me all about it. And please, no matter if you think it important or not, tell me every detail."

CHAPTER THIRTY-TWO

About eighteen miles to the south of the White House, four men and two women met in a secure conference room at Fort Belvoir off of Telegraph Road in Alexandria, Virginia.

The group consisted of two generals, one admiral, and three high-level officials from the CIA, FBI, and the NSA. So concerned was this group about security and the risk of their conversation being recorded or overheard, the general in charge of the meeting had the room swept three separate times for listening devices before ordering all of the phones disconnected.

Beyond that, he stationed six armed guards at the door with instructions to turn away any and all visitors. That included the full-bird colonel who was the garrison commander for the base. If any visitor refused to take no as an answer, then they were to be shot on the spot.

"Things are moving very rapidly now," said the four-star general running the meeting.

"Yes," said one of the two women, who was director of the National Clandestine Service at the CIA. "You said we would have more time."

"Well I was wrong," responded the general in a raised voice.

"Let's not start barking at each other," advised the assistant director of the Office of Counterterrorism at the

FBI. "We've got a mission to complete. I'd suggest we all focus."

"Agreed," said the four-star general. "Sorry," he said as he looked at the woman.

"That's okay. As things are moving faster, does anyone have any immediate thoughts?" the woman said to the general and the group as a whole.

"Yeah," said the deputy director of the National Security Agency. "As my group has been running a tap on all of these guys for the last few months, I'd say we pretty much know as much as we need to know. It's time to act."

"Meaning?" asked the four-star general.

"We need to take them out before they strike. Our operative in the Middle East said they are on the move."

The general looked at the five people at the table with him. "Are we agreed, then?"

All five nodded without speaking.

The general stood. "Very well. Let's take them out and pray to God that we are right."

CHAPTER THIRTY-THREE

The more Rachel spoke, the more Campbell felt he had to get out of the building. When she took a breath to continue her story, he held up his hand.

"Stop. Do you feel like taking a walk?"

Rachel was aware of the sweat on her body that still had not completely evaporated from her almost-jog to the White House. "Not really."

Campbell stood and smiled down at her. "Well, humor me. Let's go get some fresh, stagnant, humid air. It has to be good for something."

Ten minutes later, both were seated on a park bench in Farragut Square. A small oasis of grass that was situated between two metro stops, the Army-Navy Club, and Seventeenth Street, and was the dominion, mostly, of the homeless.

Rachel mopped the now-flowing sweat from her forehead as she looked over at Campbell who seemed as fresh as a piece of lettuce. "Don't you sweat?"

"I've been known to," he said as he looked around the park.

"So, why couldn't we continue speaking in your comfortable, air-conditioned office?"

"No reason. I just felt like taking a walk."

Rachel draped her jacket over her knees. "Pardon me,

Ian. But that's bullshit. Something I said back in your office spooked you."

Campbell sighed as he looked down at his always clipped short fingernails. "Actually, not too much spooks me anymore. At a certain point, your capacity to digest the incomprehensible reaches overload and even the most horrifying or bizarre of events blend into the white noise of normalcy."

"I wasn't a psych major, Ian. What's that mumbo jumbo supposed to mean?"

Campbell looked back up at her and cracked a smile. "I don't have the foggiest notion."

Just as quickly as it came, the smile vanished. "Rachel, are you positive that the boats that intercepted you were U.S. Navy?"

"Yes. It was not only spray-painted all over them, but the lieutenant went out of his way to make sure we knew. He didn't say, but it looked like the men under his command were Navy SEALs."

Campbell looked off into the distance as his mind flashed back to an earlier time. "Yeah, if they came up on you in Swicks, then the guys he had were SEALs."

The unrelenting sun momentarily went behind a cloud bank and Rachel felt the muscles around her eyes relax. "Ian. Before I called you, I read as much about you as I could find. From your official White House bio, to your bio from your Hill days, to news stories, to even looking at some TV clips of you online. I know about your tough childhood, I know about your six years as a Navy SEAL, I know about your battlefield citations, I know that within this very conservative, very rigid, never-able-to-admit-to-a-mistake administration, that you still have a reputation as a straight shooter. And that's the reason I called you today. Something bad happened to my brother and all available evidence seems to indicate that whatever did happen to him was at the hands of our government."

"Look," said Ian slowly as he continued to play his cards tightly to his chest. "I honestly don't have a clue what happened to your brother. I'll nose around and see if I can find out anything on the QT."

Hiatt grunted in disgust. "Sorry. That's not good enough. At the end of the day, I'm still a reporter for the most powerful newspaper on the planet earth. At the very least, I can write a stor—"

Before she could finish, Campbell spun around, grabbed her wrists in his hands and squeezed so hard that she let out a shriek of pain.

"Rachel," he hissed. "Don't even think of doing that. This isn't a fuckin' game. I honestly don't know what's going on. You have to give me some time. You have to take a step back and calm down. You can't start to threaten me or anyone else by saying you are going to run a story. In fact, I'm begging you here and now, not to mention any of this, or our conversation, to anyone. If you do . . ."

Rachel looked down at his incredibly strong hands and saw that they had turned white from the pressure he was exerting. As she looked back up into his eyes, she was certain that not only was he not aware that he was hurting her, but that in spite of what he said earlier, something had terrified him.

"If I do . . . w-what?" she stuttered.

Campbell unconsciously increased the pressure on her wrists until a tear fell from her eye. "You'll be killed."

"Ian, please," Hiatt pleaded as she struggled to free her wrists.

Campbell looked down and instantly released his vice-like grip. "Oh, my God, Rachel. I'm so sorry."

Hiatt massaged her wrists and then quietly began to sob. The stress of the moment and the last few days demanded a release. Her body softly shook as the tears flowed down her face.

Every instinct was telling Campbell to slide closer to her and put his arm around her somewhat sunburned shoulders. But, after having just been the cause of her physical pain, he doubted that comforting her would be warmly received.

In lieu of that, he took a clean paper napkin from his pocket, placed it in her hand, and let the process play out.

After another minute of gasps and gulps, Hiatt got her breathing under control, used the napkin to wipe her eyes and nose, and then stared without blinking at Campbell. "What are you keeping from me?"

Campbell kept two phones with him at all times. One was his official White House cell and one was his personal iPhone.

"Do you have a private e-mail address?" he asked as he took out the iPhone.

She nodded and gave him the e-mail.

After a minute of typing he looked back up at her. "I just sent you my address and a time for tonight. Be there. Maybe," he said as he stood to walk back to the White House, "we can help each other."

The second Campbell sent the email from his iPhone, it popped up on a computer at one of the nation's intelligence agencies. One second after it did, the analyst assigned to monitor Campbell's e-mails picked up the phone to call his supervisor.

CHAPTER THIRTY-FOUR

Hours after Campbell and Hiatt met on a park bench in Washington, six of the world's leading Islamic terrorists were killed at almost precisely the same time.

The number-two man for the Al-Aqsa Martyrs' Brigade was driving in his armored SUV in the West Bank with his bodyguards in front and behind him, when a Hellfire missile sent from a Predator drone seconds earlier made contact with his vehicle and blew it and him into smoldering fragments of flesh and metal.

In the apartment of his mistress in Beirut, the number-three man for Hezbollah was just about to reach climax as he sweated atop of a woman who turned her head to avoid his putrid breath, when the apartment, and those above, below, and to the sides, ceased to exist in a powerful blast that rocked Lebanon's capital city.

In Sanaa, Yemen, the number-two man for the Aden-Abyan Islamic Army was gathered with six of his lieutenants in one of their many safe houses, when a bullet from a silenced .50-caliber M82 series long-range sniper rifle splattered his head onto the faces and bodies of his men.

At 17,000 feet and descending into Imam Khomeini International Airport in Tehran, the brigadier general and deputy commander of the Iran Revolutionary Guard marveled at the new Gulfstream V he had just purchased for cash with money stolen from his nation's people. He had packed it with every luxury item and toy imaginable and felt it was now ready to be shown off to those who envied his position and power.

At 1,500 feet, the general's jet was hit by a cruise missile and disintegrated into a blinding fireball that spat out hundreds of chunks and bits which rained down on the outskirts of the airport.

In Tripoli, Lebanon, the number-three man for Asbat al-Ansar sat down on the toilet in his private bathroom and started to flip through the latest issue of *Playboy.* As he began to pull out the centerfold, the motion-activated bomb hidden behind the water tank detonated with such forward force as to propel him through the closed door, through the wall across the hall, and out into the street below. Residents found his right hand first, because it still clutched the forbidden magazine.

In an outdoor café in Islamabad, Pakistan, which was open 24/7 for the leadership of Al-Qaeda, the moneyman for that organization slowly took a sip of his espresso. At first, he savored the strong taste of the hot liquid. But then, his eyes went wide as his sense of smell detected just a hint of bitter almond. An odor that was an identifier of cyanide.

As he started to foam at the mouth and bounce off the cobblestone floor, the irony of his poisoning was not lost on him. Just the day before, he had transferred enough money to his masters to allow them to continue making the cyanide bombs they hoped to unleash on New York and London. It was his last transaction.

Back in the United States, a general stared at a text message that had just come across his BlackBerry:

SIX CHAPTERS COMPLETED. EXPECT THE END OF THE BOOK TO BE BLOODY AND EXPLOSIVE. REVENGE ON ORDER.

The general smiled with the information as he continued his daily walk while speculating on next steps. Both his and theirs.

CHAPTER THIRTY-FIVE

At 11:30 that evening, Campbell and Hiatt sat on his balcony and silently looked across the river at a quiet Washington, DC, as the latest Michelle Wright CD played in the background. Each held a glass of white wine and each was somber.

After another minute of reflection, Rachel reached over and touched Campbell's hand. "A penny for your thoughts."

Campbell took a quick sip of his wine and then placed it on the small glass table that sat between the two chairs. He continued to look at Washington as he answered her. "Trust me, you don't want to hear what I'm thinking."

Instead of pulling her hand back, Rachel enveloped his in hers and gently squeezed. "You're wrong. In fact I'm desperate to hear what you are thinking. I'm desperate to know what's going on and I'm desperate for someone to tell me that everything is going to be all right."

Campbell snorted breath through his nostrils as he turned to face her. "Okay. You want to know what I was just thinking. I was looking at DC and the monuments—the hunks of granite and marble that are supposed to epitomize all we stand for as a nation—and I was trying to imagine what they would look like after being hit by a nuclear weapon. Would there be anything left? Would the Washington Monument just be a nub on a charred hillside? Would the Jefferson Memorial just be a few blackened rocks next to the evaporated Potomac River? Would the World War II Memorial become superheated into a piece of flat glass?"

"And why are you thinking all of that?"

Campbell stood up and turned to face her as he leaned back on the railing of his balcony.

"Why? Because nothing is going to be all right. Nothing. Just two weeks ago I was a deputy chief of staff in the White House wondering what my next steps would be as this administration winds down, and now I'm trying to estimate how much longer we, our country, and the world have before we're all vaporized."

"Ian, I'm not sure what's going on in your everyday life, but aren't you blowing whatever it is way out of proportion?"

Campbell paused to look at her before answering. She had changed since their meeting on the park bench. She was now wearing mid-heel black boots, snug jeans with a black belt and gold buckle, a long-sleeved white collared shirt, and a simple gold chain around her neck. As the lights of the cars passing below reflected off her dark eyes, Campbell was both impressed by her strong and simple beauty, and saddened with the timing of his newfound—and to his surprise—genuine interest.

"No," he finally answered. "All the opposite. Look, I'm on thin ice even talking about this stuff, but a large part of me really doesn't care anymore. Without saying how or why, I'm basically positive that your brother and his buddy went missing because of our government . . ."

She started to speak but he held up his hand.

". . . No. Wait a minute. In the last number of days, I've had the data dump of all data dumps hurled at me. I need time to think. I need time to digest what I've been told and what I've just seen. I need time to reacquaint myself with the concept of good versus evil and why and if it really matters if good triumphs over evil. As we have learned all too painfully since September eleventh, one man's good is another man's evil."

Out of nervousness and a touch of fear, Rachel stood to face him. "Without revealing top secret information and all that, can you fill in any of the blanks with regard to what you just said? Because if it's your plan to leave that up to me, then I'm wondering if I wouldn't be better just jumping off this balcony."

Campbell laughed and pointed at the table. "Let me get the rest of that bottle into me, and I'll hold your hand on the way down."

Instead of answering, Rachel just looked into his eyes until the smile left his face.

"Okay," he said. "What are you thinking?"

Rachel stepped a foot closer. "I'm thinking that even though we don't know each other, we *know* each other. I'm thinking that for you to say the things you just said, then maybe something truly catastrophic is about to happen. I'm thinking that, at this precise moment, I could really use a hug."

Campbell looked at her for several seconds, nodded his head, extended his arms, and pulled her into him. With the heels she was wearing, she about matched his six-foot-one frame and folded nicely into his body.

The hug was anything but sensual. As she placed her head on his left shoulder, he rested his atop of her head and her thick black hair. They held the pose for over two minutes. Neither talking, neither thinking, with both just enjoying the fleeting comfort of a fellow human being facing a shared unknown.

As they separated, they both seemed more relaxed and open to continuing a discussion that was not only implausible, but insane.

"Can I pour you some more wine?"

"Yes," answered Rachel. "And as you're doing that, can you point me in the direction of the ladies' room?"

"Sure. Just walk back into the living room and when you hit the wall, take a right."

When she left, Campbell filled both glasses, put the wine back in the ice bucket, and then walked into his living room. Seconds later, he emerged with a pair of binoculars.

As he stood on his balcony, he put the binoculars to his eyes and started to scan anything and everything. He had no idea what he was looking for. Only that his instinct was telling him that he had to start morphing his mind back to when he was in battle and to focus on the fact that the slightest thing out of the ordinary could mean everything.

Campbell looked down from his tenth-floor perch at the cars in the parking lot, he looked over at the cars on Route 110 whipping past, he looked at some of the boats on the Potomac, he looked across the river toward the Kennedy Center and some of the restaurants that dotted the far bank, he looked at a few of the balconies adjacent to his, and finally, he trained the binoculars off toward the right to look at the park that was home to the Iwo Jima Memorial.

As he heard the toilet flush, he placed the binoculars behind his chair on the floor. One minute later, Rachel walked out to find him standing where she had left him. He motioned her to sit, and then joined her.

After sitting, he handed her the glass of wine.

"Are you religious?" Campbell asked as she sat back in her chair.

Rachel closed her eyes as a warm breeze momentarily swirled around the balcony. Upon its departure, she opened her eyes, took a sip of her wine, kept the glass in her hand, and looked slowly over at Campbell. "Am I religious? That's a question out of the blue."

"Yeah, but it seems to be the question of the hour, so I thought I would ask it of you."

"Why?" asked Rachel as she motioned toward DC and its illuminated white monuments. "Because we, and all this, are going to disappear in a radioactive flash, so I had better prepare myself to meet my maker?"

Campbell laughed at the response. "Not exactly, but I'm happy to see that I've got your mind focused now."

"This isn't funny, Ian," said Rachel as her eyes began to moisten.

"No, it's not. Not at all. Death is a very serious business. For some it's a petrifying thought. For others, it's the natural conclusion to the circle of life. And for a small, twisted percentage, it's something that is not only eagerly anticipated and welcomed, but something that must be hastened for the greater good of God."

"And which category do you fall in?"

Campbell shrugged his shoulders. "I guess I'm marginally in the second. I understand it's part of the circle of life and there is nothing any of us can do about it. I do happen to believe in God and the concept of Heaven and Hell, so there is some comfort in that . . . as long as I don't stagger into the down elevator by mistake when it's all over."

Rachel did not respond to the little joke so Campbell quickly continued.

"But, and no pun intended, what really does scare the hell out of me is the small percentage that falls into the third category. During my time in the navy, I was up close and personal with fanatics who twisted their faith to justify the most heinous actions on Earth. My team and I fought Islamic terrorists who thought nothing of blowing up a school full of children, thought nothing of blowing up a bus full of desperately poor men on their way to a job site, and especially thought nothing of blowing up a sacred mosque. All for the most obscene reason of all. They killed the innocent in the name of God."

"That kind of thinking seems to be on the rise."

"My point exactly," agreed Campbell. "So, back to my question. Are you religious?"

"Why? 'Cause you want to figure out if I belong with the nut jobs?"

"Not at all. Just the opposite."

Rachel stood, picked up her chair, turned it to face Campbell, and then sat back down.

"Not particularly. My brother and I are Jewish and were raised by two parents who, while not orthodox, still had and have a strong faith. My dad's a doctor and my mom's an architect. Unlike you, I come from a somewhat privileged background. I'm not ashamed that I come from some money but I do believe that because I do, I have an obligation to give back . . . as corny as that may sound."

"I think that's quite admirable, actually," said Campbell as he looked at her silhouetted by Washington in the distance.

"With regard to my faith, my mom and dad both thought it very important that my brother and I visit Israel right after high school. My brother went years before me and had a great time. When it was my turn, I really had to be pushed."

"Why?"

"Terrorism. Speaking of buses, suicide bombers had blown up a few buses two weeks before my trip, so I was pretty nervous."

"But you went."

"Yeah," said Rachel with a smile. "In the end, I still felt it was important to go. My dad had arranged the trip with a group called Birthright-Israel. It's a wonderful group that organizes free trips for Jewish young adults. For years, I listened as my mom and dad spoke of their pride in the State of Israel. That it symbolized everything about the ability of the Jewish people to renew themselves after the horrors of the Holocaust. For my family and most of my friends, Israel became a daily reminder that Judaism as a religion is alive and well and that Jewish nationalism and culture are equally important. And all of that pride manifested itself in Israel."

"So, in the end, how was the trip?"

"Great . . . I guess. I went for six weeks. I got to live and work in a kibbutz, saw the beaches of Tel-Aviv, went to Rabin Square, went to Independence Hall where Israel was created in 1948, went to Jerusalem to visit the Temple Mount and to see the Western Wall, met with a number of 'regular Israelis' such as soldiers and vendors, and went to a mega-event for all the young adult groups visiting at the time. There were rock bands, light shows, and speeches from some of Israel's leaders."

Campbell offered a small smile. "For what sounds like a fantastic time, you don't seem too happy about it."

"I was . . . I am. It's just that I still feel somewhat guilty about the whole thing."

"How so?"

"I guess . . . because I came home. I got to come back to the relative safety of the United States. My six weeks in Israel was like a glorified camp. Almost everything was scripted. For the most part, we just saw the best of Israel. The shining part of the state that those of us who don't live there romanticize from thousands of miles away. We didn't get to see the very poor Israelis. We didn't get to see the immigrants who struggle everyday to not only survive the terrorism, but to survive financially. We didn't have to live with the constant fear. We got to leave while the Israelis we met had to stay, struggle, fight, and die. Understanding that, I feel most guilty because I, like most of my group mates, have never gone back. It's like, on the list for being a good Jew, we were able to check off the trip to the homeland, and then move on with our lives. That aspect of it still troubles me."

Campbell rubbed his eyes as his body sought to remind

him how desperately tired he was. "Yeah, well I guess that begs a whole new question. Are you an American or are you an Israeli?"

"An American. But in one way or another, all Jews feel that we are part of Israel. As an American and a Jew, I am deeply proud of the fact that Israel has survived all of these years in the face of such danger. I never really talk about it. I don't talk about it at work and I don't talk about it with my friends."

"But you think about it."

"Yes. More and more of late. As a little girl, I used to ask my dad why so many people seemed to hate us. What did we do to the world to make it despise the Jewish faith. As far as I knew, my family and relatives worked hard, obeyed the laws, tried to educate themselves, tried to help others, and tried to stay out of the way. And yet, the jokes were still there, the looks were still there, the accusations were still there."

"And what answer did your dad give you?"

"He said the insecure and the ignorant needed to blame someone for their failures. That it was much easier to blame an ugly, stereotypical myth than to look into a mirror and admit the person they saw was the real reason for their ineffectiveness to succeed."

"Did you buy that?"

Rachel stood and started to pace on the small balcony. "I did as a child. But now as an adult, as a reporter, it's much harder to brush off anti-Semitism as just a failing of the insecure and ignorant. Especially when I see it on the rise in Europe, South America, and other parts of the world. Especially when I see my elderly father break down and cry with the thought that the evil that enabled, so many decades earlier, to kill his family and try to exterminate a race, is alive and well in certain governments today."

Campbell looked off toward Reagan National Airport

and softly spoke as if almost in a trance. "Yeah, evil is alive and well in certain governments. And if you buy into the hype, then God has already diagramed the carnage about to come."

"What?"

Campbell jumped up from his chair and walked over to her. "Nothing. Just mumbling. Sorry."

"You're not mumbling and you're not sorry."

Campbell reached out and took one of her hands in his. "Well, I'm not sorry you stopped by my office today. I am sorry that I hurt you in the park. I'm not sorry that you came by this evening. I am sorry about your brother. I'm not sorry that we talked and I got to know you a little better. And I am sorry that I have to ask you to leave."

Rachel shook her head as she looked into his exhausted blue eyes. "I've got more questions now than when I walked in here. Why did you ask me to come? You haven't told me a thing."

Campbell placed his right hand on the small of her back and gently directed her toward the living room. "I've told you what I can. I need you to trust me. I need you not to talk with anyone about this or to write any stories."

As soon as he said that, Rachel looked down at the small black and blue marks on her wrists.

Campbell followed her gaze and then looked back up at her face. "I'm so very sorry about that."

Hiatt leaned over and kissed him on the cheek. "I know you are, Ian. So, what's next?"

"Next, I walk you down to your car, give you a quick hug and kiss good night, and then come back up to collapse in my bed."

"And when you wake up?"

"Pray to God that the world will survive the coming day."

CHAPTER THIRTY-SIX

Commander Rob Rutten stood in the control room of the USS *North Carolina,* ran his left hand over his dark brown flattop hair, and contemplated the orders he had just been given.

For years, he had busted his ass, conspired, and crossed more than a few lines, to get his command of a Virginia-Class fast-attack submarine. Now that he had it, he was seriously considering resigning his commission.

The boat was everything he had dreamed about as a student fresh out of the naval academy. Almost four hundred feet long, thirty-four feet wide, with a crew of fourteen officers and 120 enlisted men, it was all about technology and the kill.

The *North Carolina* was an advanced stealth multi-mission nuclear-powered submarine designed for deep ocean antisubmarine warfare as well as shallow-water operations. It had a fly-by-wire control system and two Photonics Masts that housed color, high-resolution black and white, and infrared digital cameras atop telescoping arms. No more bulky barrel periscope that forced the builders to place the control room near the curvature of the hull. With the advent of the Photonics Masts, the control room was now placed one deck down which afforded it more room and a vastly improved layout.

As for armaments, the *North Carolina* was at the top

of her class. She had twelve vertical launch tubes and four 533mm torpedo tubes. The vertical launching system had the capacity to launch sixteen Tomahawk cruise missiles in a single salvo. The torpedo tubes could fire conventional and nuclear-tipped torpedoes as well as harpoon antiship missiles.

Beyond the lethality of its weapons systems, Rutten especially liked the fact that his boat had a chamber built into it that could house the Advanced SEAL Delivery System minisubmarine that could deploy SEAL or marine reconnaissance teams for counterterrorism operations anywhere around the world. As terrorism and the states that sponsored it continued to multiply, Rutten knew that that capability made his boat even more invaluable to the modern navy in fighting a cowardly, but increasingly dangerous enemy.

That was the fight Rutten had signed up for. As countries like China, Iran, North Korea, Venezuela, and other dictatorships started to build, buy, and deploy more and more diesel-electric/air-independent propulsion submarines with the express purpose of infiltrating United States waters, Rutten knew that—while he, his crew, and the *North Carolina* still had to worry about the Russian ballistic missile submarines—the name of the game was now protecting the homeland against these rogue nations.

What he was being asked to do now was anything but that. His orders were diametrically opposed to the best interests of the United States.

But there was no mistake. Nothing had been lost in translation. The admiral himself had delivered the orders in person one hour before they sailed.

As he waited for his executive officer to appear in the control room, he took a sip of black coffee from a blue mug emblazoned with the name of his boat, and slowly looked at the young sailors manning their posts. Did they have a right to know? Would they be better off if he kept the information from them?

Rutten considered himself a very religious man, but the orders seemed to be in direct conflict with what he had been taught.

"Since when were there two United States navies?" Rutten whispered to himself as he thought of the unthinkable.

Surely someone would stop him from using a nuclear weapon. Surely an EAM FLASH message will come in to stop the madness.

CHAPTER THIRTY-SEVEN

At 5:10 in the morning, Campbell woke to a gentle but insistent pounding on his condo door.

As he swung his legs over the side of the bed, he tried to get his bleary eyes to focus on his alarm clock with no success. He then sat there for several more seconds and actually started to fall asleep sitting up. Before his mind could accomplish the feat, the pounding grew louder.

Campbell opened his eyes, turned his head toward the living room and screamed, "Shut the fuck up! I'm coming!"

He then stood, opened the draw of his nightstand, took out a scraped and scarred commando knife, and walked to his door.

This summer morning, like most, he was shirtless and actually wearing reindeer pajama bottoms his sister had bought for him a few years earlier for Christmas.

When he got to his door, he stood to the side. "Who is it?"

"Secret Service," answered the muffled voice.

Campbell was physically and mentally tired enough to be paranoid. "Yeah. Well, how about you slide your ID under the door."

Five seconds later, a black billfold squeezed between the bottom of the door and his plush gray carpet.

Campbell picked it up, opened it, read the name, and snapped it closed. He then took the chain off the lock, turned his deadbolt lock, opened the door and waved the man in.

"You want some coffee?" asked Campbell as he stood in the living room.

Per his training, David Langworthy looked first at Campbell's hands before he looked anywhere else. Upon seeing the commando knife, he offered an appreciative smile.

"Mean-looking knife. A tool from your previous life?"

Campbell looked down at the knife, which he still had partially hidden behind his right leg. "Yeah, I sort of forgot to give it back when I left."

Campbell then placed the knife on a shelf in his entertainment center as he started to walk toward the kitchen. "So, how about that coffee."

"Sure," said Langworthy as he closed the door behind him. "Cream and sugar if you've got it."

As Campbell walked into the small kitchenette, Langworthy took a quick glance into the bedroom and bathroom to see if they were alone. He then walked back out into the living room and sat down on the sofa.

During his career with the Secret Service, Langworthy had only drawn his weapon twice and never had to fire. The file he read before he came to see Campbell confirmed to him that the man now making his coffee had more than likely killed at least twenty people and wounded that many or more.

Campbell, he knew, like so many veterans who had killed in combat, was, as Sir Winston Churchill would say, "a bit of a riddle wrapped in a mystery inside an enigma." How could one take the life of a fellow human being, sometimes in the most vicious and brutal of ways, and then come back and be a productive member of society? Langworthy knew that the tragic answer to that question was that many could not.

Be it World War II, Vietnam, or Iraq, many who killed in those wars were emotionally scarred for life because of the experience. Many a combat soldier could not make the transition from killing the enemy one day, to being barked at by a fat supervisor from UPS the next. One moment they are literally saving the lives of their buddies, and the next, they are getting chewed out because they misplaced a package.

Langworthy knew that Campbell was well above the average combat soldier in terms of training, intelligence, skill, psychological makeup, and numbers killed. When he read Campbell's background, he felt fairly certain that, as a Secret Service agent, if he had to kill a potential assassin to save the life of the vice president, he would not lose much or any sleep over it. But, he also wondered how his mind would cope with the knowledge that he had taken the lives of a couple of dozen human beings. Did Campbell see their faces? Did he look into their eyes? Did he see the fear? How could such things not haunt a person? And yet, every indication was that Campbell had that part of his life tightly sealed off in a part of his brain that he could control.

Langworthy knew that to compartmentalize like that was also a skill set. And that most likely, Campbell had developed that skill long before he became a Navy SEAL. His childhood of poverty, squalor, and pain would have trained his mind to lock things away. If it had not, he would not have risen to his current level in life.

Langworthy had been around some dangerous individuals in his time, but no one quite like this former SEAL. He would tread lightly.

Campbell walked back out of the kitchenette and asked, "You want some toast to go with that coffee?"

Langworthy crossed his legs and shook his head. "Nope. I'm okay."

Campbell laughed. "Good. Because that was basically

a bluff. The bread turned green about three days ago. I haven't been to the store in a while."

Langworthy looked up at Campbell and noted the heavily muscled arms and chest. "How often do you work out?"

With the question, Campbell realized that he was shirtless. "Not as much as I should. Let me go grab a shirt and I'll be right back."

Twenty seconds later, Campbell was back, wearing a white Boston Red Sox T-shirt.

Langworthy laughed at the sight. "The red letters are a great match for your reindeer pajamas."

"Hey, give me a break. I'm a bachelor. I just wear what's clean."

"Well," said Langworthy, "at least we've got the same baseball team in common."

"Yeah? Where you from?"

"Originally, the Cape. My parents moved from Massachusetts to Texas when I was about eleven, but I still consider the Sox to be my team."

"Great. I'm from Dorchester."

"I know."

Campbell nodded. "Of course you do. So what exactly does the Secret Service want of me at five fifteen in the morning?"

Langworthy adjusted his Glock 9mm, which was digging into his side a bit. "The Secret Service? Nothing. Me? I wanted to chat with you about some things the vice president mentioned."

CHAPTER THIRTY-EIGHT

President Robertson sat in the Roosevelt Room with General Mitchell, Kent Riley, Julia Sessions, and Graham Kinahan, the director of the FBI. The Roosevelt Room was directly across the hall from the Oval Office and was so designated because of the memorabilia it showcased from the two Roosevelt presidencies. Not the least of which being the Nobel Peace Prize awarded to Teddy Roosevelt in 1906 for brokering the war between Russia and Japan. A prize that was the furthest thing from Robertson's mind or aspirations.

"General Mitchell tells me that six of the top Islamic terrorists in the world have just been assassinated. Is that what your people are telling you, Graham?"

Kinahan adjusted his wire-rimmed glasses, patted down his thinning reddish blond hair, and looked over at Robertson. "Yes, Mr. President. That is the information my people are picking up."

"Well, seems like welcome news to me."

"Yes, sir," agreed the FBI director. "Those killings will most definitely lead to the activation of several Islamic sleeper cells both here and in Europe."

"Excellent," said the president with a smile. "And when these cells hit, what are our expectations of casualties here in the United States?"

"Satellite phone traffic we have intercepted the last

few months indicates that the Islamists have smuggled enough explosives and radioactive material into our country to kill upwards of fifty thousand Americans."

That number was met by silence from the four others seated around the table.

After another few seconds of introspection, the president spoke up.

"Excellent. That's very good news indeed, Graham. Just the sort of chaos and results we were looking for. I suggest we get our contingency plans in motion."

"I have already gotten those under way, Mr. President. Among other things, I have ordered that our people start their respective journeys toward Neptune," said General Mitchell.

The president stood and all followed his lead. "Thank you, Wayne. I should have known you would be on top of this. Now, if you would, I would ask that we all bow our heads and thank our Lord for His guidance, His support, and His generosity in bringing us one step closer to His plan for this world."

CHAPTER THIRTY-NINE

As Ian Campbell hosted David Langworthy, Vice President Dale was looking across the table at Paula Hanson, the director of the Central Intelligence Agency.

Like Dale, Hanson had served in the United States Senate, with the beginning of her Senate career seeing her claim a coveted seat on the Senate Foreign Relations Committee. She was given that plum assignment mostly on the strength of her sixteen years of employment as a clandestine operative for the CIA.

While running for president and shamelessly pandering for the female vote, Shelby Robertson promised to appoint a woman to head up the nation's top spy agency. Once elected, he reached out to Hanson based on the strong recommendation of his vice president. While he harbored no great respect for Dale, he was thankful for her help on the campaign trail and decided to reward her with this crumb. This particular morning, Dale was not only very grateful that he did, but appreciated the irony of it all.

"What do you think?" asked the vice president as she reached for her bagel.

The DCI shook her head as she looked out the window toward the sloping lawn of the naval observatory. "I don't know, Eileen. We are really in uncharted waters here. This is a very dangerous path we are now walking. It's one thing to feel the president of the United States has frozen you out of his administration because he's grown tired of you. It's quite another to suggest that he's engaged in conduct that could very well morph from unethical, to criminal, to traitorous."

"That's the point, Paula. While I haven't figured out what he's up to, I do have enough intelligence and political common sense to know that it's far more than freezing me out of government. This is not about my ego. I couldn't honestly care less. This is about the fact that over the last number of months, President Robertson has shrunk his circle of advisors to a small cadre of religious zealots . . ."

The vice president pushed her chair back, stood, and started to pace back and forth in front of the table.

"Paula, you've known me for a long time. We're close friends. You know that I don't have flights of fancy. I consider myself to be a very good person and a very good Christian. But when you hear Robertson's handpicked group of advisors talk, it makes me sound like I'm a proabortion atheist. There is a finality in their remarks. They oftentimes communicate in fatalistic terms but seem to be serenely peaceful with regard to the subject. Ironically, it sounds very much like one of your briefings when you describe the motivations of the terrorists who target our nation. As I told someone recently, I have a gut feeling that something is coming to a head."

Hanson looked alarmed with that last bit of information. "Who have you been talking to about this?"

"I'd rather not say at this point."

Hanson laughed derisively at the response. "You have to be out of your mind if you think I'm going to accept that answer. Given what we are talking about, if you are not prepared to lay every card on the table, then I really don't see the point in continuing this discussion."

Dale crossed her arms across her chest and looked

down at her longtime friend. "Fine. You are right. It was Ian Campbell."

"The deputy chief of staff?"

"Yes."

"Isn't he part of this inner circle that has you so concerned?"

The vice president nodded as she sat back down to drink some orange juice. "Yes and no," she answered once she placed the glass back on the coaster. "As far as I can tell, the president is convinced that Campbell is a true believer. While that snake Kent Riley may have his doubts, the president seems ready to bring Campbell in even closer."

"And what if you're wrong? What if Campbell is really part of the team and he's ratted you out to the president?"

The vice president lowered her head and spoke softly but deliberately. "I don't think I'm wrong, but if I am, it may be the last mistake I'll ever make."

"Yeah, well if you're right about your nonspecific but ominous signs, then the last thing any of us have to worry about is just making our final mistake."

The vice president raised her head and seemed to have a bit of fire in her contact-lens-covered, bright blue eyes. "I am right. I don't know what I'm right about, but I know something is going on and that something is moving rapidly. That's why I reached out to you several months ago. You've got the resources that can confirm some of this. You've got the people who can tell us who, beyond Riley and Sessions, are in on this with the president. They speak in shorthand as if they are expecting an attack. But if that were so, you would, or should, have intelligence to confirm it."

"As you know, our friendship doesn't mean jack to me at the moment. Whatever I do or don't do will be based solely on my responsibility to this nation. As silly as this may sound to some people, when I first joined the agency on the covert side, then when I first became a senator, and finally, when I was sworn in as the director of the CIA, I took an oath to protect our nation from all enemies, foreign and *domestic*. That oath means something to me. It's not a collection of hollow words. Even before we talked a few months ago, some of my people had come to me privately with concerns regarding the Christian Ambassadors. Over the last couple of years, General Breck, Admiral Thomas, and the president's former classmate and best friend, General Mitchell, have quietly assumed a larger profile within our government. They have really stepped up the evangelical rhetoric as they have reached out to nonmilitary, high-ranking officials in our government. People who, as you and I have discussed, have this six degrees of separation when it comes to their ultrastrong religious beliefs. Obviously, the president is at the head of that class."

"Yes," answered the vice president. "It seems their tentacles reach into every branch of government."

"Almost," Hanson said with a smile.

"Yeah, that's right. Why not CIA?"

Hanson squinted her hazel-green eyes almost closed. "I don't have a clue. Maybe we just don't have the right mix of Christians for them. I'm a nonpracticing Catholic. The director of the National Clandestine Service is a practicing Mormon. Who knows. Maybe they decided they had enough without taking a chance on co-opting our agency."

"Maybe they have co-opted enough to do whatever they have in mind."

"Well," said Hanson as she reached for the pot to refill her coffee cup, "one person they *have* co-opted is the director of the FBI. He's another one of those guys who goes way back with the president and Mitchell. Seems so obvious now, but when the administration was being put together, our focus was on Al Qaeda, Iran, China, and other threats. We never stopped long enough to connect the dots on how Robertson was really building his administration. Wasn't our bailiwick. Just seemed like the usual mostly white boys club to us."

"Yeah," said the vice president with a smile. "White boys with dangerous toys."

"With regard to Graham Kinahan, my people tell me he was at the White House earlier this morning. Well before the normally scheduled intelligence briefings."

"So, you are keeping an eye on—pardon the joke—all the president's men?"

The director of Central Intelligence nodded her head. "Illegally, yes. I'm in violation of our charter regarding domestic spying, but you got me nervous enough earlier to decide that I was not going to trust this task to anyone else. I need my people reporting directly to me."

"And they told you that Kinahan went in for a predawn meeting?"

"Not just him. General Mitchell is still in town and he was present as well."

"Does that tell you anything?"

"One more piece of the puzzle. Again, against the very laws of our nation, I have several of our paramilitary teams operating here in the United States. One of those teams was out at Andrews and photographed the president, General Mitchell, and your boy Campbell, getting on a C-40 heading south. The trip was not on the president's schedule and he was back in the White House in time for a three o'clock meeting."

"I had no idea. Where did they go?"

"Why don't you ask your new boyfriend?"

"Ian?"

"None other," said Hanson. "If you're wrong about him, he won't tell you anything. But if you're right, then you maybe learn something and buy us some more life insurance."

When Paula Hanson got back to her office at CIA headquarters in Langley, Virginia, the director of the National Clandestine Service was waiting for her.

"Did you tell her?" These were the first words out of her mouth when the soundproof door was closed.

"Did I tell her what?" asked Hanson as she maneuvered behind her desk to sit in her chair.

"Did you tell her about the Judas Club?"

Hanson shook her head as she moved her mouse to wake up her computer. "Did I tell the vice president of the United States that we have covertly assembled a government within our government to monitor and potentially neutralize the government within our government that now worries us?"

"Yes. I thought we agreed you would based on the agenda for the last meeting of the club."

"Well I didn't."

"Why not? We are way out of our element here, Paula. We are messing with the Constitution and the line of succession. Many, if not most, in and out of government, would already label us as traitors. We need to kick this up to the vice president to cover our asses."

"I know. I agree. But not yet. She's not ready to be told. I could see it in her eyes. She is not a professional operative. She may not buy into our argument that the end justifies the means on this one. She doesn't have the poker face to deal with Robertson and his thugs."

The director of the National Clandestine Service—the person in charge of the human intelligence agents who spied overseas for the nation and the paramilitary operatives that supported them—shrugged her shoulders. "Who gives a shit if she has a poker face?"

"I do. I'd rather not have her assassinated."

"You really think they'd go that far . . . to kill the vice president of the United States?"

"Much, much farther, in fact. They've already killed a three-star general. That was the signal to me that there is no going back for these people. Their insanity has reached a level that quite possibly has no parallel in history. And guess what? We've got ringside seats to the circus."

"Yeah," agreed the deputy. "And we know exactly where they have pitched their shiny new tent. Did you tell the vice president that?"

"No."

"Why not?"

Hanson opened her secure Outlook page and then looked up at her deputy. "Because I want to see if Campbell tells her."

"Yeah, he's on the list of e-mails and phones we've been tapping."

The DCI nodded at the update and then said, "If he does tell her, we may be able to use him."

"And if he doesn't?"

"Then he's one of them and we'll have to have one of our teams deal with him . . . quickly."

CHAPTER FORTY

Three days later, Harrods in London, Macy's on Thirty-fourth Street in New York, Marshall Field in Chicago, and fifty-plus-story residential towers in San Diego, Los Angeles, and San Francisco, were brought down to the ground at basically the exact same time, by a coordinated series of powerful explosions.

As it was a busy Saturday evening in London, its world-famous department store was full of locals and tourists trying to find the best deals in a place where celebrities often went to see and be seen. Scotland Yard's first estimate on the dead and wounded was something over two thousand.

That store, like Macy's in New York and Marshall Field in Chicago, had been infiltrated months earlier by Islamic terrorists masquerading as part of the cleaning crew. With regard to Harrods, they had strategically placed ten powerful bombs at the basement level with the sole purpose, upon detonation, of imploding the building into rubble, dust, and unimagined carnage.

The planning, timing, and execution was carried out to perfection. Soon after Harrods fell, Macy's, and then Marshall Field, collapsed upon themselves in fiery explosions that blew out windows for tens of blocks around, and when the last bits of brick and mortar had settled to the ground, over seven thousand people had been killed and wounded.

When the casualties from the residential towers in San Diego, Los Angeles, and San Francisco were added to the count, the number of dead and wounded had soared to over forty thousand. Revenge had been achieved, a twisted version of honor reclaimed, and forty thousand pawns had just been sacrificed for the greater good of warring faiths.

The worst was yet to come.

CHAPTER FORTY-ONE

Like most of the essential personnel in the United States Government, Campbell had rushed back to his office when he was informed of the bombings. The nation, as it had been with more and more frequency over the last few years, was once again at Code Red.

When Campbell walked into his office suite, his assistant was already at her desk. One look and it was clear to him that she had been crying.

"Hi, Janice. Thanks for coming in."

The blonde-haired and bespectacled assistant almost wailed at her boss. "Have they told you what's going on? It's like an armed camp outside. I've never seen so many agents and ERT guys on the grounds. Do they think the White House is going to be hit next? This is the worst one yet. Most of the phone lines are jammed. People are fleeing the city. My husband cried this morning as he begged me not to come to work and to quit my job. Should I quit, Ian? Should my husband and I drive to South Carolina to be with our daughters and their families? These monsters have just killed tens of thousands of people. Tell me what to do."

At the completion of her impassioned and frightened remarks, she burst into uncontrollable sobbing.

Campbell walked over to her desk, got down on one knee beside her, and gently pulled her head into his chest and held her for the next couple of minutes as the terror of the moment cascaded from her eyes and nose.

When she finally pulled back, she looked at the blue blazer he was wearing and her eyes went wide. "Oh, Ian. I'm so sorry. I've covered your jacket with tears and . . . stuff."

Campbell looked down at the shiny collection of liquid that had attached itself to the left side of his sport coat. "Yikes," he laughed. "Well, I wanted to waterproof this coat anyway, so the mucus should certainly help."

In spite of the moment, Janice laughed at the remark as she reached for the box of tissues on her desk. She pulled out a handful and proceeded to try and dry the front of Campbell's jacket.

Campbell stepped back out of arm's reach. "No, no. Don't worry about it," he said as he looked at the multitude of blue tissue flecks that had now attached themselves to the liquid and his jacket. "It's nothing that can't be dry-cleaned."

After saying that, he took it off and went to hang it on a coatrack in the small reception area.

He then walked back over to his assistant who was now blowing her nose into her Kleenex.

"Look. At this point, I don't know much more than you. I suspect what's done is done. Meaning I don't think they are going to hit us again . . . at least for this wave of attacks. At the moment, you can tell your husband that I think the White House is about the safest place you can be. And he should be perfectly fine out in Glen Burnie."

He started to walk into his office and then stopped and turned back to look at her. "Do I think you and your husband should move to South Carolina to be with your daughters?"

He went silent for a few moments as the last few days flashed across his mind.

"Yeah. You know what? I do think you ought to move.

It's up to you to decide as to when you think you are ready. But when you are, I think it would be a great place to be for a while."

Janice sucked in her breath in preparation of another crying jag. "Why? You know something you're not telling me. Please tell me what it is?"

Campbell stood in his doorway and shook his head. "I honestly wish I could. If I knew something concrete, I'd tell you. Barring that, my best advice is that you should take early retirement and join your daughters and grandchildren."

"Now?"

"No," said Campbell with a smile. "Not quite yet. Right now, I'd like you to find Tammy Han and ask her to come to my office."

CHAPTER FORTY-TWO

Five minutes later, Han was seated in Campbell's office with the door closed. She was wearing sneakers, blue warm-up bottoms and a gray Princeton T-shirt.

"Tam," Campbell pleaded, "can we please put our personal lives behind us. I can't exaggerate how weird and out of control all of this is getting."

Han smiled and reached over to offer her right hand. "With what's going on . . . done."

Campbell shook it and seemed relieved with the response. "Great. Thanks. Look, the fact is, I always thought you were the best when you were back in naval intelligence and I don't think anyone comes close to you for talent or instincts in this building. So with that buildup, tell me something. Tell me anything."

"Okay," answered Han. "I'll tell you something. Speaking of weird, the president does not seem all that concerned with the bombings. He's been holed up in the Oval for the last hour or so with Kent Riley and Julia Sessions. He's kept our entire intelligence team cooling their heels in the Situation Room for over two hours."

"Where's the vice president?"

"Last time I heard, she was on her way to the Sit Room as well."

Campbell had not seen the vice president since they

had dinner, but his conversation with Langworthy made it very clear that her interest in him had only increased in the interim.

"How come you're not down there?"

"No room. Between my boss, the CIA, FBI, and Homeland Security types, it's standing room only."

Campbell laughed. "Yeah. All with competing theories and all trying desperately to cover their asses just in case they missed something blindingly obvious."

Han's long hair was in a ponytail and it bounced about as she nodded her head in agreement. "Other than that, communications traffic in the Middle East is at an all-time high among the rank-and-file terrorists. They are all congratulating each other and praising Allah for the blow he has dealt to the satanic infidels in England and the United States. Beyond that, the leadership of the top terrorist groups have gone into hiding. Actually, they've been burrowed into their rat holes since somebody whacked their six deputies."

Campbell stopped her. "Yeah, speaking of that. Do we have a clue who did the hit? I know the Israelis are getting very nervous, but I wouldn't think they'd take a chance like that. Not with the possibility of a Palestinian State being as close to reality as it is . . . or was."

Even though the door was closed, Han still felt the need to lower her voice. "Oh, it wasn't the Israelis."

Campbell wrinkled his forehead. "The Brits?"

Han shook her head.

"Us?" asked a disbelieving Campbell.

Han now offered her first smile of the meeting.

"Not exactly."

"Come on, Tammy. The world's on the brink of total anarchy, so just tell me what you know."

"Sorry. Well, ever since my days in the navy, I've had sort of a unique hobby."

"What's that?" asked Campbell as he unbuttoned the cuffs of his light blue dress shirt, and rolled up the sleeves.

"I like to keep tabs on the intelligence traffic for our side."

Campbell smiled. "Your hobby is to spy on our spies?"

"More or less. I mean, I like tennis, golf and certain, ah, inspirational movies . . . as you used to know . . . but this is the hobby I find most fun and challenging."

"And?"

"And of particular interest of late, has been that freak collection of Christian crazies operating out of the Pentagon."

Campbell leaned back in his chair and closed his eyes. "Not just in the Pentagon, Tammy."

"No shit," exclaimed Han in a louder voice. "For my money, there's three of them meeting in the Oval Office right this second."

Campbell was well beyond the pretense of trying to protect the president or anyone else in the administration.

"You don't know the half of it."

"Maybe not," said Han as her unlined face lit up. "But I know this. Right before and right after those six fanatics got wasted in the Middle East, General Breck got some cryptic e-mails that seemed to indicate that the mission was first, commencing, and second, was successful."

"Tammy, I don't really care how you got the information, and I most likely wouldn't understand anyway. Just tell me. How sure are you?"

Han looked down toward her feet, saw that the laces on her right sneaker were loose, lifted her foot up off the floor, and retied the sneaker. Once done, she looked over at Campbell.

"Very. As in positive."

"Fine. I take your word for it. In fact, maybe we are betting our lives on your word."

Han did not seem concerned with the statement. "There's more."

"What?" asked Campbell in a tone that tried to communicate that he was tired of her histrionics.

"The group that communicated with Breck from the Middle East seems to be part of a team comprised entirely of former Special Forces, SEALs, and marine recon. A friend of mine at NSA has been working this with me, and we've got their communications traffic on tape and locked away."

"You've been driving *way* outside of your lane on this one."

"So what. Maybe I'm involved in more ways than you can imagine."

Campbell let the veiled remark slide, so Han continued.

"The world has been on the edge of going to Hell in a handbasket for the last few years and I'll be damned if I don't try to compile a list of all the bad guys—theirs and ours—and try to figure out what they're really up to and how it impacts the lovely Tammy Han."

"Well," laughed Campbell. "Like I said. You're the best."

Campbell started to stand when Han reached over and grabbed his arm. "Wait, Ian. I haven't told you the worst."

Campbell sat back in his chair and just stared at Han. His mind being too numb to ask the question.

"Aside from our former people operating out of the Middle East, my friend and I came across an even larger group operating here in the United States."

Campbell still did not say anything.

"It's a private army, Ian."

Campbell found the power to speak. "Anything else?"

"Yeah," answered Han as she stood. "It's on the move."

CHAPTER FORTY-THREE

Rachel Hiatt was sound asleep when her editor finally raised her on her cell phone.

"Rachel. It's Gail Dowd. Get your ass down here. We've been hit by terrorists again and we need to know what the White House knows."

Hiatt jumped out of bed, turned on her television, switched to CNN, and then watched the mass confusion as she quickly got dressed. Once dressed, she went to the bathroom, brushed her teeth, grabbed her laptop, and exited her apartment building on Massachusetts Avenue to find the city gridlocked on a Saturday morning.

As a native New Yorker, she had never felt the need to own a car, and even if she had one, it or a taxi, were clearly going nowhere. To the blare of car horns and screaming matches between boxed-in and terrified drivers, Hiatt started to power walk to the Washington bureau of the *New York Times* located at 1627 I Street.

As soon as she got to her desk, Dowd pounced on her. "Look, I know you're the rookie around here, but I've got everybody churning trying to get anything out of that Cro-Magnon-like White House. You've been over there a few times by now. Have you struck up even a hint of a professional relationship with one of those cave dwellers?"

Rachel had not told a soul about her conversations—or budding friendship—with Ian Campbell.

"Not really. I went to a couple of briefings with other beat reporters, but as of yet, haven't clicked with anyone over there."

"Fuck!" screamed Dowd as she stormed off toward her office. "End of the world or not, we can't get scooped again by the fuckin' *Washington Post*."

Rachel watched her recede into madness and then paused as she tried to figure out what to do next. At this point, she knew her first obligation was to herself, her brother, and family and not to her employer. With that in mind, she knew that the only thing she could do was to reach out to her contact in the White House.

With the phone lines of most of the nation still overloaded and jammed by Americans calling other Americans in a panic, Rachel decided to try and e-mail Campbell and hope for the best.

To her utter amazement, twenty seconds later, Campbell replied:

PARK. ONE HOUR.

Rachel immediately deleted the e-mail, deleted her sent e-mail, and then went to the deleted file and deleted both from there. Once done, she looked at her watch, made a note of the time, and wondered what the next hour would bring to her, the country, and the world.

CHAPTER FORTY-FOUR

As thousands of people fought to flee a city they feared may once again be targeted by those bent on the destruction of the United States, twelve men figuratively swam upstream against the human riptide. They did not fear an attack. They did not fear death. Their only fear was failing in their mission and, as a result, failing their Lord.

The team was divided evenly into four black SUVs and was led by the African American "homeless" man who, with his sergeant from his Special Forces days, had been trolling in front of the Mayflower Hotel days earlier. At the moment, they were just crossing the Memorial Bridge from Virginia, and were ever so slowly making their way toward their ultimate destination.

Each of the SUVs was equipped with police lights and sirens. Each of the twelve men possessed authentic FBI identification.

Almost as common as taxis in Washington were the black SUV "war wagons" that populated the motorcades which protected the sometimes hundreds of government and foreign leaders who crisscrossed the city daily on the way to meetings that ultimately served no one and solved nothing. Four more black SUVs thrown into the mix would be as good as invisible.

The former Special Forces captain, who commanded this particular group, sat in the passenger seat of the first

SUV. His entire being was now consumed with only one job. To avoid having any of the SUVs in his little convoy inadvertently hit one of the hundreds of potholes that littered the DC roads.

He was not worried in the least about damaging any of the tires or having his men bounce around on the lunar landscape that passed for roads in Washington. Rather, he was riveted with the thought of the immediate extinction of him and his men should the one thousand pounds of explosives packed into his SUV be jarred into ignition.

His vehicle and the third were each packed with one thousand pounds of C4, and each also carried two 105mm artillery shells which were wired to go off with the high-grade plastic explosives. During his three tours in Iraq, he and his team had dodged and been hit by more than their share of improvised explosive devices (IEDs). While they hated these weapons of terror that had been responsible for the majority of U.S. casualties, they also understood that it was to their benefit to learn as much about them as possible.

What they discovered was that Iranian intelligence agents were designing and then building the most lethal of these explosives. While primitive compared to the might and technology of the U.S. military, they were still highly effective in urban combat when the targeted vehicle would be at its most vulnerable. As it was his team's intent to decimate a vehicle, primitive was just perfect.

The former captain looked down at his watch. If the operation went as planned, he and his men would be racing to their new home under the sea less than twelve hours from now. A new world was coming and it was his job to tie up some of the loose ends.

CHAPTER FORTY-FIVE

As Campbell walked quickly down Seventeenth Street toward Farragut Park, he wondered, as he had many times since his nation was first hit on September 11, 2001, how the people of London did it during the constant bombardment they endured during World War II.

The German blitz of England by the Luftwaffe lasted from September of 1940 until May of 1941. During that time, the Nazi air force bombed London for fifty-seven consecutive nights. By the time the blitz had wound down, over forty-six thousand men, women, and children had been killed by the indiscriminate bombs and incendiary devices.

And yet, through the unrelenting terror, the British demonstrated to the world the resolve of a people who would not be intimidated. Every night they would be bombed and every morning they would get up, dust themselves off, and go to work. They would not give in to evil.

As Campbell looked at the traffic that clogged the DC streets, he wondered if that was the future of his nation. Like Israel now and England before, would they have to accept terror strikes as an everyday part of life? Would they have to fool themselves into thinking that the odds were in their favor? That while the terrorists may kill twenty, forty, or sixty thousand Americans at a time, in a nation of over three hundred million, that maybe they would live to make it home and then start the process all over again. Was that the future of America? Was that a future anyone could really accept?

As Campbell walked across I Street, he spotted Rachel sitting on a bench with her right leg jumping like a jack-hammer. As he got closer, he was not surprised to see, other than a circle of homeless men at the far end of the park, that she was alone.

When she saw Campbell approaching, she sprang off the bench and almost sprinted to intercept him. When they collided, she wrapped her arms around him and held him tightly for well over a minute.

After they separated, he looked into her eyes and was somewhat surprised not to see any tears. Maybe she had hit rock bottom as far as her emotions.

"Ian," she finally said. "Can you please tell me what's going on?"

Campbell pointed to the bench next to them and they both sat down.

"Are you wearing your Rachel hat or your *New York Times* hat?"

Rachel shook her head and her face turned serious. "Thanks for the trust."

"Oh, come on, Rachel. That's a totally legitimate question. You can't get pissed over me asking something like that. Truth be told, I've yet to deal with a reporter who hasn't screwed me or this administration over."

At the conclusion of the sentence, Rachel stormed off the bench heading back toward I Street.

Campbell quickly ran after her and grabbed her by the right arm. She yanked her arm from his grasp and spun to face him in one motion. "What!" she yelled. "Is the Navy SEAL going to abuse me again!"

Instead of getting angry or responding in a harsh way, Campbell blankly stared at her as a sense of profound sadness washed over him. He then slowly shook his head and whispered, "Sorry I bothered you," as he started to walk back to the White House.

Hiatt watched after him and was at a loss as to what to do. Her pride was telling her one thing, and her common sense was screaming another. As she gazed at the evolving panic around the park, she shoved pride to the back of her mind and ran after Campbell.

"Ian," she said as caught up with him on the side of the street waiting for a break in the traffic jam. "I'm sorry. You have every right to ask that question. I'm a reporter. That's my gig. But from the minute we talked, I told you this wasn't about the *New York Times* and it wasn't about reporting. It was about my brother, and now"—she paused and pointed to the confusion all around them— "it's about something much larger. Something much larger that you are dealing with and something much larger that our nation is dealing with. Having said that, can you cut a girl some slack and come back and sit down with me and tell me *anything* that will make me feel even a tiny bit better?"

Campbell looked at her infectious and sincere smile, nodded his head, and gently took her left hand in his right as he turned to walk back toward one of the benches.

When they sat, Campbell leaned his head back, closed his eyes, and let the morning sun warm his face as he organized his thoughts.

Hiatt looked at him and knew that she needed to wait for him to speak. She was desperate to know what he knew and also petrified that he might tell her and confirm her worst fears.

As Campbell sat with his eyes closed, he thought of the phrase, "out of sight, out of mind." As he listened to the background noise of the traffic, the occasional horn, the throng of pigeons cooing around them, and the rustle of the branches in the soft breeze above his head, he allowed his mind to transport him back in time to his dysfunctional childhood. When he was about five or six years of age and his mother and father would engage in one of their drunken screaming matches, or another sheriff or constable would pound on their front door to throw them and their meager possessions out onto the street, he would grab his Bugs Bunny flashlight, run into his bedroom closet, turn on the flashlight to banish the scary darkness, and then cover both ears with his hands and hum little songs until either the screaming stopped or his older brother would pull him out of the closet to pack his things to move, once again, into a seedy motel, or the back of their car until his father could scam the next landlord into giving them an apartment.

With those depressing thoughts filling his mind, Campbell raised both hands to his head, covered his ears, and quietly hummed a song.

As Hiatt watched this eccentric behavior, she felt a pang of nervousness as she ran her hands up and down her own thighs. After thirty more seconds of his humming, she could take no more and tapped him on the arm.

Campbell stopped humming, lowered his hands, and slowly opened his eyes. After another few seconds, he sat up straight on the bench and turned to face her.

"Yes?" he asked with the beginning of a smile.

"What in the world are you doing? You're starting to scare me a little."

Campbell shook his head. "Nothing to worry about. Just confirming to myself that you can't always hide from bad things and pretend they don't exist. It didn't work when I was a child and it sure as hell won't work now."

Rachel did not have the energy nor inclination to engage in a philosophical discussion. "Okay. If you say so. Whatever."

Campbell smiled more broadly at her response and the expression on her face. "Don't worry. I haven't snapped . . . yet."

Hiatt returned the smile and unconsciously reached for his hand.

"I really don't want to know, but since you just brought it up, can you please tell me what horrible things we are facing now? I'm guessing that whether I know or not . . . I'll be the one to snap."

Campbell looked down at his watch. "I've got to get back to the White House in a few minutes. As it is, someone is going to be looking for me. Not exactly the best time to pull a disappearing act from the building."

"So why did you?"

Campbell placed his right hand on top of her hand covering his left. "I think you know. It's what you said on my balcony. We don't know each other, but we *know* each other. Aside from the little background you gave me, I really know next to nothing about you. I don't know your politics, don't know if you're ultraliberal or just liberal . . ."

"Hey, watch it," said Hiatt with a smile. "Not everyone at the *Times* drinks the leftist Kool-aid."

". . . don't know if you've been married," he continued. "Don't know if you're seeing someone, and don't know . . . anything, really."

"And yet you slipped away from the White House during a national emergency to meet with me."

"I did."

"So again. Why?"

Campbell ever so faintly began to rock back and forth on the bench. Years earlier, when he went to see a naval psychologist about nightmares brought on by post-traumatic stress syndrome, the doctor noticed the rocking and told him that it was a defense mechanism employed by his mind to deal with stress overload. When

Campbell told the doctor he had been rocking like that since he was a child, the doctor quietly explained to him that his PTSS began during and because of his highly traumatic childhood. His combat experiences had merely piled on to an existing problem.

"Because, I've come to the conclusion that most of it is just bullshit. The last few days has confirmed to me that a universe of about two thousand people are the puppet masters for the three hundred million rest of us. They jerk the strings and we obediently dance to their self-serving and choreographed dance. We don't matter. We think we do, but we are so wrong. Real life inside the White House, like all of government, is about circulating useless information that never leaves the building and never really matters. The two thousand don't care. They keep their own counsel and have their own experts. They already have the answers they want. They have already decided the best course of action and you, me, and every-one else in this country are irrelevant to them. In fact, I could make the argument that we are much more of a hindrance to them than a help. We are the herd and the herd has grown much too large and must be thinned. They don't have the resources or the time to keep an eye on all of us and still do what they have to do. I suppose I always knew that, but the last few days has made that the truth above all others in my mind."

Rachel slid closer to him. "And that made you want to come talk with me."

Campbell nodded forcefully. "Yes. More than any-thing. At the end of the day, all that really matters in this mostly ugly and painful world, is a human connection. Faith is wonderful and faith matters to me, but I still need a connection. In one way or another, I've been alone for all of my life. Part of that was a way to protect me from anyone else hurting me and part of it was because of the career path I chose. You never wanted to get too close to a person because you didn't know when you'd lose them on the battlefield."

"Ian. We are not on a battlefield now."

Campbell laughed. "Of course we are. Look around you. Look around the world. The entire planet has become a battlefield. Our two thousand have declared war on their two thousand who declared war on the next nation's two thousand and so on. It's not going to stop. The fanatics have taken over and the global herd is going to pay the price. Well, before they inflict the final damage, I wanted a connection. I want to be part of a real human connection. A real human relationship. I don't want . . . I don't want to be alone anymore."

Hiatt looked at him and tried to see anything in his eyes that would tell her he was playing her for reasons yet to be learned. The harder she looked, the more she felt he was simply opening up to her.

Campbell turned on the bench to better face her. "Look. I'm sorry about all of this. I apologize for dumping this mental dreck all over you. You don't know jack-shit about me other than discovering now that I'm a head case in so many ways."

"Who isn't?" Hiatt smiled. "And no need to apologize. I want to learn more about you. I want to know what in your background and life created the person sitting next to me now. And I'm happy to know that if I'm a fellow sheep on the way to the slaughter, that this big, tough sheep is not only there next to me, but seems to care about me . . ."

Rachel shrugged her shoulders as she continued. "I'm no different than you. We all pretend our job is so important. Especially those of us in the media. We work and work and work, and for what? Does it really make a difference? Does it make any difference to the two thousand puppet masters you just talked about? I guess the answer is, not one bit. We work and push and try to succeed and all the while we are petrified to look behind us and see the truth. We are petrified to acknowledge that the truth is that what we do, in the grand scheme of things, does not matter. To continue with your 'herd' analogy, we are the hamsters on the wheel, the rats in the maze. Life goes by in the blink of an eye and we wake up one day and we are very old people who have lost the ones we love, lost the capacity to work and oftentimes lost the capacity to physically take care of ourselves. And at the end of our time on earth, what mark did we really leave? Take a look back and we will see a new hamster on our wheel, a new rat in our maze and a new sheep in our place about to be slaughtered . . ."

Hiatt stopped for a second to get the next words right. "I can't believe that we are both talking this psychobabble, but the real truth is that I'm on this bench for the same reason you are. I'm alone in life and I'm scared beyond comprehension. My brother is gone, my parents are up in New York, and the 'friends' I have at work are superficial at best. I do think we have a real connection. I do feel something. Maybe this will turn out to be the ultimate shipboard romance and as we really do get to know each other, we will each say, 'What in the world was I thinking?'"

Campbell blinked his eyes rapidly to deal with his emotions as he spoke. "Maybe. I don't think so. Look, Rachel. As mentioned, you don't know much about me. I know you've read things about me and think you understand certain aspects, but you really don't. I'm not a choirboy. I've hurt people. I've taken human life on the battlefield. I've been with quite a few women. I gave none of them the respect they deserved. If we're going to keep talking, going to keep exploring, then I think it's important that you know that."

"Thank you," was all that Rachel could think to say.

"That's just some of what I want you to know. There's

much more baggage. But I mostly want you to know that for the first time in my life, I feel it's incredibly important to get to know the person in front of me. Shit. I've opened up more to you now on this bench than I have to anyone else ever. So, to wrap up this stream-of-consciousness conversation, I do know what I'm thinking. I do know that I want to try and grow this relationship with you. I do know that. And at this point, that's the one thing I'm sure of . . ."

Campbell then stood. ". . . and I do know that I have to leave before I make a complete ass of myself."

Hiatt stood with him and smiled. "Anything but, Ian. Circumstances are accelerating our friendship much faster than normal and you know what?"

"What?"

"That's the only thing I'm thankful for in this whole mess. No matter what, I got to meet you."

Campbell reached down and held both of her hands. "Me too. Look, not to bring this back to the serious, but the president is up to something and he thinks I'm going to want to be part of it. Without getting into the details, I may be about to go to the 'undisclosed location' of all time. I have nothing to base it on other than a discussion with a colleague of mine earlier today, but my gut tells me this latest attack on the homeland was caused by our puppet masters pulling their strings."

Rachel looked panicked as she ignored the last part of his sentence. "You're going away? When?"

"I still don't know for sure. Could be soon." Campbell then smiled. "Maybe I can stop by for dinner tonight and we can talk further and see if we've come to our senses by then."

"Please. I'd like that very much. I need to see you again."

Campbell leaned in close to her and gave her a gentle kiss on the lips. "Absolutely."

As he turned and started to walk back to the White House, he stole a quick glance at four black SUVs moving up Seventeenth Street toward Connecticut and the general direction of the Mayflower Hotel.

He didn't give them a second thought as he rushed back to his office.

CHAPTER FORTY-SIX

Midafternoon found Paula Hanson and the rest of the Judas Club gathered in a large conference room at CIA headquarters. Among their number, and seated at the far end of the table, was Tammy Han.

Hanson looked at the now fifteen other faces in the room and said something that she thought would only haunt her worst nightmares and never enter into the realm of reality.

"Are we all agreed then, that the president of the United States has acted, and is about to act, in ways that are in direct violation of the laws and the Constitution of the United States of America . . ."

She then held up her hand in a stop signal before finishing. ". . . If anyone at this table does not agree with that statement or would like to voice an objection, it is imperative that you speak up now."

Hanson's request was met with resounding silence and looks of resolve.

"Fine," she continued. "Based on that, and our earlier meetings, I have decided that we will have to fully brief the vice president and the Speaker of the House tomorrow at the latest."

"Tomorrow is Sunday," said the representative from the NSC.

"Oh what, John?" offered the irreverent Han. "Because

it's the Lord's Day or something, we can't try to save the nation? That's how those dickhead zealots think."

"Ms. Han," scolded the director of the CIA, "as this meeting is being recorded, I'd suggest, and greatly appreciate, if you kept your remarks professional and on topic."

"Yes ma'am. My apologies," said Han as she lowered her head and pretended to look at her notes.

Hanson nodded at Han and then went silent in reflection as she marveled at their current situation. As women in government, we have come so far and yet, are backsliding so fast, she thought. The United States has a female vice president, a female Speaker of the House, a female head of the CIA, and at least four very accomplished women preparing to run for president to succeed Shelby Robertson. And for what? To bear witness to their progress and the very security of their nation, threatened by a group of men who would so twist their religion, as to make it unrecognizable, grotesque, and a vehicle to do the unthinkable?

Hanson frowned slightly, shook her head as if to clear it, and then looked around the table at the men and women gathered together to anticipate the next move of those who had no doubts and were, quite likely, anxious to enter into battle.

"What do we know, Tim?" she asked of the assistant director of the Office of Counterterrorism at the FBI.

"What do we know? Aside from my boss being one of the leaders of the Christian Ambassadors? Too much and next to nothing. People seem to be disappearing. Several flag officers from the Pentagon have gone missing as well as various colonels, majors, ensigns, and enlisted personnel. All people we have tagged in the past. Beyond that, at least a quarter of the president's hometown church have vanished. Men, women, and children. Entire families. They are just gone."

208   Douglas MacKinnon

"Any ideas as to where?"

"Sure. The underwater Shangri-la. We know that General Mitchell has been busy the last few days trying to shepherd some of their believers in that direction."

"And what's your best guess as to why?"

The assistant director looked around the table at those who already knew the answer to the question.

"Because for them the game clock is winding down to its final seconds."

Hanson fought to disregard the negative thoughts that just flooded her mind. "And to conclude your sports analogy, what happens when the buzzer sounds?"

"You tell me."

CHAPTER FORTY-SEVEN

David Langworthy walked quickly into Campbell's suite unannounced. As Campbell's assistant had just gone to the restroom, Langworthy kept walking straight into Campbell's office and quickly closed the door behind him.

"Hey, what are—" said Campbell as the agent's shadow fell across his desk.

"Quiet," said Langworthy. "We don't have much time."

Campbell looked at his closed door and half expected it to burst open. "Don't have much time for what?"

"For me to deliver a message."

Campbell waited and Langworthy remained silent.

"What?" Campbell said in a raised voice. "Why does everyone have to be so fuckin' melodramatic? Can't people just speak anymore? What message?"

Langworthy tapped the top of Campbell's desk. "You need to be home tonight. Don't go anywhere, don't make any phone calls, keep your shades down, and stay off your computer."

Campbell's first thought was of Rachel and their tentative plans for dinner.

"Why?"

Langworthy laughed. "Well, at the risk of sounding melodramatic, the fate of the nation may depend upon you being home."

Campbell's mind raced to try and figure out the reason. Within seconds, he thought he had solved the mystery.

"I'd like to see how you're going to pull this one off."

Langworthy still had the traces of a smile on his face. "Pull what off?"

Before Campbell could respond, his phone rang. He looked down at the screen and saw that it was his assistant.

"Yes, Janice," he said as he picked up the handset.

"The president wants to see you right away, Ian. What do you think that's about? What could he want? I'm scared."

Campbell looked up at Langworthy and raised his eyebrows before answering his assistant. "Nothing to be scared of, Janice. Things will be fine soon. I promise."

"Nothing's ever going to be fine again," said Langworthy after Campbell hung up.

Campbell stood up and looked at the agent. "That's not a very positive attitude. I thought it was your job to make sure everything was fine."

Langworthy shook his head. "Nope. You've got me confused with the fuckin' tooth fairy, or Spider-Man, or a camp counselor. I'm all about the power of negative thinking. I try to think of the worst thing possible and then work my way back from that to try and figure out some answers or find an escape hatch."

"Ten-four on that."

Langworthy nodded his head toward the phone. "So what's up? The master calling?"

"Yup. Maybe this is the command performance."

Langworthy turned toward the door. "If so, it may come in useful tonight. Please stay put."

CHAPTER FORTY-EIGHT

When Campbell walked into the Oval Office, he was greeted with the sight of the president, General Mitchell, Kent Riley, and Julia Sessions all sitting in a tight little circle near the center of the room. All, but the president, seemed unhappy with his entrance.

"Thank you for coming everyone," said Robertson as he looked at those around him. "Ian and I are going to have a heart-to-heart discussion."

As he stood, Kent Riley openly shook his head in contempt at the president's remark. He lingered for a second, clearly conflicted as to if he should say something to the president before leaving. He decided to bite his tongue as he glared at Campbell on his way out of the Oval Office.

When they were alone with the door closed, the president patted the sofa next to him. "Come on, Ian. Come take a load off. It's been a tragic day and I'm sure you're tired."

Campbell walked over to the sofa, sat, and turned to face the president. All without saying a word.

"Would you like a coffee? A Coke? A stiff drink?" asked the abnormally effervescent president.

"No sir, Mr. President. I'm good."

"Well, I'm not," said the president with a smile. "After what our nation has just been through today, I'd say I'm entitled to have a scotch and water. Sure you won't join me?"

Campbell shook his head. As he did, the president picked up the phone and put in his order with his assistant.

Upon hanging up, the president looked over at Campbell with a face that could only be described as beaming. While Campbell did not have much experience with it as a child, he imagined the president now had a face that was mostly the domain of little children just about to burst from their rooms to tackle the multitude of presents arrayed under the Christmas tree.

"Kent Riley doesn't like you," said the president as he waited for a reaction.

Campbell remained silent.

"I'd like you to respond to that statement, Ian."

Campbell chewed on his lower lip for a second or two before answering. "All right. Riley is a fat, pampered rich kid who has never done an honest day's work in his life. He's a troll who, like the bully in the school yard, abuses the power that was given to him but not earned. He's an ivory tower academic who has zero idea of how the real world works. And for my money, his fat ass wouldn't last ten seconds outside of the protective bubble you have built for him."

The president burst out laughing and actually slapped his knee. "Gee, don't sugarcoat it, Ian. Tell me what you really think."

Campbell was on the middle of the tightrope and was taking risks that were not warranted. He knew that, but was almost powerless to stop the words from leaving his mouth.

"I'm sorry if I crossed a line, Mr. President."

"Nothing at all to apologize for, my boy. All leaders need useful idiots, and Riley is one of mine. He's much more interested in power than faith, but as long as I know that, he can still be of great service to me . . . and the Lord."

"Yes, sir. If you say so."

The president looked down and saw a piece of white lint on the right sleeve of his suit coat. As he had once read that in the eight years Ronald Reagan had been president, he had never once taken off his suit coat in respect to the office, Robertson thought that a fine example to emulate. He brushed off the offending lint with one quick motion and then looked back up at Campbell.

"What about you, Ian? Which do you value more? Power or faith?"

Campbell had no doubts that he was being administered the most important oral exam of his life, and flunking it would have consequences like no other. His only thought was how to further ingratiate himself to the president and his cause.

"I've never been one to crave power, Mr. President. I'm just not built that way. Maybe it's because of my childhood, or my military career, or just my DNA. I guess I've always defined success as doing something with my life that is meaningful to me."

The president smiled. "Well put, Ian. So, are you successful now? By your very definition, is what you are doing today, right this second, meaningful to you?"

Campbell was momentarily saved by a knocking on the door as the steward had arrived from the White House Mess with the president's drink order.

"Enter," said the president as he continued to look at Campbell.

The slightly curved and very heavy white door swung open and a Filipino steward walked in carrying a silver tray.

"Good afternoon, Mr. President."

"How are you, Fred?" asked the president warmly.

"Very well, Mr. President. If I may say so, thank you again for the money you sent to me and my wife. We were able to keep our house and we owe everything to your kindness."

The president waved his hand in the air. "Please don't give it a second thought. My assistant told me of your daughter's illness and how that had put you in a tight spot money-wise. Jesus Christ teaches us all that we are our brother's keepers. It was the least I could do. I'm happy to hear your daughter is fine and that you've caught up financially."

"Yes, sir," answered the glowing servant. "Thanks to you. Mr. President, I brought your scotch and water, and just in case, a very hot pot of coffee and two Cokes."

"Thank you, Fred. Most thoughtful as always."

After the steward left, Campbell quickly tried to factor in what he had just heard. The more he thought about it, the more sense it made. Monster or not, Robertson, like most people, was a complicated human being. Campbell remembered that when he was in combat, one of his team members took almost a psychotic pleasure in killing the enemy. To the point where he had to almost be brought up on charges because of his brutality. And yet this same man had found a small field mouse in the outskirts of Baghdad, and cared for it like it was his child. Campbell had become convinced that his colleague would have given his life to save that field mouse from harm. Why? What manner of thought pattern would allow a man to gleefully take a human life, but protect a tiny field mouse . . . or humble servant?

As Campbell thought, he heard the president snap his fingers almost in front of his face.

"Ian. Wake up. Like Elvis, has your mind just left the building?"

The president then pointed to the pot of coffee. "Why don't you pour yourself a cup, get some caffeine into your body, and then answer my question."

Campbell quickly did as he was instructed and then took a sip of the steaming black coffee. He chose to keep the small white cup in his fingers as he answered the president.

"Yes, sir. To answer your question, 'is what I'm doing right this moment meaningful to me?' Yes it is, Mr. President. Very meaningful. The more I think about all of this, the more I have come to realize that our time on Earth is merely a test that determines our place in the afterlife. If we pass, we spend eternity with the Lord and all of His glory. If we fail, like Lucifer, we are cast down to Hell where we will rightfully be damned for all time."

Campbell had never taken any acting classes, but he had once read that the Oscar-winning actor Michael Caine had said that the best acting lessons he had ever gotten were from his childhood of abject poverty when he had to spin tales to various bill collectors on behalf of his mother hiding in the next room. Campbell had those same lessons forced upon him as a child and he was hoping the quality of his acting would now fool a dangerously demented president clearly looking for any telltale sign of doubt, revulsion, weakness, or betrayal.

The president picked up his scotch and water and slowly swirled the drink in his glass to the subtle chimes of the ice cubes inside.

"Again. Well put, Ian. One can only hope that you believe it."

Campbell shifted on the plush white sofa. "I'm sorry, Mr. President. I don't think I understand."

"Allow me to make things clearer. Out of the four people that were here just before you came in, I'm the only one in your fan club. It seems to be the consensus among them that I should not take you into my confidence. All the opposite in fact. That certainly gives me pause."

Campbell shook his head. "It should not, Mr. President. We have already discussed Kent Riley. As for the general and Julia, your guess is as good as mine."

The president looked hard at Campbell, appraising him. "Well, I do have a guess, Ian. Kent is a weakling who has a real fear of your strength. General Mitchell, while a longtime friend, has grown soft over the years and has never been involved in your type of combat. You make him nervous because you are the real deal and he is not. Julia? Well, let's put it this way. Julia is extremely loyal to me and has grown a bit overprotective these last few years. So you see, I can come up with very good reasons why you would make each of them insecure. I never try to fool myself, Ian. I'm the president of the United States and as such, I inadvertently collect sycophants like some people collect stamps or baseball cards. It goes with the territory."

"Yes, sir."

"Ian," said the president as he stood and moved to the sofa opposite Campbell so as to get a better look at him. "You have three things in your favor at the moment. First, is that my instinct tells me you are one of us. That you are a true believer. And as you know, my instinct comes straight from the Lord. With our numerous conversations this last year, you and I have bonded. Second, Senator Webster James swears by you. Tells me he has never known a better, more dedicated, or more loyal person. I happen to agree. Webb is a man of quiet strength. Like you, he has seen extensive combat, which puts him in a rare class. His opinion has always rated high with me. As you know, that's why you got the job. Third, I believe you to be a man of conviction. You have demonstrated that to me time and again while here in my White House. You are a man of tremendous strength. A man . . . well, a man like myself. We are not like the weaklings, Ian. We are human shepherds sent to Earth to deal with the Lord's growing flock."

The president stopped talking and just stared at Campbell with eyes that radiated their own light.

Campbell was not sure if the president wanted a response or not, so he offered a tepid, "Yes, Mr. President."

When the president next spoke, it seemed to Campbell as if he had made a final determination.

"I see you as a man who is prepared to do whatever it takes to serve our Lord. Does that sound about right, Ian?"

"Yes, Mr. President," said Campbell with no hesitation.

"When I say, 'whatever,' Ian, I mean 'whatever.' Are you truly prepared to do whatever is necessary to carry out our Lord's mission?"

"Yes, Mr. President," answered Campbell with the total conviction of one who was now telling the exact truth. "I am prepared to do *whatever* is necessary. Of that, you have my word."

"I never had a doubt, Ian," said the president. "Now let me tell you exactly what is going to happen and why I need your expertise for Neptune."

CHAPTER FORTY-NINE

While Campbell was behind the closed door of the Oval Office with President Robertson, General Mitchell and Kent Riley were quietly conversing in the Roosevelt Room across the hall.

"I just don't trust that guy, General," whispered Riley.

The general leaned across the conference table. "The president has always been the most capable, most pious man I have ever known. He has literally been touched by the hand of God. That said, he is still human. And like all humans, he has flaws. He has always been a bit of a swashbuckler in his mind, and has somehow attached himself, vicariously, to the combat exploits of Campbell. I think the fact that a real-life war hero works for him gives him a bit of a thrill. Plus, as close as he and I have been over the years, he and Web James have forged an even closer friendship. James signed off on Campbell, and that's always been good enough for the president. As Campbell has never given the president any reason to doubt his loyalty, he mentally decided that Campbell would head up security for Neptune over six months ago."

Riley's round face looked dejected. "So what? As we prepare to change the face of the world forever, we have to accept the fact that Campbell is the teacher's pet and there is nothing we can do about it."

General Mitchell smiled and displayed his yellowing teeth. "We don't have to accept anything. While we can't openly challenge the president on this one, that does not mean we can't take precautions."

"Like what?" hissed a now-hopeful Riley.

"Oh, in this chaotic and dangerous world, we all need as much insurance as possible. With that in mind, I've just taken out an extra policy to insure us against one Mr. Ian Campbell . . . just in case."

CHAPTER FIFTY

The president drained his scotch and water, wiped his mouth with a napkin, and looked contently at Campbell.

"Ian. For some time now, the Lord has been speaking to me through my dreams. He has blessed me as the one and true conduit for His voice here on Earth. Me. Not that idiot pope in Rome. Not some Christ-bashing rabbi in this country or Israel. Not some rag-head mullah in the Middle East. Not some fat Buddha in Asia. None of them. The Lord chose me because only true fundamentalists will be with Him in Heaven. Only us. The Lord has made it clear to me in my visions that all of the others are false religions. The Catholics, the Jews, the Hindus, and even a number of so-called Christian faiths have failed the Lord's test. As such, they will never pass through the pearly gates."

The president then paused and spread his hands before Campbell.

"Ian. I'm relaying the word of our Lord, here. Are you truly prepared to accept it as Gospel and welcome it into your heart?"

"I am, Mr. President."

The president seemed to bow his head for a moment before looking up at Campbell. "I'm so very happy to hear you say it, Ian. I'm glad because I am now going to tell you His number-one message to me. And that is, more than the Jews, more than the Catholics, the one false religion that dishonors him the most, is Islam. The Lord has told me point-blank that the Islamists are winning the war against Christianity. That because they are barbarians they can never be stopped by conventional means. The Lord has shown me that they will very quickly take over the world. They multiply like rabbits as Christians have fewer and fewer babies. They are literally a disease growing out of control. And once they conquer us, they will impose their false religion on all the peoples of the Earth. If we do not succumb, they will kill us all. Ian, quite clearly, these people are vermin to be exterminated. They are less than human so anything we do to them will not be a sin. The Lord has told me that."

Campbell immediately thought of the over one billion Muslims in the world. The vast majority at war with no one and at war with no religion. Just people trying, like everyone else who was not part of their particular "two thousand," to make it to the next sunrise and get one more day with their children.

Campbell then thought of two close friends of his who happened to be Muslim. Brothers who were naturalized citizens from Jordan. They came to the U.S. with nothing, worked two or three jobs each until they saved a little money, opened their first Subway franchise in DC years earlier, and now owned six. Campbell had been to dinner at their homes a number of times and had rarely seen such good or more "human" families.

"Yes sir, Mr. President. It's amazing the Lord has told you so much."

The president stood from the sofa and began pacing between the coffee table and the fireplace.

"Amazing is not the word, Ian. I think it's a miracle. He chose me for a specific reason, and that reason is why I will sit next to Him in Heaven."

Campbell decided to probe a little. "Mr. President. Has

the Lord made it clear to you if He has a time frame in mind for you to . . . do whatever He needs you to do?"

Robertson looked down at Campbell. "Possibly. But not in so many words. But . . . if it's tomorrow, I will be thrilled. If it's twenty years from now, I will be thrilled. For whenever it is, it will be His plan and His timing."

"Of course, Mr. President. Please excuse the ignorance of that question."

"No apologies necessary, Ian," said the president as he stopped in front of the fireplace and faced Campbell. "All that is required of any of us now is that we carry out our duties to the Lord. There can be no doubt and no hesitation. For what He has asked of us is well beyond the capacity of all but a handful of people on the entire planet to understand and implement."

"And what has He asked of us, Mr. President?"

The president walked quickly from the fireplace and sat in the chair next to Campbell. Once seated, he placed his left hand on Campbell's right forearm.

"He has asked us to honor Him and prove ourselves. He has directed us to cleanse the Earth by fire, Ian. He has asked us to wield His sword to vanquish the Islamists, the atheists, the sinners, and all the nonbelievers. He has asked us to do this to bring on the end-times. To bring on the Rapture so that we may meet with Him in the sky and that we will know a millennium of peace and tranquility here on Earth under His rule."

Campbell tried to swallow but a lack of saliva kept him from completing the task.

"How has the Lord directed this to happen, Mr. President?"

The president had not removed his hand from Campbell's arm and now squeezed hard as he answered the question. "When the Lord asks us to accomplish something very difficult or even something impossible to comprehend, He always gives us the tools to carry out His wishes. This case is no different. Quite simply, we have gained complete control over a relatively small percentage of our nuclear arsenal. While small, it is more than enough to enforce our Lord's will and cleanse the Earth by fire."

At that very moment, Campbell was aware of only three things. First, that he was becoming nauseous. Second, that his heart was beating at an abnormally high rate. And third, that the beats seemed the strongest exactly where the president was squeezing his forearm.

Without realizing the words were coming out of his mouth, Campbell said, "What do you plan to do with these nuclear weapons, Mr. President?"

The president's eyes closed as if he was envisioning his answer.

"We have targeted Iran, Iraq, Syria, Lebanon, Libya, Egypt, Saudi Arabia, Pakistan, Afghanistan, Sudan, Yemen, the UAE, Indonesia . . . hell . . . the truth is any country that is majority Muslim will cease to exist. We have also targeted Moscow and parts of Russia, Beijing and parts of China, Caracas, parts of France and England, and . . . well . . . General Mitchell has the whole list."

Campbell put his left hand down on the sofa cushion to steady himself. "There's more?"

The president released his hold on Campbell, snapped open his eyes, and then folded his hands in his lap. "Yes, Ian. Of course. There are sinners and nonbelievers all over this Earth. Sadly, millions of them reside right here in the United States. Understanding that, the Lord has asked us to strike along our border with Mexico, to strike Mexico City, to strike Los Angeles and San Francisco, to strike South Florida, and to strike New York, Boston, and most of the Northeast. He has asked us to rid our nation of the vipers in our own nest."

"Mr. . . . Mr. President. I have no doubts of what you say, but won't this action destroy the Holy Land and make the rest of the world uninhabitable?"

Robertson shook his head and smiled. "The Lord works in mysterious ways, Ian. He would not have asked us to carry out this action if it meant bringing permanent harm to the Holy Land. Again, General Mitchell has the particulars, but we are using a combination of conventional nuclear and neutron warheads to carry out the Lord's will. The Holy Land will be spared from physical destruction."

"I see."

"Make no mistake, Ian. The Lord's mission must and will be enforced. The Earth *will* be cleansed. And when we are done, I'm told that over two billion will perish. Either directly from the blasts, or from the radiation, starvation, or cannibalism to follow. Now you understand why the Lord also directed us to build His fortress under the ocean. And why its security is everything."

"Yes, Mr. President," Campbell said in a robotic voice.

The president stood. Campbell tried to stand with him but found that his legs would not let him. He grabbed the armrest and forced himself to an erect, if slightly trembling, position.

"Ian. Because of circumstances out of our control, we have had to accelerate our schedule. But"—the president smiled—"as the Lord is calling the shots, I guess nothing is out of our control. Understanding that, I need you to be in your office by 5:30 A.M. tomorrow. Bring whatever personal belongings are important to you and will fit in one suitcase. And in the meantime, you are directed not to tell a soul of this conversation. Do I make myself clear?"

"Yes, Mr. President."

The president turned and started to walk toward his desk. He then stopped and faced Campbell.

"Should you attempt to tell anyone, or betray us, please

know one thing. The Lord will smite you where you stand."

Campbell could not feel his legs or feet as he walked from the Oval Office, turned right, walked down the hallway past the Cabinet Room on his right, and then took a left down the hallway that led to the West Wing Lobby. Before getting to the lobby, he stumbled into a small bathroom, locked the door behind him, turned on the water in the sink full-force to make some noise, fell to his knees in front of the toilet, and proceeded to throw up until painful dry heaves signaled that he had emptied his stomach.

CHAPTER FIFTY-ONE

Commander Rob Rutten stood off to the side of the bridge of the USS *North Carolina* and spoke in a whisper to his executive officer, George McNeil.

"Yes, George. I'm sure. COMSUBLANT himself gave me the direct order."

McNeil was still not confident in what he was hearing. "Vice Admiral Robert McKinney told you this personally?"

"Yes."

"The commander of the submarine force in the Atlantic told you one-on-one."

"That's a big ten-four," said a frustrated Rutten. "He actually grabbed me by the arm and wouldn't let go until I acknowledged his order."

"But there is no precedent in naval history for that order."

"That's right."

McNeil nodded toward the men. "What are you going to tell the crew?"

Rutten shook his head. "Nothing until I have to. And when I do, as little as possible."

"Skipper," said a now-troubled McNeil. "When and if the time comes, can you do it? Can you do what Admiral McKinney is asking of you . . . asking of us?"

Rutten felt a sudden chill and put his hands in his pants pockets. "Honestly, I have no idea."

Both remained silent for a good twenty seconds before McNeil spoke up.

"Okay. I guess we have to run this to its natural conclusion. If no one calls us off at the moment of truth, then I wouldn't want to be in your shoes."

McNeil smiled to rob some of the offense from the words, but they both knew he was serious.

"A month of Our Father's won't be enough to save my soul," said Rutten as he moved to the center of the control room.

"Okay, George," said Rutten in a normal tone. "Let's get this thing into gear. We're officially about to hunt a boomer. A boomer that only has *one* job."

"Yeah . . . stay hidden from the world until they are ready to launch. A task they excel at."

Rutten lowered his voice again. "Look, I know Gerry Donovan. Some people were pissed that he got the command of the *South Dakota* because they figured someone pulled some strings. If strings were pulled, I'm guessing it was by Admiral Thomas. But BFD. Gerry is one of the best I've ever seen. He deserves a command. He has a sixth sense as a submariner that is second to none. I don't give a shit if he believes in God or not. That's irrelevant to the mission at hand. If we are within six thousand meters of that bastard and one of our guys passes gas, he's gonna hear it, send a couple of fish our way, and then launch his missiles."

The XO grinned. "So what you're telling me is to not fuck up?"

"Not in those *technical* terms, but yes."

McNeil pointed down toward the deck. "You want us to dive the boat under the thermocline?"

Rutten nodded. "Yeah, for the moment. Let's get beneath

the warm-water boundary to the *really* cold stuff. Once we are under the semipermeable barrier, it will be much harder for anyone to bounce sonar off of us. I'd rather come up from under him than have him down there waiting for me."

"Aye, aye, Skipper." McNeil then turned to look at a very young-looking sailor. "Diving officer. Make your depth fourteen hundred feet."

"Aye, aye, sir. Fourteen hundred feet. Twelve degrees down angle on the planes."

For the about the fifth time that day, Rutten paused to appreciate the professionalism of his crew. A crew that might turn on him if and when they knew his orders.

"Let's kick her in the ass, XO," said Rutten.

"Aye, aye, Skipper," answered McNeil. "All ahead full. Let's get down to where the whales fear to swim."

CHAPTER FIFTY-TWO

Campbell was basically camped next to his condo door at 11:20 P.M. when he heard two soft knocks.

He yanked the door open to see Langworthy, and a woman with blonde hair and draped in a long tan raincoat, standing in the hallway.

Campbell quickly ushered them into his living room and closed the door behind them.

As soon as he turned to face his visitors, Langworthy had a smile on his face. "I should have bet you earlier today."

Campbell did not return the smile. Nor did he reply. Instead, he went to sit on his sofa and then grabbed the beer that was resting on his coffee table.

"What should you have bet, David?" asked the woman.

"Oh, nothing, Madame Vice President. Ian did not have a great deal of confidence that I could get you here tonight."

Vice President Dale slowly took off her wig, patted down her auburn hair, and slipped out of the raincoat to reveal a light blue skirt and jacket framing an expensive-looking white blouse.

"Well," said Dale, "not all the credit rests with David. While it was his idea, my butler, Thomas, deserves a pat on the back as well. Not only did we use his car, but he drove us with David and I basically lying on the floor behind the front seats."

Upon completion of the vice president's sentence, the agent turned behind him to lock the door.

"Yeah," said the still smiling agent. "I got the idea from an old book I read about a previous administration. According to the author, the then president used to sneak out of the White House that exact same way from time to time. I figured if it was good enough for a president, it was good enough for a vice president."

Langworthy looked from the vice president to the glum and unresponsive Campbell and then back to the vice president before shrugging his shoulders.

"Speaking of keeping things unnoticed and off the record, in advance of our meeting here now, I had a team come in earlier today and sweep this place."

That got Campbell's attention. In light of his Oval Office conversation, he could think of nothing that could upset or unnerve him. Least of all, the break-in of his home.

"And?"

Langworthy pointed to the phone on top of the bar in the living room. "Someone is keeping tabs on you. Your phone is bugged. Once we found that, we ran a check on your BlackBerry and home computer. Both being monitored."

"Did you figure out who?" asked a mildly curious Campbell.

"Basically. It's us. Meaning the USG. Who in the government we have not found out yet, but I'm leaning toward CIA."

"Why?" asked Campbell and the vice president at the same time.

Langworthy shook his head. "Nothing brilliant or clever on my part. One of my people used to work there and was recently approached about joining a very special 'club.' A club comprised of high-level government officials that may or may not be involved in . . . whatever's going on."

The vice president walked over and sat in one of the two chairs that flanked the ends of the coffee table.

"What 'club' is that, David?"

The agent turned one more time to double-check that the door was locked, then sat in the other chair. "With all due respect, Madame Vice President, I was hoping you would tell me."

"Really," asked an amused Dale. "And why is that?"

"Because . . . it's headed up by Paula Hanson. As in the director of the CIA who just visited with you."

The vice president seemed to recoil a little from the statement. "Listen, David. I'm not sure what you are hinting—"

"Pardon my language, Madame Vice President," said Campbell in a harsh tone as he spoke for the first time, "but who gives a rat's ass what he's hinting at? The world is literally about to be incinerated so I don't think who's spying on who in our government is going to matter for very much longer."

The vice president took a long look at Campbell. Like most in the White House, she knew he had been tested by adversity that few would know. Because of that background, she also knew—and appreciated—that he generally kept his composure. The fact that he now looked like he had seen a ghost and was going off on her only signaled to her that she needed to remain calm and let him vent and tell his story his way.

As she prepared to gently prod him, she thought of a joke her husband had often told. *"If you can keep your head while all those about you are losing theirs, then you don't know what the fuck is going on."*

"I'm sorry, Ian," Dale said very softly. "I was going to ask you some questions about the president and the trip you took with him to Florida, but now I think it would make much more sense if I just listen to anything you have to say."

"I'm sorry for my lack of manners, Madame Vice President," offered a contrite Campbell. "My mind is not working right at the moment, but still, you didn't deserve that."

The vice president reached over and touched Campbell's hand holding the beer bottle. "Don't give it a second thought, Ian. I guess none of us knows how to act or what to say. We each have knowledge of a piece of a frightening puzzle that is near completion. If you feel like it, why don't you tell us about your piece."

Langworthy held up his hand. "Whoa. Before you do, bub. Mind if I grab a brew?"

"Feel free."

As Langworthy walked toward the kitchen he said, "Madame Vice President. May I get you something?"

"A water please," she answered as she continued to look at the lifeless face of Campbell.

When the agent returned, he placed a bottle of water before the vice president, a new beer before Campbell, and kept his bottle in his left—and nonshooting—hand.

Fifteen minutes after Campbell had finished recounting the horror story revealed to him in the Oval Office, as well as the details of his field trip to Neptune, the vice president and Langworthy were still frozen in the positions they had taken before Campbell spoke. Neither had touched their drinks, neither had moved a muscle, neither could think of a coherent sentence to utter.

Finally, it was the vice president who broke the silence. "I guess in the endless bad movies we are subjected to on television and at the theaters, the hackneyed, always predictable line recited at a moment like this is, *'I don't believe it.'* But, of course, I do. I believe every word of it."

Langworthy laughed the laugh of one climbing the few last steps to the gallows. "Yeah. For all these years, we've worried about, and tried to defend ourselves from, having the Islamic fundamentalists nuke the planet in the name of their God, and now we are faced with the reality that our own fundamentalists are going to beat them to the punch."

The vice president stood and walked over to one of the bar stools where she had placed her wig and coat.

"Please excuse us, Ian. I've got to get back to a secure phone and call Director Hanson. Assuming she's still on our side, we need to start moving some assets tonight."

Campbell and Langworthy stood.

Just telling his tale seemed to have sapped Campbell of most of his energy. "What can I do, Madame Vice President?"

"Go with the president," Dale answered assertively. "You must. It's your duty. At least if you do, we will have someone on the inside to do anything . . . and *everything* necessary to stop this."

Campbell contemplated her last words. "Yes, ma'am."

Dale shrugged into her coat. "Ironically, and in an amazing bit of timing, the president has asked me to meet him in the Oval Office tomorrow at six A.M."

"You're not going after what Ian just told us, are you?" asked her protector.

Dale paused before putting the wig on her head. "I have to, David. You know that. I now have to give him an ultimatum. I have no choice. I know that the president has all the cards—or at least thinks he does—but that still doesn't mean that he can't slip up, or that I can't say something, anything, that will make him realize that he is about to extinguish at least hundreds of millions of God's children . . . in the name of God. . . . Pardon my language, but Hell would be ashamed to claim this asshole."

"Madame Vice President," said an increasingly worried Langworthy. "Let's think this through. He's not calling you down there to let you in on his demented plan. He's not calling you down there to make you president in his absence. He's most likely calling you down there to kill you or otherwise get you out of the way."

The vice president patted her wig into place and imagined how silly she looked in what had once been part of a old Halloween costume.

"No, David. I think if he wanted to kill me, he would have done it already. I suspect he wants to gloat and rub my face in it for good measure . . ."

The vice president stopped to suddenly take in a deep breath as she almost slipped into an emotional ravine that would never see her stop screaming and crying in disbelief. She let out her breath slowly, steadied herself, and smiled at the two men.

". . . and besides, so what if he does kill me? It would be a blessing if it meant I would be spared seeing the master plan of the new master race carried out."

CHAPTER FIFTY-THREE

Ten minutes after the vice president and Langworthy left, Campbell was down in the mail room in the lobby of his building using the pay phone. He knew the number of Red Top Cab by heart and punched in the digits as quickly as possible.

He had to see Rachel before the morning, but did not want to use his phones to call her. More than that, he was no longer sure that her phones weren't tapped.

The next best answer was to race over to her place so he could just hold her in his arms. So he could just have a moment's peace before . . . the end.

The vice president had just basically ordered him to sacrifice his life for the greater good. If the opportunity presented itself, he had no doubt that he would do just that. While a SEAL in Iraq and elsewhere, he had put himself in suicidal situations to save various team members. Not to do so to save two billion fellow human beings would be to expand upon the definition of insanity already drafted by President Robertson.

As he waited outside for the taxi, Campbell did not think himself a hero or remotely altruistic. He could even make the argument that if he did have to give his life to try to stop the president, he would simply be taking the coward's way out. But, he thought as the taxi made its way through the gatehouse of his complex, the vice president just articulated why that way was the road best traveled.

As the taxi pulled up before him, Campbell reminded himself that he truly did believe in God. As such, he hoped and prayed that divine intervention would prevent the all but inevitable from happening. Unfortunately, that image was quickly erased by the realization that that's exactly what tens of millions of innocent people thought throughout the ages—right before they were slaughtered by men embraced and defined by evil.

Campbell had to tap repeatedly with his keys on the glass of the front door of Rachel's building before he could wake the snoozing security guard. When the guard did raise his head off the desk, he angrily pointed to the keypad outside the door.

Campbell shook his head and tapped on the glass some more.

The exasperated guard walked over to the door. "I'm not allowed to let you in!" he yelled through the glass. "If you're not a resident, then you have to call to have someone come and get you!"

Campbell quickly pulled one of his business cards out of his wallet and plastered it against the glass for the guard to read.

The guard didn't even get to "Deputy Chief of Staff" before he nervously started to nod his head and push on the door to open it. Just the words "The White House" at the top of the card were enough to do the trick.

Campbell slipped through the opening and into the lobby before the guard had even fully opened the door.

"I need to see Rachel Hiatt right away. Can you please call her and let her know that she has a guest? Tell her it's an emergency."

The guard suddenly looked very sad. "I'm sorry. Are you a friend of Ms. Hiatt's?"

Campbell felt his heart skip a beat. "Yes . . . I am."

"Tragic," said the immigrant from India who moon-lighted as a security guard. "Some other men from the government just came for her about an hour ago. They said she was delusional and had been saying crazy things about the government. They said she was a danger to herself and needed to be hospitalized. It was horrible. She was screaming the entire time until they placed her into the back of the ambulance."

Campbell was having a difficult time with the guard's accent.

"Could you make out what she was screaming?"

"Oh, yes," said the cooperative guard. "It was 'Ian.' Over and over, she just kept screaming that name."

During the last number of days, Campbell had allowed himself to pour his entire being into the fantasy that was this woman. For reasons he could not fathom, a few con-versations had turned into the most precious moments of his life. A life that was now begging for the sanctuary of dementia to free his mind from the unstoppable and un-bearable pain.

For the first time since his childhood, Campbell slowly sank to the floor in paralysis. He could not think, could not breathe, and could not move. As his eyes began to water, he pressed his face against the cool marble, closed his eyes to the world, and began to hum.

CHAPTER·FIFTY-FOUR

Sixty feet beneath the surface of the Earth at F.E. Warren Air Force Base in Wyoming, Captain Arthur Benson looked around at the self-contained living space he shared with First Lieutenant Chris O'Flinn.

For twenty-four hours at a time, they slept, ate, worked, and *waited* in their crew capsule. Their "work" being an all-but-forgotten career path . . . even in the air force.

Benson and O'Flinn were the launch crew for a Minuteman III nuclear missile site. Part of the intercontinental ballistic-missile force spread out over three states. Missiles that were dispersed in 150 hardened silos to protect against attack and connected to an underground launch control center through a system of hardened cables.

During normal times, a variety of communication systems provided the president and scretary of defense with highly reliable, virtually instantaneous direct contact with each launch crew. As these were not normal times, Benson and O'Flinn were not concerned about other launch crews or what the secretary of defense had to say. Their focus lay only with their launch site and *their* president.

Captain Benson sat in his launch chair in front of the control station and stared at the monitors and computers. A station from which—if the orders were given—he and O'Flinn would insert their launch keys and send nuclear missiles on their way to gouge out a chunk of the planet and melt a sizable portion of the world's population. Some in the air force referred to the launch crews as "Key Turners," but Benson, like all launch crew members, preferred the title, "Missileers."

The two launch chairs were attached to a rail that allowed them to slide up and down in front of the control station. Benson turned his head to the right and saw O'Flinn lying under a blanket on the only bunk, watching a DVD with his headphones on.

Seeing the blanket reminded Benson of the one part of the job he hated. As a way of protecting the sensitive electronics—and he was sure, as a way to keep the crews awake—the temperature in their crew capsule was a constant sixty-two degrees. No matter how long he was down there, he never got used to the cold.

Benson blew into his hands to warm them as he pushed himself with his left leg and quietly slid the length of the rail until he was in kicking distance of O'Flinn. Once stopped, Benson reached out with his right foot and tapped O'Flinn on his knee.

O'Flinn immediately took off his headphones and looked over at his senior—both in rank and in age. O'Flinn was twenty-seven and Benson was twenty-nine years of age. While most would consider them shockingly young to be entrusted with the most disturbing job in the world, both men felt they were wise beyond their years and fully prepared to launch their missiles when the time came.

While both men—like all launch crews—were graduates of the missile-launch officer school and had been extensively screened by air force psychologists, there was still no guarantee that they would launch when the time came. It took a highly disciplined—and emotionally detached—person to understand that the action he or she took would kill, at the minimum, a few hundred thousand fellow human beings.

Understanding that, the air force would run the occasional drill where the launch crew was convinced that they were really going to launch. When the reports from those drills came in, a full 30 percent of the crews refused to turn their launch keys. No matter how well-trained, or how motivated, they could not have such devastation on their conscience.

Benson and O'Flinn were not part of that 30 percent. They had proven time and again that when the president gave the order, they would send their Minutemen on their way.

"Is it time, Ben-o?" asked O'Flinn.

Benson looked down at his watch. "Almost . . . Isn't it amazing?"

O'Flinn sat up on the bunk. "Isn't what amazing?"

"That General Mitchell not only introduced us to the Christian Ambassadors, but brought us together for this holy purpose. All the while assembling teams at the other launch sites in North Dakota and Montana. Simply amazing."

The baby-faced lieutenant nodded his head. "I guess it's all part of God's plan for all of us."

The captain looked down at his watch again. "Whoops . . . it's time."

With that, the lieutenant grabbed his Bible off the shelf above the bunk and the captain removed his from his right pocket.

Both men then knelt on the floor, opened their worn Bibles, and silently began to pray. Discipline was everything when you were a launch officer, and now was a time to give thanks.

CHAPTER FIFTY-FIVE

Eileen Dale sat at her desk in the small study off of her bedroom and finished her handwritten note to her husband. She then softly blew on the ink to dry it, folded the paper in half, and placed it in a small white envelope.

Once done, she turned in her chair to acknowledge the breaking of dawn outside her window. As she stared transfixed at nothing and everything, she allowed herself a minute to feel sorry for herself and to cry. But only a minute.

She had not slept since leaving Ian Campbell's condo. Throughout the early morning hours she had been on her secure phone with the director of the CIA as well as various members of Congress and a few trusted military officers.

She had done her job—was doing her job—and felt she was entitled to be an enormously frightened human being for at least sixty seconds. Surely her country could allow for that.

Dale dabbed her eyes with a tissue and then raised her stress-racked body out of the chair. She then pulled the chain on her green-glass-shaded desk lamp to shut it off and quietly walked back into her bedroom.

Once there, she smiled at the sight that greeted her. Her husband was curled up on his side of the bed, contently snoring away. During the night—like every night

during the summer—he had kicked off all of the sheets
and the blanket. He was wearing his favorite blue pajamas, the bottoms of which he had cut into shorts a
couple of years earlier after he had worn holes in both
knees.

She stepped closer to him and gently covered his fetal
form with the sheet. Once done, she leaned down, kissed
him on his cheek, left the note on his nightstand, and
walked quickly and forcefully out of the room.

The vice president walked out of her residence and was
greeted by the dour-looking face of David Langworthy as
he held the door open to her car. She nodded at him without saying a word as she took her place in the back of the
vehicle.

She and Langworthy had argued the entire drive back
from Campbell's about her personal security and she—to
the disgust of the loyal agent—pulled rank and insisted
that she would not postpone or cancel her meeting with
President Robertson. After another five minutes of "it's
my professional opinion . . ." and "it's highly irresponsible . . ." she gave in to him on what she considered to be
one minor point. Beyond that, she was going to the White
House for the meeting.

Langworthy got in the opposite door next to her and,
when sitting, turned to look at her with a voiceless plea
for her to change her mind.

She felt his gaze but refused to turn toward him. While
still staring straight ahead, she said, "Isn't it time to go
now, David?"

Langworthy looked at her for a three count, compressed
his lips, slowly shook his head, and then spoke into the
microphone hanging just outside his left sleeve coat.

"Redwood is secure. Let's roll," said Langworthy in ref-
erence to the vice president's Secret Service code name.

Five minutes later, the vice president's motorcade, with

its full complement of DC police and Secret Service escort vehicles, was speeding down the almost empty Connecticut Avenue on its way to the White House.

As the motorcade was approaching the block that contained the Mayflower Hotel, two men sitting in the cab of a Filene's Basement large-panel delivery truck took a quick look at each other and then steeled themselves for the task at hand.

The driver kept careful watch in his side-view mirror of the fast-approaching motorcade. When the second of the eight DC motorcycle cops flew past him, he suddenly yanked his truck hard left from its parking spot to block most of the entire lane. With that one maneuver he instantly killed two of the six trailing motorcycle cops and—as planned—caused a chain reaction that brought the vice president's motorcade to a screeching halt basically in front of the Mayflower Hotel.

As a number of foreign dignitaries often stayed at the Mayflower, the sight of two Secret Service-like war wagons parked in front and directly across the street from the hotel would not strike anyone as unusual or suspicions. A false and last assumption for those whose time had come.

As the motorcade braked to its forced stop, Secret Service agents in front and behind the vice president's vehicle boiled out of their SUVs with assault weapons and pistols drawn.

While those agents were the first to die, their deaths preceded the others by a millisecond at best. The blast from the two explosive-packed black war wagons was like nothing the District of Columbia had ever experienced.

Not only did the two thousand pounds of high-grade plastic explosives detonate at the exact time, but the four massive artillery shells did exactly what was expected. Each shell was positioned to do the maximum damage to the vice president's vehicle and her motorcade.

The explosions were so incredibly powerful that not only was the vice president's armored limo completely destroyed, but every vehicle—since they had bunched up when forced to an unexpected and complete stop—was shredded beyond recognition.

The entire front façade of the block-long Mayflower Hotel had collapsed into the street as well as the entire front of the Bender Building across Connecticut Avenue. Any and every guest asleep in the front of the hotel, as well as the bellmen and the fifteen or so taxi drivers patiently waiting in line for a big-paying fare, were killed instantly.

As for those in the motorcade, most were reduced to bits and pieces of smoldering bones, flesh, and material. No one, not the protectee, not the Secret Service agents, not the DC police, not the loyal staff, and not even the two men who blocked the street, had survived. All had been turned into reddish-white blobs of gelatin.

That section of Connecticut Avenue looked like the worst part of Berlin during World War II after days and weeks of Russian artillery fire had reduced it to rubble, dust, and rotting corpses trapped under what had been spectacular buildings and bustling streets.

Five minutes later, to the blare of car alarms, building alarms and the screams of the wounded in and around the hotel, police, firefighters, and ambulances rolled to the scene in a futile gesture to save the vice president of the United States.

CHAPTER FIFTY-SIX

As pieces of the vice president's motorcade were still floating down into the dual blast craters that marked its last position, miles to the south, two separate military teams were on the move.

At Fort Bragg, North Carolina, the U.S. Army's First Special Forces Operational Detachment-Delta (SFOD-D) had four squadrons in buses and ready to be transported to the adjacent Pope Air Force Base, where four C-130 Hercules were waiting to get them airborne and on-site at their just-given operational targets.

Just as the buses started to roll, four HH-60 Seahawk helicopters roared by the base on their way to waiting transports at Pope Air Force Base.

The four helicopters had recently taken off from Dam Neck, Virginia, and contained team members from the United States Navy Special Warfare Development Group (Dev Group). The successor to the famous SEAL Team Six.

As both teams were the U.S. Government's premier units tasked with counterterrorist operations outside of the United States, their commanders were more than a little shocked when they got their orders. After some "chain-of-command" conversations back and forth, they were convinced that this was not a drill and that their targets were what they were told they were.

Per their job description, Delta and Dev Group did not get to choose when and where they would be needed. For that reason, they had trained for any and every eventuality. As the elite members in the buses and the helicopters neared the C-130's, never in their wildest imaginations had they anticipated going up against the targets now assigned.

CHAPTER FIFTY-SEVEN

After finally composing himself and leaving Rachel's building, Campbell mentally struggled through the night as to what to do.

His honest first instinct was to go down to the White House and kill the president. To literally kill a madman in the hopes of cutting off the head of the coiled snake. For the first half hour he was home, he contemplated a few scenarios that he had little doubt would conclude with him successfully taking the life of Robertson.

While he could not get a weapon into the building, he knew . . . he knew what he was. He knew what he could do. That he was more than capable of carrying out a justified execution. While those not in the business of taking another human life would never understand it, he was supremely confident that his training and actions of years earlier had honed him into such a person. His training and battlefield experiences allowed him to adapt to any situation and to use anything as a weapon. Himself included. With regard to the president, Campbell felt it would be relatively easy to snap his neck, kill him with a letter opener, with a pen, or even with a rolled-up newspaper.

Between his past life, his will, and the "weapons" at his disposal, he knew he could take the president's life before the Secret Service took his. But to what end, he thought.

Would killing Robertson stop the plan? Surely Mitchell would follow through. And if not Mitchell, some other member of the Christian Ambassadors.

Beyond that, what of his own selfish motivation? How would killing Robertson help him to find Rachel? Was she still alive? As he gave that question more and more thought, he was convinced that she was alive and being held by those he hoped to defeat.

Like the terrorists he fought in Iraq and Afghanistan who thought nothing of using women and children as human shields, he was sure that Mitchell or Riley had taken Rachel to use her as leverage against him. Tactically, it was a good move and in their positions he may have done the same thing.

Killing the president would also not get him inside Neptune. That underwater fortress was now the nerve center of this fundamentalist operation, and he had to get inside that facility to gather intelligence, learn their weaknesses, and then go operational.

It was not until four in the morning that he came to his senses and reached that conclusion. At that point, he rushed into his shower, ran the water as hot as he could take it for as long as he could take it to relax his muscles, then turned it as cold as it would go to wake him up and get his exhausted mind at least momentarily focused.

One hour later, Campbell was getting into the back of another Red Top taxi to take him on what would be a fifteen-minute ride to the White House.

Before leaving his condo—most likely for the last time, he thought—he had thrown some clothes, a small box of Ritz crackers, and a jar of peanut butter into a green canvas travel bag he had gotten for free years earlier when buying some Ralph Lauren cologne.

With the bag now resting next to him on the seat, Campbell began to run options, obstacles, and personalities through his mind as the taxi proceeded across the Key Bridge, took a right on M Street, made its way onto Pennsylvania Avenue, before dropping him off at the corner of Seventeenth and Pennsylvania.

As Campbell quickly walked past the Eisenhower Executive Office Building on his way to the northwest gate of the White House, he gave little notice to the two Presidential Protection Division agents talking to themselves across the street in front of the Blair House. That was part of their territory and their presence was expected.

As Campbell presented his White House ID to the Uniform Division agents inside the gatehouse, one of the Secret Service agents in front of the Blair House spoke into his sleeve.

"He's coming your way. Check him for weapons, but be very careful when you do."

Campbell walked into his office and was instantly met by the sight of a six foot five inch, two-hundred-and-fifty-pound Presidential Protection agent, whom he remembered as being a regular on the president's detail.

Campbell stopped short, looked into the agent's eyes and then at his massive hands hanging down by his side, and decided on the spot that sudden moves should not be on the menu.

Campbell had his travel bag in his left hand. He extended his right and smiled up at the towering agent.

"Hey, good morning. It's Bruce, isn't it?"

The agent stepped closer as he moved himself into an offensive position.

"Mr. Campbell. I'm going to need to pat you down and then search your bag. I hope that's okay with you."

Just as Campbell was about to answer, the White House

rocked, windows cracked, pictures fell off the walls, glasses and cups crashed to the floor, and the ground literally moved from the massive explosion that just took place less than a mile away in front of the Mayflower Hotel.

The sound of the explosion was deafening as Campbell dropped his bag and grabbed on to his door frame with both hands to steady himself. As he did, part of the ceiling out in the hallway fell loudly onto the deeply carpeted floor where it proceeded to make a cloud of white dust that almost instantly merged with the dust from other parts of a West Wing that was threatening to collapse upon itself from the shockwave.

After another ten seconds of movement, the building seemed to steady itself.

Campbell lowered his hands from the doorway and looked over at the agent, who did not seem the least bit concerned.

"What the fuck was that?"

The imposing agent offered Campbell a confident and knowing smile. "Part of the Lord's plan, Mr. Campbell. Part of our Lord's plan."

"Where's the president? Where's Riley? I need to speak with them. The president asked me to meet him here."

The agent moved quickly, snagged Campbell's bag from the floor, and then stepped back out of range.

"The president's not here, Mr. Campbell. Neither is Mr. Riley or anyone else who should be of concern to you. They are safely at the facility. They left early this morning. My orders are to get you there as quickly as possible. But first, I need to make sure that you are not a threat to yourself . . . or anyone else. Can you please turn around, get down on your knees, cross your ankles, and then interlock your fingers above your head. I'm sure you remember this drill from the battlefield, Mr. Campbell."

As the fine dust from the ceiling started to coat his throat and nose, Campbell slowly lowered himself to the floor to submit to the pat down.

CHAPTER FIFTY-EIGHT

Just beyond DuPont Circle, Eileen Dale sat frozen in the backseat of her car as the world before her ceased to exist.

She, David Langworthy, and two other Secret Service agents in the front seat had been riding a quarter of a mile behind her motorcade in an armored town car with heavily tinted windows when the explosions took place. After a night of arguing, it was the one concession she had made to Langworthy.

After the initial shock wore off and as soon as she could hear herself think, Dale screamed in horror.

"Carol! My chief of staff was in that car! Oh, my God! Carol!"

During the night of no sleep, Langworthy decided that he needed a look-alike to take the place of the vice president in the back of her limo. For years, the gossip page of the *Washington Post* and other publications had made fun of the fact that the vice president seemed to have cloned herself when she hired her chief of staff. That coincidence in appearance had just cost the middle-aged mother of three her life.

"She's gone!" yelled the agent. "They're all gone. Take a good look, Madame Vice President. 'Cause what you're looking at is our immediate future if we can't stop Robertson. You just underestimated him now. We can't afford to do that again."

Instead of getting angry at the impertinence of the head of her detail, the vice president merely nodded her head slowly up and down. "You're right, David. I did underestimate the president. I won't do it again . . ."

She then reached across the backseat of the car with a trembling hand and tried to take his. As she did, she was surprised to see that it was already filled with his Glock 9mm as his, and the eyes of the agents up front, nervously scanned everything within their view.

". . . Before I get to prove that, I need to thank you and to apologize for questioning your security instincts."

The agent angrily shook his head. "No thanks or apologies necessary. It's my job. It's what the American people pay me to do. Now, with all due respect, Madame Vice President, we've got to get out of here right this second. Where would you like to go?"

Without hesitation, but with a voice choked with emotion, she answered, "The CIA and Paula Hanson. Let's get to CIA headquarters at Langley. It's time to assert the full, rightful, and Constitutional authority of this nation."

CHAPTER FIFTY-NINE

Commander Gerry Donovan took the greatest of comfort in knowing that all of the officers on his Ohio-Class ballistic missile submarine were members of the Christian Ambassadors. It had taken a while for him and Admiral Thomas to pull it off, but he was now secure in the knowledge that his officer corps pledged its allegiance not to him, and not to the United States of America. Rather, they pledged their entire allegiance to the Lord and the mission at hand.

Because he ruled over an Ohio-Class submarine, Donovan was aware that he commanded more firepower than almost all of the nations on earth combined. His boat was designed to do one thing and one thing only. And that was to single-handedly kill millions of human beings and lay waste to their nation or nations.

While the Ohio-Class had been built as the ultimate deterrent to a first strike by the former Soviet Union, its role over the years had evolved since the fall of that Communist nation. What had never changed, Donovan knew, was the lethality of his boat. If anything, it continued to be improved upon by the leaps and bounds of technology.

The USS *South Dakota* was a self-contained small town that was constantly on the prowl under the surface of the ocean. At 560 feet long and with a beam of forty-two feet, it was the largest submarine in the U.S. fleet.

His Ohio-Class submarine was capable of being out of port for many months, with a typical mission lasting about seventy days at sea. Donovan was well aware that the only limits placed on his killing machine were human. The length of time under the ocean was dictated solely by the amount of food that could be stored and the tolerance of his crew. The nuclear power plant for the submarine could run 24/7–365 for decades. The massive amount of power it supplied allowed his boat to convert seawater to oxygen for breathing, and fresh water for food preparation, drinking, showering, and toilets.

As the commander of an Ohio-Class submarine, Donovan was finely tuned to the fact that morale was everything on his boat. For that reason, his crew had to have the best. The best food, the best movies, the best sports DVDs, the best video games and the best of everything and anything the navy could send his way. And the fact was that because their job was so crucial to the security of the nation, and the hardships they endured so unique to the human spirit, the U.S. Navy was only too happy to give them every conceivable luxury.

Before this particular mission, Donovan had his boat stocked with ninety days' worth of food, consumables, and entertainment packages. He made use of every single nook and cranny on the *South Dakota*. That included the area between the missile silos and underneath the grated walkways. With this deployment, his men would need to be pampered and satisfied as never before.

Donovan took immense pride in knowing that his boat was going to serve as the main instrument for his Lord's plan to rid the Earth of the nonbelievers, the sinners, and those who practiced false and—with the irony totally lost upon him—violent religions.

For that exact purpose, the Lord could not have picked a

better tool than the USS *South Dakota*. She had twenty-four Trident II D-5 submarine-launched ballistic missiles. Each Trident missile carried eight multiple independently targeted reentry vehicles (MIRVs).

This all-but-undetectable stealth-launch platform carried 192 nuclear warheads that it would deliver to each target with extreme precision. Each warhead with dramatically more killing power than the nuclear bombs dropped on Hiroshima and Nagasaki during the darkest days of World War II.

The USS *South Dakota* was the supreme doomsday machine for the Supreme Being worshipped by Donovan and the other members of the Christian Ambassadors.

Donovan almost ached in anticipation of carrying out the Lord's wish. He prayed hourly that the president would give the signal so he could let loose Hell on Earth and then get his crew back to Neptune.

CHAPTER SIXTY

Rachel Hiatt ever so slowly woke up and tried to get her bearings. She was aware that she was lying on a bed. She turned her head to the right and saw what looked like a small hotel room lit by brass, white-shaded lamps on two nightstands, and a desk. She moved her head back to center too quickly and felt as if she was going to pass out. The room started to rotate as some kind of vertigo took hold.

After several minutes, the spinning subsided and she tried to sit up. As soon as she did, it felt as if someone had placed a hundred-pound weight between her ears. She fell to the floor and once again waited for the vertigo to wane.

When she finally felt more steady and had the nausea under control, she tried to push herself back up off the floor and onto the bed. She placed her left hand on the blue carpet, but when she tried to do the same with the right, she noticed that it was chained to a metal ring attached to the wall next to the headboard.

With her left arm and wobbly legs, she managed to get herself back on top of the narrow bed. As she lay there dizzy from the effort, she had flashes of memory.

Men at her front door, a struggle in her lobby, a needle being pushed into her arm in the back of an ambulance, the sensation or dream of flying, the sound of a helicopter, and then nothing. Nothing until her waking now.

As she lay on the bed and tried to connect the memory dots, she heard a sound at the entrance to the room. She lifted her head from the pillow to look at the door, saw it open and a heavyset man in a blue uniform step in, and then dropped her head back on the pillow exhausted from the effort.

The man walked over until his round face was looming over her.

"Hello, Ms. Hiatt. My name is General Wayne Mitchell. Welcome to Neptune."

Rachel blinked a number of times in succession until some of her blurriness went away.

"Welcome . . . welcome to what?" she asked in a somewhat slurred manner.

The general grabbed the chair from in front of the desk and spun it around to face the bed. He then sat down, crossed his legs, and rubbed his hands together.

"Welcome to Neptune. It's the name of the facility that you now find yourself."

Rachel's mind was finally starting to clear. "What have you done to me? Why am I here?"

"All in good time, Ms. Hiatt."

Rachel tried to control her erratic breathing. "This is some kind of government facility?"

The general smiled as he shook his head. "Well, yes and no. It was built by our government with taxpayer dollars, but it serves a much higher calling."

Hiatt frowned at the answer. "So this is a government facility that is not answerable to our government."

"That's right."

Hiatt ran her tongue over her teeth and then rubbed the outside of her mouth with her left hand. Everything felt dirty. Everything felt as if it were covered in some kind of film.

"But you're a U.S. general. Air force, it looks like."

"Right again."

Rachel closed her eyes as she fought to keep her coherent thoughts coming. "I'm sorry. If you're a general in our government, and you and our government don't control this place, then who does?"

The general clasped his hands in his lap. "Our Lord and Savior, Jesus Christ."

Rachel wondered if she was still asleep and dreaming as her eyes opened wide. "Our Lord and . . . you've got to be kidding me."

Mitchell's face instantly went dark as he reached over and grabbed her by the throat.

"Oh, I'm not kidding you, Jew. I'm not surprised that you don't understand or would answer me in a disrespectful way. As you and your kind killed Christ in the first place, the last thing I expect you to do is understand . . ."

Mitchell then leaned down and applied more pressure to her throat as Hiatt used her left hand to try and pry his fingers off her.

". . . All I expect is for you to pay for your sins. Your time is coming, Ms. Hiatt."

Mitchell released his grip and Rachel instantly sucked in air to feed her starving lungs.

As she did, Mitchell stood, adjusted his jacket sleeves that had ridden up in his attack on Hiatt, and smoothed some stray hairs back into place.

While Rachel continued to draw in air and allow the blood to flow back into her brain, Mitchell leaned over her once again.

"I apologize for that, Ms. Hiatt. I plead the stress of the moment. I should not have done that. My Lord would not want me to do such a thing. While you are indeed a sinner, I should still remain respectful."

As he spoke, Rachel slid as far away from him on the bed as possible. "Where exactly are we?" she asked while rubbing her throat.

Mitchell started to walk toward the door. When he

reached the handle, he turned back to face her. "You are approximately nine hundred feet beneath the surface of the Atlantic Ocean, Ms. Hiatt. As an aside, you will—I'm quite sure, since it's occupied so much of your time of late—be happy to know that your brother is alive, but not so well. We have him, along with others who stumbled across this location, locked up in cells at Guantanamo Bay in Cuba. He has been labeled an 'enemy combatant' and will be able to await the end of the world from the extreme discomfort of his prison cell."

A combination of the drugs in her system, the stress of the last few days, the physical assault she just withstood, and now the news of her brother, proved too much for Rachel. She flipped over toward the edge of the bed, leaned her head over the side, and threw up all over the floor.

"Oh, don't worry about that," said the general with a grin. "We'll have someone come in to clean that up. Maybe even . . . Ian Campbell."

Rachel wiped her mouth and face with the edge of the sheet. "Ian? Is Ian really here?"

"He soon will be," said the general, who then thought of one more way to torment her. "He's one of us, you know. He's in charge of security for this facility."

Mitchell then contently laughed to himself as he left the room and locked the door behind him.

CHAPTER SIXTY-ONE

Ian Campbell sat in the wide leather seat of the U.S. Air Force version of a Gulfstream V and stared vacantly out the window as it made its final approach to Homestead Air Reserve Base in South Miami Dade County. From there it would be a quick Blackhawk ride to the USS *Ronald Reagan* and then the descent into Neptune.

While he knew his mind should be entirely focused on finding any possible way to slow down or avert the coming calamity, he was not surprised to find his thoughts drifting to Rachel instead. Just to think of her gave him the modicum of hope he needed to push forward. As he learned in combat, without hope and something to go home to, the need to succeed—or even live—became irrelevant.

As the wheels of the private jet bounced off the runway, Campbell reviewed the questions that played in his mind on a loop. Was Rachel alive? He was fairly certain she was and that gave him hope. Was she being held at Neptune? If she were alive, he felt she would be there and that gave him hope. Was there any chance that the two of them would survive the coming hours and days? Campbell was as equally certain that they would not.

For most of his years on the planet, Campbell knew that his life had been a series of fairly normal events punctuated by moments of sheer terror. One day, he would leave from his family's apartment in Dorchester to go to school, and when he came home that same afternoon, would see all of their possessions scattered all over the sidewalk after another heartless eviction. One second, he was taking a break on the banks of the Euphrates River in Basra as he and three team members made their way back from the successful assassination of a local Al Qaeda leader, and the next, they were taking heavy gunfire from both sides of the river that instantly killed two members of the team and forced him and the others deep underwater as they tried to swim for their lives.

Fear and terror had been the two constants in his life. While he never welcomed them, he often found himself a bit disoriented if too much time had passed and neither had paid him a visit.

One of the gifts of his childhood had been the ability to think fast on his feet. That, in turn, made for a very successful career as a Navy SEAL. That career reinforced and enhanced talents that were never called for in the civilized world.

What he was going to now was anything but civilized. He would die down in that world. Of that he was positive. Either he would die in the act of killing those about to do the unthinkable, or the United States Government—through the person of Vice President Dale—would figure out how to destroy the all-but-impenetrable Neptune before those inside could destroy the planet.

Should that not happen and Robertson and Mitchell succeeded, then Campbell also had a plan. He would take his own life rather than survive Armageddon. If he were with Rachel, he would offer to take her life before his. Were he not with her, then he hoped God would forgive him and let them meet in Heaven.

Hope. In the calm before the firestorm, Rachel Hiatt represented the sole reason Campbell forced himself to take the next step.

CHAPTER SIXTY-TWO

Back in the large conference room at CIA headquarters, the Judas Club was joined by Vice President Eileen Dale and Speaker of the House Patricia Lopez. While from different political parties and opposite ends of the ideological spectrum, both had left partisanship at the door in favor of survival.

Paula Hanson had ceded her chair at the head of the table to the vice president as she now sat to Dale's immediate right.

"Madame Vice President," started Hanson, "the media is reporting nonstop on every television channel that you were killed in a terrorist assassination this morning. They are also starting to create some degree of panic in the nation as they openly speculate as to why the president has not addressed the nation and if he is in hiding for security reasons. My intelligence counterparts from around the world have checked in with me to ask if you have been killed, and if we have any leads of real substance. Heads of State have been contacting the White House for confirmation and to offer condolences and have become angry or worried that the president has not been there to take their call or has not called them back as of yet."

"Yes, Paula. Thank you," said the vice president.

No matter the expert security offered by the CIA, Dale had insisted that Langworthy be allowed to join them in the conference room. Knowing he was there gave her some peace of mind as she faced the unknown.

"I think for the moment it's best if we let the world—and especially Shelby Robertson—think I'm dead," continued the vice president as she thought of the pain her husband was now going through.

"I agree, Madame Vice President. And with your permission, I'd like to give some background that I think is crucial to the Speaker of the House, and our invited generals and admirals, in understanding this situation in the shortest time possible."

The vice president nodded in agreement as she looked at Speaker Lopez and the four flag officers who were rounded up based on all available evidence that indicated they were not members of the Christian Ambassadors.

The director of the Central Intelligence Agency took several large sips from her bottle of water before beginning.

"Now is not the time to assign credit, but I wanted to thank the assistant director of the FBI for helping to gather the information I'm about to relay. Let me preface this by saying this information is as chilling as it is accurate.

"President Shelby Robertson, General Wayne Mitchell, General Peter Breck, Admiral Frank Thomas, various members of Congress, a number of high-level White House aides, a vast amount of political appointees throughout our government, and surprisingly, more than a few influential journalists, are members of an organization known as the Christian Ambassadors.

"President Robertson and General Mitchell are basically charter members. Back when they were freshmen together at the United States Air Force Academy, they fell under the strong influence of the then commandant of cadets. A brigadier general by the name of Johnny Wedman. It seems the general felt it was his purpose in life to aggressively proselytize his crop of cadets. Our people have learned that when Robertson and Mitchell were attending their first orientation at the academy, they were led by a group of ten young, exclusively evangelical chaplains, who literally stood shoulder to shoulder and screamed at them that if they did not receive Jesus as their savior, they would 'burn in Hell.' It should be noted that no priest, rabbi, or mainline Protestant was allowed to participate in this orientation.

"Beyond the evangelical chaplains on campus, the air force academy was then, and is now, surrounded by evangelical megachurches. When the regular chaplains weren't working over Robertson, Mitchell, and the other cadets, the academy would bus in members from these megachurches to continue the nonstop indoctrination.

"After the megachurch people were finished, the sports coaches at the academy would run with the 'evangelical' baton. In the locker rooms populated by Robertson and Mitchell, the coaches would hang signs that read, 'Competitor's Creed: I am a Christian first and last . . . I am a member of Team Jesus Christ.'

"And finally, if that were not enough, for the four years Robertson and Mitchell were at the air force academy, the school newspaper ran an ad which read, 'We believe that Jesus Christ is the only real hope for the World. If you would like to discuss Jesus, feel free to contact one of us! There is salvation in no other name under Heaven given among mortals by which we must be saved.' The ad was then signed by sixteen department heads, nine permanent professors, the dean of faculty, and the athletic director . . ."

The vice president held up her hand. "Okay, Paula. Thank you. Clearly the president, General Mitchell, and the others, were influenced at a very early age. I get that. I really do. But at the moment, I couldn't care less. Right now, I just want to stop them. When and if we accomplish that, then we can write the history of how they warped their minds and, in truth, dishonored Jesus Christ and all that he represents."

"I understand that, Madame Vice President," answered the DCI. "But what I'm telling you is not a history lesson. It's a blueprint that shows how large, how entrenched, and how dangerous the Christian Ambassadors have become. It . . ."

As Paula Hanson continued to talk, David Langworthy looked not at her, but at Vice Admiral James Wilson, the director of the Defense Intelligence Agency. As Hanson and the vice president spoke, he seemed to fidget more and more in his seat.

When scanning a crowd for threats to the president or vice president, Presidential Protection Division agents were drilled to look for certain keys. Certain "tells" that would alert them to the fact that a particular person may represent a threat to the protectee. Admiral Wilson was exhibiting more than a few of the keys. Had he not been in CIA headquarters, and if Wilson were not a distinguished and highly decorated admiral, Langworthy would have already had him up against a wall to be searched.

As the admiral continued to shift his eyes from the vice president to Hanson and back, Langworthy unbuttoned his suit coat, slowly removed his weapon from its holster, kept it hidden from view under his jacket, and slipped off the safety.

". . . This is a disease that has gone unchecked for years," continued Hanson. "There is no part of our government that is not infected, with the military being the worst . . ."

Langworthy kept staring at the director of the Defense Intelligence Agency. As Hanson continued to speak, it looked as if Wilson was starting to mumble something to himself.

". . . and the air force being the worst of the military.

I guess these Christian Ambassadors in the air force forgot part of their code of ethics which reads: 'Military professionals must remember that religious choice is a matter of individual conscience. Professionals, and especially commanders, must not take it upon themselves to change or coercively influence the religious views of subordinates.' Obviously—"

The vice president shook her head. "Paula. Please. We understand that this is a problem, but we also have to remember that the Christian Ambassadors that have twisted their faith represent a minute percentage of our military. The vast majority of evangelicals are wonderful people and patriotic Americans."

Hanson was not prepared to cede her ground so quickly. "A minute percentage of the military? Maybe. But if that is so, why did the Pentagon try to send 'freedom packages' to our troops in Iraq and Afghanistan that contained no letters from home, no baked goods, no sports DVDs, and no body armor. Rather, these 'freedom packages' contained Bibles, proselytizing material in English and Arabic, and a computer video game entitled, *Left Behind: Eternal Forces*. A game in which 'Soldiers for Christ' hunt down nonbelievers. A game that was derived directly from a series of very popular post-Rapture novels. A game—"

"All right, stop," said the vice president angrily. "We need a plan of action . . . now. We can't waste time disparaging the finest military in the world because of certain Christian supremacists. I need to know . . ."

With the words, "Christian supremacists," Wilson grew more agitated and more vocal. At first, no one could understand him. But after a few seconds, it became clear that he was saying, "Forgive them, Lord. They know not what they say. Forgive them, Lord, they know not what they say. Forgive . . ."

Langworthy saw that both of Wilson's hands were

before him, folded together on top of the conference table. For the Secret Service, a subject's hands were everything. That is where they would hold the weapon. That is what they would use to strike out at the protectee. It was all about the hands and Langworthy knew it.

He looked at the table in front of Wilson and saw a yellow legal pad and Mont Blanc fountain pen with its cap removed. He then looked back at Wilson and saw his body start to tense.

As it became obvious to everyone at the table that Admiral Wilson seemed to be having some kind of nervous breakdown, Vice President Dale turned in her chair to look back at her protector. As she did, Admiral Wilson launched himself across the table at her with the fountain pen now in his right hand.

In less than two seconds, Langworthy shoved the vice president to the floor with his left arm and fired four rounds into Admiral Wilson. Hitting him twice on the top of his head, once on his right shoulder, and once on his right calf that had become extended in flight.

As the lifeless body of the admiral crashed to the table, Langworthy swept the vice president up from the floor and placed her behind him as he leveled the gun at everyone else in the room.

"Hands!" he screamed. "I need to see some fuckin' hands right now!"

CHAPTER SIXTY-THREE

Ian Campbell was trying to match the long strides of his Secret Service escort as they walked down a hallway on the first deck of Neptune.

Even though he had been through it on his quick tour with the president, Campbell could still not get over the immense size of the facility and the technology that it possessed. Five decks with over 400,000 total square feet. It's the eighth wonder of the world and basically nobody on the planet is aware of its existence, thought Campbell.

Halfway down the hallway, they came to a security post manned by four commandos.

"I've been instructed to drop off Mr. Campbell to you," said the large Secret Service agent. "You are to bring him to his quarters, have him stow his gear, and then bring him to conference room six."

"Aye, aye, sir," answered the lead commando. "We will take it from here."

After the Secret Service agent had turned and was almost back at the elevator bank, the commando in charge looked at Campbell and smiled.

"Well, well, well. Looked what the cat dragged in."

Campbell looked at the man for several seconds before returning the smile. "Shit, is that you, Taylor?"

The almost-forty-year-old ex-Navy SEAL smiled even

wider. "One and the same, Your Highness. Last time I saw you, you were crawling onto a C-130 at Baghdad Airport for a flight to sanity."

Campbell looked at the three other commandos who had nothing better to do but pay attention to the conversation, and then back at Taylor.

"Yeah, well I seem to have missed my stop," answered Campbell as the smile left his face.

Taylor stepped from behind the counter and out into the hallway with Campbell as he took the travel bag from Campbell's hand.

"Well, welcome to the starship *Enterprise*, fearless leader. No green alien babes that we've seen quite yet, but the food's good and the establishment seems to be filling up fast. Let me show you to your quarters."

They walked another fifty yards down the hallway until they came to his room. Campbell had treated himself to a transatlantic crossing on the *Queen Mary 2* after his discharge from the navy, and while Neptune was not nearly as luxurious as that "lady of the seas," its setup still reminded him of a cruise ship. At least a cruise ship on steroids.

Taylor pulled a key card out of his pocket and inserted it into the horizontal opening above the door handle.

Same as the cruise ship or a hotel, thought Campbell as Taylor pushed open the door to reveal a windowless suite of about 250 square feet.

Taylor waved him in and then followed with the bag. Once inside, Taylor closed the door behind him, put the bag on the floor, and took a long look at Campbell.

"What's up with the look?"

"Nothing much," answered Taylor. "I understand that you are here to take over security of the facility."

Campbell grabbed the bag off the floor and placed it on top of the small sofa. "Yeah, that's what they tell me. Why? Am I taking your gig or something?"

Taylor shook his head as he started to look around the suite that contained a small living room with a moderately sized bedroom behind it. "Not me, bro. I'm just one of the worker bees. After I left the navy, I went to work for BlackOps security. Went right back into Iraq, but the pay was a hell of a lot better."

"Is that who runs security for Neptune now?"

Taylor shook his head again. "Not really. A number of their people are here, but it's not because of BlackOps. It's because of their Christian beliefs."

Campbell quickly reminded himself that he was now in the belly of the beast and had to choose his words carefully. "Isn't that why you are here? Although, I must say, I don't remember you being one of the most religious guys I ever served with."

Taylor slowly scratched his face that hadn't been shaved in two days. As he did, Campbell focused on the M-4 that he carried in his left hand as well as the sidearm strapped to his leg.

"Not really . . . No offense, by the way," he quickly added.

"No offense taken, Don. If you're not a holy roller, then why are you here?"

"Shit," said Taylor with a grin. "It was a gig, man. One of my former BlackOps buddies recommended me and next thing I know, I'm 20,000 leagues under the sea. But you know what? The pay is fantastic, and these people seem real nice."

"Yeah," said Campbell in a harsh tone. "*Seem* being the operative word."

As soon as the sarcasm dripped out of Campbell's mouth, Taylor put his finger to his lips and pointed to the table next to the desk. He then motioned Campbell over and had him look under the circular table until he spotted the small listening device.

"Yeah," said Taylor in a normal voice. "Let me show

you your bedroom and bathroom real fast. We got to get you to your meeting."

Taylor then motioned him into the sleeping quarters as he walked over to the narrow door that led to the bathroom.

"As you may have guessed," said Taylor still in a normal voice, "everything here was built by one of those companies that builds the cruise ships. All of the rooms are modular and can be switched out if something goes wrong. Here, come check out your bathroom."

With that, Taylor quickly turned on the water in the sink and then whispered to Campbell.

"Big Brother is listening all the time, Ian. You may already know that and for all I know, you were the one who ordered the placing of all the bugs."

Campbell lowered his voice to match Taylor's. "Wasn't me, man. I'm just here to try and do the *right* thing."

Taylor looked at him quickly and Campbell saw recognition in the former SEAL's eyes.

"Things are moving too fast around here. It's like the former Soviet Union. Everywhere you turn, there is a Christian Ambassador making sure you are keeping it real. I was told that I was just temporary until they had their full complement of *followers*. With all of the shit going on, no one seems to know who is on first base and for the moment I seem to have fallen through the cracks. I just signed on for a paycheck, man. Not a crusade."

Campbell stared at him for a couple of seconds, imagined he saw a glimmer of hope, and then nodded once.

"Well, that's it for the tour," said Taylor as he shut off the water. "Let's get you up to the executive suite."

CHAPTER SIXTY-FOUR

The vice president, the Speaker of the House, the director of the CIA, several members of the Supreme Court—including the chief justice—a majority of the cabinet members, and the majority and minority leaders of Congress, as well as other congressional leadership, were now squeezed into yet another conference room at CIA headquarters.

An hour earlier, mass pandemonium had ensued as Langworthy had struggled to protect the vice president above all others.

After the shooting, he grabbed his two fellow agents who had been cooling their heels in the lobby of the CIA. They had been in the car with him and the vice president when her motorcade had been destroyed, and he trusted them implicitly. Of the two—one man and one woman—he had known Colleen Corbett longer, but both were outstanding agents.

He had basically carried the vice president across the hall to the director's office where he stationed his two agents outside with orders to shoot anyone who tried to enter without his explicit permission.

As soon as he vocalized that order, Paula Hanson screamed at him. "I've got my own people to provide security! We don't need you running around here like some kind of goddamned cowboy!"

Langworthy was about at the end of his rope. "Oh really, Director. Is that a fact? It seems like *your* people allowed Admiral Wilson in to try and kill the vice president. Let's just cut the pompous shit, okay? At the moment, we don't know who the fuck we can trust . . ."

Langworthy stopped in midsentence and looked over at the vice president as an idea dawned on him. ". . . Madame Vice President. Do I have your permission to call my director and bring in some people?"

Eileen Dale had never heard a gun fired in her presence in her entire life. To see the admiral's head splatter before her eyes all over the conference table was too much to bear. She was sitting at Hanson's desk as she tried, once again, to get her hands to stop trembling as the adrenaline coursed through her system.

"I'm sorry, David . . . what did you say?"

"Do I have your permission to bring in a security team I believe we can trust?"

Dale looked back and forth between Hanson and Langworthy. "Of course, David. Do whatever you think is best."

Thirty seconds later, Langworthy was on the phone with the director of the United States Secret Service.

"Chuck, it's me again. We had a shooting here. Yes, she's fine. Admiral Wilson from DIA. Turns out he was one of the Christian Ambassadors. Flipped out and tried to stab the Veep. Yeah. I just told you. She's fine. Look . . . I've got a very strange request to make of you, but it's critically important that you follow through. I'm acting on orders of the vice president. Great. Well here it is . . . I need you to round up every Jewish, Catholic, and Muslim agent we have in the DC area and get them over to CIA headquarters right away. I know, I know. Believe me, getting fired is the least of my worries. Just do it, please. Thanks."

As soon as Langworthy hung up, he looked at Paula Hanson. "Sorry about my outburst, Director . . ."

Hanson nodded her head for him to continue but said nothing.

". . . Okay. Back to who we can trust. I think I read in one of our briefings that the CIA hires more Mormons as agents than any other religious denomination. Is that correct?"

Hanson saw where he was going and was already picking up the phone. "Great idea," she said as she smiled at him and the vice president. "Frank," she said when her call was answered. "This is an emergency. Get some paramilitary teams up here to help protect the vice president and the Speaker of the House, and the other guests on the way. And before you send them this way, make sure they are Mormon, Jewish, Catholic, or Muslim . . . what . . . fuck political correctness. Just pick the right teams and get them up here . . . now."

With the security situation settled for the moment and her nerves more calm, the vice president was better able to conduct the meeting.

"You were saying, Mr. Chief Justice?"

John Rickman looked around the room and had a flash of memory back to the Kennedy assassination and the famous photo of then Vice President Lyndon Johnson being sworn in aboard Air Force One as the thirty-sixth president by Federal Judge Sarah T. Hughes. The photo captured the same fear, confusion, and desperation he was observing in the conference room he had been escorted to minutes earlier.

"I'm saying that if what you say about President Robertson is true, then the articles of impeachment will be useless to you. The Constitution allows you to seek impeachment of the president, the vice president, and all civil officers of the United States. They can be removed from office because of treason, bribery, or other high crimes and misdemeanors. I would say leading a religious cult planning to destroy the world passes as a 'high crime.'"

"But you're saying we can't impeach?"

As the first Jewish chief justice of the Supreme Court, Rickman had secured his place in history. Understanding that, he worried about getting too far out on a limb when the subject of the day was a Christian cabal headed up by the president of the United States.

"No, Madame Vice President. I'm not saying you can't impeach. What I'm saying is if everything you just told us is accurate, then you don't have the time to use impeachment as a tool to remove Robertson from office. Article One, Section Two of the Constitution specifies that 'the House of Representatives . . . shall have the sole power of impeachment.' Once you get past that qualifier, which could take days or weeks to accomplish, then once impeached, as specified by Article One, Section Three, the Senate would then have the power to try the president. And if the president were tried in the Senate, I, as the chief justice, would have to preside. Again, you are talking about a relatively lengthy process to arrive at the conclusion you are seeking."

"Shit," said Paula Hanson as she slapped the table and made more than a few people jump. "We may not have two days left, let alone two weeks. What's plan B?"

"The Twenty-fifth Amendment," said the vice president with no happiness in her words.

"Exactly," said John Rickman. "With the Twenty-fifth Amendment, you can remove the president from power at this very meeting."

"Please tell us how, John," said the vice president as she leaned her head back against the high-backed chair and closed her eyes.

Rickman opened his briefcase and took out bound copies of the Declaration of Independence and the Constitution with all of the amendments. After thirty seconds or so of flipping pages, he spoke.

"Here. The Twenty-fifth Amendment. Section One. *'In case of the removal of the President from office or of his death or resignation, the Vice President shall become President.'* Now, if we jump down to Section Four, we have this: *'Whenever the Vice President and a majority of either the principal officers of the executive departments or of such other body as Congress may by law provide, transmit to the President pro tempore of the Senate and the Speaker of the House of Representatives their written declaration that the President is unable to discharge the powers and duties of his office, the Vice President shall immediately assume the powers and duties of the office as acting President.'*"

The vice president massaged her temples. "John. Can you break that down to us in layman's terms? Clearly, Congress is not here."

"No, they're not," said Rickman with a slight smile. "And guess what? You don't need them. All you need is a majority of 'the principal officers of the executive departments' to write a quick report to the president pro tempore and the Speaker. As I look around the room, all of the ingredients are here to invoke the Twenty-fifth Amendment."

The vice president sat up and looked around the room. In fact, the majority of the president's cabinet was present—two were missing and assumed to be at Neptune. The cabinet represented "the principal officers of the executive departments." Eileen Dale looked to her right and saw that president pro tempore was there in the person of Senator Brendan Alston of West Virginia. A very old man who met the qualification as the most senior senator of the majority party. Seated next to him was Speaker Lopez.

Forty-five minutes later, Vice President Dale placed her hand on a Bible being held by the Speaker of the House and took the oath of office for president of the United States, as administered by Chief Justice John Rickman.

All of the proceedings, from their private discussions to the swearing-in ceremony, had been filmed and recorded per the orders of now President Eileen Dale. She wanted to leave nothing to chance when and if she got the opportunity to present their case to the nation and the world.

Ten seconds after receiving tepid and nervous congratulations by those in the room, she gave her first orders as president.

"Before I go on television to speak to the American people, I need to speak with all of our allies. I especially need to speak with the presidents of Russia and China. It is critical that we convince them that it is not the intent of the United States to harm them in any way. We must make them—and all of our allies—understand that what is happening is the action of sick individuals who have twisted a peaceful religion into a rationale to sanction mass murder and genocide. While we are getting those calls ready, I need to speak with any members of the Joint Chiefs of Staff who are not part of the Christian Ambassadors. I need to speak with any flag officer who will stand with me and our republic to put down this treasonous and blasphemous act. And I need all of this to happen . . . instantly."

CHAPTER SIXTY-FIVE

Taylor stepped aside as the elevator door opened upon reaching deck five. After he followed Campbell out into the hallway, he pointed to the right toward the end of the hallway where eight heavily armed commandos and several Secret Service agents were stationed.

"Welcome to the executive suite," said Taylor. "The president's holding court in the meeting room at the end of the hallway and my orders are to deliver you to that meeting and then assist with your ongoing orientation of Neptune."

As they walked down the long hall toward the massed group of professional killers and bodyguards, Campbell tapped Taylor on the arm and whispered.

"Do you have any idea what's really going on here? Do you know what this place is for?"

Taylor smiled as a show to the guards as he answered Campbell. "We were told from day one that this was the new super-duper bomb shelter for the government. Same as the one they built way back in the fifties. Told us that in case the terrorists or some foreign government hits the U.S. in a real bad way, that the government can function down here until it's safe to go topside again."

Campbell and Taylor were now about one hundred and fifty feet from the conference room.

"And what did they tell you about all the people that have been sent here the last few days?"

Taylor slowed his gait to give them more time to talk. "Said it was just a dress rehearsal. That they wanted to test everything under realistic conditions to make sure the place operated as advertised."

Campbell had never been much of a gambler, but he knew he had to roll the dice on Taylor. Either he was a true Christian Ambassador, or he was what he said he was. A hired gun who had slipped through the cracks. If he guessed wrong, he was sure he'd find out in the next one hundred feet.

"Bullshit, Don. This is no dress rehearsal. This is it. The president and his crazed evangelical followers are about to blow up the world in the name of the Lord. I don't know the timetable, but I guess I'm about to find out. I know this sounds crazy, but you have to believe me. I don't know if there is jack-shit we can do about it, but we've got to try."

Taylor slowed even more. "You're the new head of security, man. You're one of the president's top boys. You are talking some serious smack, now."

"Look," answered Campbell as he pleaded with his eyes. "It's a long story. Use your judgment. You used to know me. You fought with me. Either I'm crazy, and who gives a shit, or I'm telling the truth and everyone you love topside—your family, your kids, your friends—are about to be killed. Time to pick a side."

Taylor let out a genuine laugh. "Fuck. I'll think about it. What you're saying is too crazy to be crazy. I'll talk to you after you get out of your meeting."

Fifty feet short of the meeting room, Taylor motioned Campbell to stop. When he did, he confirmed Campbell's worst fear and his overriding desire. "Based on what you told me, you should know that Mitchell had a woman brought into the facility against her will. She was drugged and a little beat-up when we locked her in her room. But she did mumble one thing that makes all the sense in the world now."

Campbell knew the answer, but also knew hearing it would kick-start his adrenaline.

"What?"

"Ian," said Taylor as he looked to the floor to hide his mouth from the security team. "She just kept saying, 'Ian.'"

CHAPTER SIXTY-SIX

President Dale looked across the table at U.S. Army General James Mullen, the chairman of the Joint Chiefs of Staff.

"Welcome to our nightmare, General," said Dale. "What can you tell me that is of immediate use to us."

"Thank you, Madame President," said Mullen as he made eye contact with Dale and some of the others gathered around what was now the command post for the United States Government. "Obviously, as you stressed to me on the phone, time is of the essence. It will please you to know that we have not been operating in a vacuum with regard to the Christian Ambassadors. For whatever reason, these guys have exhibited pretty lousy operational security as they have gone about their business. Maybe it was because of conceit, maybe because the president was behind them and they didn't feel they had to really cover their tracks, or maybe . . . they truly believe that since they are acting on *'orders from God,'* that they cannot fail no matter what, as the Lord has preordained that they will succeed. Whatever the reason, we, along with some of the members of the Judas Club, have not been ignorant of their actions."

"What, if anything, have you done about it?" asked President Dale.

"Well," said the general, smiling. "More than we are

allowed by law. As you know, back in 1986, after the reorganization of the military undertaken by the Gold-water-Nichols Act, the Joint Chiefs of Staff were stripped of operational command of U.S. military forces. Responsibility for conducting military operations goes directly from the president to the secretary of defense directly to the heads of the unified combatant commanders. That said . . ."

"That said," added Dale, "you smelled a rat and decided to freelance beyond your mandated and legal responsibilities."

"Yes, ma'am. Let's just say that we have been conducting *joint exercises* with some of the Christian Ambassador units. Joint exercises that were and are known only to us. For the record, our operational security has been about as airtight as possible."

"That's nice to know, General. But can you tell me anything that is going to make me feel even remotely better about this situation?"

"Yes, Madame President. As I told you on the phone, after Secretary of Defense O'Reilly shot himself, I assumed—"

"What?" screamed Paula Hanson.

"My apologies," said the chairman of the Joint Chiefs of Staff. "Things have been happening so fast on so many fronts, I have been remiss in briefing you on this action. Approximately three hours ago, one of our Delta teams took control of Homestead Air Reserve Base south of Miami. Soon thereafter, Secretary O'Reilly landed in a C-20 that originated from Andrews Air Force Base. As you can imagine, things could not be more confusing for our troops, our intelligence operatives, or most of our government. In the military, we follow a chain of command. That chain starts with the president and goes through the Sec/Def. So, when the president and or the Sec/Def are barking orders at you, it's almost impossible not to obey that command. But, because some of us on the Joint Chiefs have—"

"General," interrupted the president. "Before you continue, can you tell us who from the Joint Chiefs is with us and who is not?"

"Yes, ma'am. The air force chief of staff, the army chief of staff, and the Marine Corps commandant are with us. Frank Thomas, and the vice chairman, have, for lack of a better phrase, gone over to the dark side. It is believed that they have joined the president and his team in Neptune."

"Thank you," said the president as she pointed at a video camera. "I just wanted that on the official record sooner rather than later. Please continue."

If the ramrod-stiff, highly decorated four-star general was having trouble taking orders from a female president, he was doing an exceptional job of keeping that prejudice under wraps.

"Yes, Madame President. Over the course of the last number of months, Secretary O'Reilly has engaged in activity that was well beyond the norm. Because of that, and because of my, ah . . . association with the Judas Club, Director Hanson and I decided to monitor and record his activities, among others. When he left Andrews this morning for an unscheduled trip, I knew where he was going."

"Thanks for telling me," said Hanson.

"Paula," said the president as she tried to keep the conversation focused.

"When the Sec/Def and his security team—all members of the Christian Ambassadors—landed, an SFOD-D team confronted—"

"A what?" asked the Speaker of the House.

"Sorry, ma'am," said the general. "A Special Forces Operational Detachment-Delta team intercepted the Sec/Def. At that moment, a member of his security detail fired upon my team. That gentleman and the rest of the security detail were neutralized and—"

"Killed?" asked the president.

"Yes, ma'am. After that brief firefight, the Sec/Def was still alive. When the team approached him and asked him to surrender himself and lie on the ground, he pulled a small-caliber pistol from his suit coat and shot himself in the head."

"General Mullen," said President Dale as she quickly gazed at some television monitors at the far end of the room. "Won't the killing of the Sec/Def and some of the other actions we are taking force the president's—that is to say Robertson's—hand, and have him accelerate his plan?"

"Quite possibly," said the general in response. "That said, he at least will find such a acceleration more difficult now than even a number of hours ago."

"How so, General?"

The general shrugged as he looked down at the notebook before him on the table. "Well, the hands of the Judas Club have not been idle. I fully understand that if we survive the coming days . . . or even hours . . . there will be investigations into our activities. I am fully prepared to resign my commission, as will the other military members of the Judas Club. Understanding that, I hope all in this room will acknowledge that the situation we are now facing is unprecedented in the history of our nation. On this one, we saw our *only* option as being, 'better to ask for forgiveness rather than permission.' Going through the bureaucracy was out of the question. Talking to anyone—my apologies, even you, Madame President—risked a leak and our exposure to the Christian Ambassadors. Again, should we survive, you will see that for the most part, we used force and bluster to get our people into position. We faked orders, we exaggerated orders, we lied, we threatened, we imprisoned, and we have killed . . ."

The general then paused and looked at the president and those in the room with more than a little pride. "... It's all well and good that former President Eisenhower warned of the misuse of military power and the military industrial complex, but at this moment, it may be the patriotic, untainted members of the military who rise up to save our nation."

"I pray that is so, General," said Dale. "Since you brought it up, how much of our military is *tainted?*"

"While it's obviously all but impossible at this moment to get an accurate number, our best guess is that about 5 percent of our armed forces are aligned with the Christian Ambassadors and upwards of 30 percent of our flag officers."

"So, who do you trust, General?"

"Our friends. Those that we know to be loyal to our nation."

"Like Admiral Wilson?" interjected Speaker Lopez.

"No, Madame Speaker. Not like Admiral Wilson. He was not working with us. And while there are no guarantees in any of this, we are confident that when the time comes to perform, our people will do what is necessary."

"The time has come, General Mullen," said the president. "Frankly, I don't care what laws or rules you have broken. I only care about the end result. Please tell us what steps—illegal or otherwise—you have taken and what the status is."

CHAPTER SIXTY-SEVEN

Ian Campbell walked into the tightly guarded conference room and saw the usual suspects. President Robertson, General Mitchell, Admiral Thomas, Kent Riley, and Julia Sessions were seated around the large conference table. The only face that surprised him was that of FBI Director Kinahan.

"Ian," said the president as he spied Campbell walking through the door. "Welcome to your new home."

Campbell felt as though his thought process was being filtered through molasses. Everything was coming much slower to him. His concentration was about shot and he knew it. His past ability to think quickly on his feet was but a faint memory. The only thought and motivation that crystallized for him was his desire to find Rachel.

"Thank you, Mr. President . . . ," answered Campbell in a tone that suggested he was on autopilot. ". . . Home?"

"Yes," said the president as he pointed to an open chair next to him. "Why don't you sit down so we can go over a few things and get you started on your new career."

Campbell shuffled over to the chair. Once seated, the president patted him on the back and then continued.

"It appears that our Lord has decided that *now* is the time for us to act on his behalf. Because of that, Neptune is going to serve as our home for the foreseeable future. I've just been told that things seem to be getting . . . more interesting . . . up on the surface. We are still not sure what some in our government know or think they know about our purpose, but as discretion is the better part of valor, we won't be waiting to find out. We will proceed with our plans and we will do so very quickly. As such, your duties are going to take on even more significance and timeliness. The security of Neptune takes precedence over any other assignment."

"Yes, Mr. President."

"When we initiate our preordained actions, we are not completely sure how long we will have to remain in our new home. Some of our scientists—who have now joined us in Neptune—tell me it could be as short as six months or as long as three years. Regardless, when we do emerge, those who would dishonor our Lord will have been vanquished. We will have fulfilled our destiny and will await the Lord's next step. Until such a time, we have also taken the necessary precautions. We have hidden food, supplies, weapons, aircraft, and advanced technologies in underground bunkers, in several strategic locations in this country and around the planet. When we emerge from Neptune, we will claim those supplies and our rightful place in the world."

Campbell looked at the president and then around the table at those who were staring in adoration at their earthly leader. "Yes, Mr. President. It seems that you have thought of everything."

The president shook his head as he reached next to him to touch Campbell on the arm. "We have thought of nothing, Ian. Our Lord and Savior has thought of everything and blessedly used me as a conduit for his wishes."

"Yes, Mr. Pres—" Campbell started to reply before being interrupted by General Mitchell.

"Mr. President . . . Ian. My apologies. If you will excuse me, I need to step outside for a moment to follow up on some logistical issues regarding Neptune."

"Of course," answered the president. "But please be quick about it. You need to get back here to brief our new head of security."

"Yes, Mr. President," answered Mitchell as he stood, exchanged an almost imagined glance with Kent Riley, then exited the conference room.

When General Mitchell walked out of the conference room he found the commandos and Secret Service agents in various subdued conversations.

"Excuse me, gentleman, but which one of you escorted Mr. Campbell to this meeting?"

Don Taylor, who was off to the side and leaning against a wall, stood straight and raised his hand. "It was me, sir."

"Oh, thank you," said the general. "Mr. Campbell is now speaking with the president, but as he is now the head of security, he wanted me to pass along some information. Why don't we walk down the hall as we speak."

"Yes, sir," answered Taylor as he sprung away from the wall and caught up with the general who had already advanced a dozen feet down the hallway.

When they were about one hundred feet from the conference room, the general stopped and grabbed Taylor's arm. "Well?"

Taylor broadly grinned in response. "It was just like you said it would be, sir. Once he saw a familiar face and I regained some of his confidence, he decided to open up to me."

"And?"

Taylor's face turned serious. "He said the president and all of us were crazed evangelicals who are trying to blow up the world."

Mitchell remained silent for a few seconds as it seemed he was doing some calculations in his head.

"Well, it's confirmed then. Campbell is a traitor to our Lord and our cause. The president has always had a blind spot when it comes to him and for that reason I soon learned not to push him on this subject. But, we have no choice now. Campbell has left us no choice."

"Yes, sir. What would you like me to do?"

The general looked down both sides of the hallway to make sure they were still out of earshot and then back at Taylor. "Did you tell him about Rachel Hiatt?"

Taylor nodded. "Yes, sir. Just as you instructed me to do if it became clear that he was not one of us. I told him just before we got to the conference room."

"Perfect," said the general as he stepped closer. "I see no reason why you can't bring Mr. Campbell to see Ms. Hiatt. The condemned are entitled to one last wish, and I have no doubt that such a visit would be the dying request for both."

"Yes, sir."

"And Mr. Taylor . . ."

"Yes, sir."

"Once they are together in the room behind the closed door . . . please kill them both."

Taylor instinctively touched the sidearm strapped to his leg. "Yes, sir. It will be my pleasure in service to our Lord."

"Thank you, Mr. Taylor," said the general as he turned to walk back to the conference room. After going about one meter, he stopped and turned back to Taylor.

"Neither the president, nor anyone else, will know about this action, Mr. Taylor. President Robertson's mind needs to be focused on the mission. When the time comes, I will tell him of the unfortunate news and explain that, for whatever reason, Mr. Campbell decided to take his own life."

CHAPTER SIXTY-EIGHT

As General Mullen continued his presentation, President Dale and the others in the stuffy conference room felt a degree of relief with the information that some part of the government had not been caught unaware.

"As you know from previous briefings, Madame President," continued the general, "the United States predicates much of its security on what is called the nuclear triad. Traditionally, the three legs of that triad consist of submarine-launched ballistic missiles, land-based intercontinental ballistic missiles, and long-range bombers carrying nuclear weapons. The theory being that no one would dare hit us with a first strike as one of the legs—most likely the submarine-launched ballistic missiles—would render such a strike a Pyrrhic victory at best. Now, while there was some tinkering with the system back in 2002 under President Bush, brought about by a congressionally mandated review of our nuclear capabilities called the 'Nuclear Posture Review,' our triad remains virtually the same . . . it's the most complete killing machine ever devised by man."

"General," said the director of the CIA. "You stated during our *unauthorized* meetings that you were only concerned with the submarine and land-based legs of the triad. Is that still the case?"

"Yes, Ms. Hanson. For reasons known only to the

Christian Ambassadors, they seem not to have tried to infiltrate the long-range bomber leg of the triad. But—"

"But," added Dale, "they have successfully infiltrated our submarine and land-based forces."

"Yes, ma'am. As you and I discussed on the phone prior to this meeting, it appears to us that they have one submarine under their command as well as a number of land-based Minuteman launch crews. Per your orders, Madame President, we have ordered all of our Ohio-Class submarines back to port, or to rendezvous immediately with another U.S. naval vessel. We also ordered all Minuteman launch crews not to go down to their underground crew capsules or to come to the surface immediately."

"And what were the results of those orders, General?" asked President Dale.

"Pretty much what we expected. All but one submarine complied, and all but one launch crew complied. Three Minuteman launch crews on the surface tried to force their way past our people and were either shot or captured. I don't have all the details. But one launch crew definitely refused to come up."

"And what of the one submarine that you have not been able to recall?"

The general shook his head and for the first time during his remarks, looked worried. "It is an Ohio-Class, Madame President. Admiral Roger Newsome, who is the COMSUBLANT and based out of Norfolk—"

"The what?" again asked the Speaker of the House.

"Sorry, Madame Speaker. Just as you have your shorthand up on the Hill, the same applies to the military. COMSUBLANT stands for, 'Commander Submarine Force, Atlantic Fleet.' "

"Please, Patricia," implored the president. "Let the general finish. All of your questions can be answered . . . if you live."

The Speaker of the House did not like being put in her place in front of the room and the video cameras recording the proceedings, but she was smart—and scared—enough to obey the request of the freshly appointed president.

"General," said the president.

"Yes, ma'am. Anyway, Admiral Newsome has been suspicious of this one particular submarine for a few months. I should also state at this time that Admiral Newsome is also a member of the Judas Club."

"Again, General," stressed the president, "I don't care if he's a member of the Mickey Mouse Club. Which submarine are we talking about?"

"The USS *South Dakota* under the command of Commander Gerald Donovan. Donovan, like most of the officers of the *South Dakota,* was handpicked by Admiral Thomas with the inferred blessing of the Sec/Def and the president."

"And what has Admiral Newsome done about his suspicions?"

"He . . . we . . . detailed a Virginia-Class fast-attack submarine to shadow the *South Dakota* and prepare to engage."

"Can we stop these people, General?"

"We think so. Mostly."

Eileen Dale was fighting herself to remain calm and focused. As she took a deep breath, she wondered how a very young John F. Kennedy dealt with the Cuban missile crisis. He played a game of nuclear warfare chicken with Nikita Khrushchev and the Soviet Union and got the "evil empire" to blink. How, she silently asked herself, would that gifted president have dealt with his own nation being compromised by religious fanatics prepared to initiate a nuclear strike?

When the general said "mostly," half the room groaned as the participants started to whisper among themselves.

As they did, Eileen Dale outwardly seemed to become more assured.

"Quiet, please," she said loudly. "What do you mean by 'mostly,' General?"

"Yes, ma'am. Even though the *South Dakota* is by far the more dangerous and lethal weapons platform, it is also the most easy to neutralize. On your orders, the *North Carolina*—which is the Virginia-Class fast-attack sub shadowing the *South Dakota*—can engage and, hopefully, sink the boomer. With regard to the renegade launch crew, that is a more difficult situation. This particular launch crew is sixty feet under the ground at F.E. Warren Air Force Base in Wyoming. There is no doubt that they are part of the Christian Ambassadors. One of our teams has already searched their homes and personal computers."

"It's just two people. Why are they more difficult than an entire Ohio-Class submarine with what—192 separate warheads?" asked Dale.

"For a few reasons, Madame President. First, the crew capsule they are now in is an underground structure of reinforced concrete and steel of sufficient strength to withstand massive weapon effects. These two officers are, at this moment, controlling, monitoring, and capable of launching fifty Minuteman III intercontinental ballistic missiles. They have their own power supply and, in conjunction with the Sec/Def and the president, apparently have their own launch codes and targeting information. They just need to go though their many times rehearsed steps and turn their launch keys, and less than sixty seconds later, fifty missiles will fly. The crew capsule's outer structure is cylindrical with hemispherical ends. The walls are approximately four and a half feet thick. A blast door protects the entry way to the capsule. They also have an escape hatch that is about three feet in diameter that is located at the far end of the capsule. The escape hatch and associate tunnel that leads to the surface are also constructed to withstand massive blast effects. At this moment, a Delta team is trying to work their way down the tunnel and into the capsule to neutralize the crew."

"And if they don't?"

"There is no sense in trying to fool ourselves, Madame President. There is basically zero chance of Delta breeching that capsule in time. Again, if they have somehow figured out a way to jury-rig the system so as to bypass all of our fail-safe systems, then you are looking at fifty warheads being launched. One bit of good new being that these particular Minutemen III's are not MIRVed."

The president smiled coldly. "Is there another bit of good news?"

The general nodded slightly. "Actually, there may be. Two years ago, this air force base switched their Minutemen from 'hot launch' to 'cold launch.' Meaning that before, the Minuteman would ignite its first-stage engines while inside the silo. With 'cold launch,' the Minuteman III is pressure ejected from the silo by a cold-gas generator which lofts the missile about fifty or sixty feet in the air before the main engines ignite. The idea being that by switching to this system it reduces damage to the silo and allows for quick refurbishment and, if needed, reloading."

Dale shook her head. "I'm sorry, General. But why might that be a benefit to us?"

"Because," answered the general as he took a quick look at the Speaker to see if she was about to interrupt him, "with the 'cold launch,' when the Minuteman is basically sprung out of the silo, it's actually suspended in midair for a split second before its engines ignite. During that one brief moment, we may be able to have our teams fire on the missile and disable it or blow it up."

"Blow it up!" yelled the Speaker. "That will set off the nuclear weapon."

General Mullen looked at the president and offered her a small smile before turning his attention to the Speaker.

"No, Madame Speaker. That won't happen. The warheads do not arm themselves until they enter the descent phase of their flight. Nothing will happen to the warhead if we fire on it and the missile at launch."

"General," said the president. "You said this particular launch crew controlled fifty missiles. Can your teams get to all fifty silos in time?"

"I don't know. The air force chief of staff is working this problem hard right now with the Delta teams and air force security. Obviously, we know where all fifty silos are. Much of it depends on if and when they launch."

"What if our teams can't disable them all?" asked an increasingly nervous Paula Hanson.

"Oh," said the general grimly. "If they launch, I have little confidence that we will get them all."

That comment was met with more groans and whispers as one participant softy started to recite the Our Father.

"Then what?" asked the president.

"Then," answered General Mullen as he held his hands up before him, "we hope that our own ballistic missile defense system can shoot them down."

"Can it?"

"Not all. No. Some will get through and find their targets."

"What God in Heaven would want such a thing?" screamed the Speaker.

"None, Patricia. None," the president said. "This is not about God. It's about some very sick individuals who are prepared to kill millions, or even billions of human beings, in the name of Jesus Christ. The Jesus I, and basically every Christian, worships would stand in front of these missiles to prevent even one person from being harmed. Clearly, in his dementia, Shelby Robert-

The Apocalypse Directive 297

son has never bothered to ask himself, 'What would Jesus do?' If he has, and has still brought us to the brink of destruction, then he will know the fires of Hell for eternity."

"Pardon me, Madame President," said Hanson. "Religion and God have never been high on my list of things to worry about. As far as I can tell, tens of millions of people have been killed in the name of your God or someone else's. There is no evil worse than that hypocrisy. If your faith brings you comfort, great. But I don't believe it should have any place in our government. Look where it's gotten us."

"With all due respect, Madame President," added the general, "I consider myself to be a man of faith, but I think Ms. Hanson makes a very valid point. If we do survive this experience, then we are going to have to have a national dialogue on religion, and its place in our government, and the world."

"*If* we survive, General. With that in mind, let's all of us—myself included—keep our eye on the ball. What do we do about the Ohio-Class submarine?"

"We kill it, Madame President."

"I assume we will give the captain and his men an opportunity to surrender," said the president.

"No. We can't, Madame President. Let me give you an example of why that is not possible. Years ago in Moscow, Islamic terrorists took over eight hundred people hostage in a opera house. They were part of the 'Free Chechnya' movement. They had already killed a number of innocent people when they stormed the building and Russian security forces knew there was no bluff about them. The security forces decided that the only way to save a majority of the hostages was to flood the opera house with a gas that would almost instantly render everyone inside unconscious. After they did this and entered the building, they found that a number of the female terrorists had suicide belts attached to them. The security team made the operational decision right then and there, that if these women woke up, they would set off the bombs. And them if they tried to disarm them while they were unconscious, then the security team might set them off."

"And what solution did they arrive at?" asked the president for the benefit of the cameras and posterity as she already knew the answer.

"The Russian security team shot each of the women in the head while they were sleeping."

"I see."

"Yes, Madame President. We have basically the exact same situation with the *South Dakota*. If we talk to them to try and convince them to surrender, then they may very well launch. And let me remind everyone in this room that the *South Dakota* has twenty-four missiles that *will* deliver 192 warheads to their targets. This one submarine can blacken and eradicate life on half the planet. I believe we have no choice. If Commander Donovan even detects the *North Carolina* on his tail, he may launch."

"Does the crew of the *South Dakota* have any idea what's going on?"

"No, Madame President. I doubt it. Only the officers. I'm sure the crew thinks they are on a normal deployment and will soon be home with their families."

"Well," said the president. "At the risk of offending Paula, may God bless them all. What is the next step, General?"

"It's the COMSUBLANT's opinion—and one that I share—that we need to put a nuclear-tipped torpedo into the *South Dakota* at our earliest opportunity."

"What is the final step needed to take this action?"

"Your order, Madame President."

Dale closed her eyes and tried not to visualize the very young faces of the enlisted personnel onboard the *South Dakota*.

"Do it," she answered as she closed her eyes even tighter.

CHAPTER SIXTY-NINE

Ian Campbell walked next to Taylor as they approached the elevator bank.

"Ian," whispered Taylor. "If you like, I can take you to see your lady friend before we do anything else."

Campbell stopped in his tracks. "Yes. Please. Let's go now."

Taylor tugged him on the arm. "Okay. Keep walking. She's down on Two Deck. Let's just pop in the elevator and get down there."

Thirty seconds later they emerged from the elevator and took a left. As they quickly walked down the hallway, they came upon another security post manned by two commandos.

"Look alive, gentlemen," said Taylor. "Our new boss is with me. He wants you alert and ready for . . . anything."

Campbell looked quickly at the two commandos as they passed. They, like all he had seen, were large, solid, and were clearly combat tested.

Another hundred feet and Taylor stopped in front of one of the many pale blue doors that dotted the cream-colored hallway. As he reached for his pass key, Campbell took notice of the large amount of civilians that were walking in and out of rooms at the far end of the hallway.

Were there really five thousand people here, he wondered. From this colony, would future Christian theologians record the next Adam and Eve? What if Robertson succeeded? What if . . . Campbell shook his head to try and clear the defeatist and wasted thoughts as he forced his mind back to the here and now.

Taylor opened the door and then stood to the side.

Campbell walked in and the first thing that hit him was an odor of vomit. He looked to his right and saw Rachel asleep on the bed with a chain running from her right arm to the wall.

Campbell quickly turned to look back at Taylor. "She's handcuffed to the bed."

"Don't worry," Taylor answered as he tapped his right pocket. "I've got the keys right here. First things first. Why don't you go over there and let her know that her *savior is* here."

Campbell nodded as he looked at Taylor. What was with the emphasis on "savior," he wondered as he turned to walk over to Rachel.

As he walked over to the bed, Taylor softly closed the door behind them.

Campbell got down on one knee next to Rachel and slowly reached out his right hand and began to gently stroke her hair. As he did, he caught the reflection of Taylor moving up behind him in the small brass lamp on the nightstand. As he continued to touch Rachel's hair, he kept his eyes on the reflection of Taylor. Two seconds later he saw his former SEAL team member reach for his sidearm.

In one blurred motion, Campbell spun on his left knee and swept his right leg into Taylor's ankles. Just as Taylor hit the deck, Campbell came down upon him with the full force of his weight and the cumulated fury that needed to strike out. He drove the point of his right elbow directly into the exposed throat of Taylor.

As Taylor gurgled and thrashed about the floor with

a crushed larynx, Campbell quickly grabbed his head between his two arms and snapped his neck, killing him instantly.

"Ian!" screamed Rachel from the bed, simultaneously thrilled to see Campbell and repulsed at what she had just seen.

"Quiet," Campbell begged as he ran his hand through Taylor's pants pocket. "Nothing. No fuckin' keys."

With that, he stood, grabbed hold of the chain attached to Rachel's arm, placed his right foot against the wall, and yanked as hard as he could. The force of his effort not only freed Rachel, but pulled the metal ring out of the wall along with a good amount of the surrounding material.

Campbell then reached down and grabbed the M-4 assault weapon next to Taylor as well as his sidearm. Just as he did, there was a loud pounding on the door of the room.

Campbell leaned over, pulled a still wobbly Rachel off the bed, placed her behind him, switched off the safety of the SIG 9mm pistol, jerked open the door, and fired three rounds each into the two commandos that were filling the hallway.

Before they had even fully collapsed to the floor, Campbell was dragging a confused and petrified Rachel down the hallway back toward the commando station. Once there, he found what he was looking for—a padlocked weapons locker.

Campbell motioned Rachel to move down the hall, placed the barrel of his SIG against the lock, and pulled the trigger. The round from the handgun split open the small padlock as the shrapnel from the bullet and the lock mostly traveled downward.

Campbell yelped as a few of the fragments imbedded in his right thigh. "Ah, shit!"

Rachel ran back in front of the counter to look at him. "What happened?"

Instead of wasting time to answer, Campbell flipped open the top of the locker and grabbed three M67 fragmentation hand grenades, two MK 3A2 concussion grenades, and two extra magazines for his pistol.

As he was doing that, screams from the civilians mingling at the end of the corridor filled his ears. Screams that were just as quickly drowned out by a shrieking alarm system.

Campbell shoved two of the M67 fragmentation grenades, each green and about the size and shape of a small orange, into his pockets. Once finished, he thrust the two MK 3A2 concussion grenades at Rachel.

"Here. Can you carry these?"

Rachel only nodded in response as fear, shock, and nausea fought for control over her body. She took the black, cylinder-shaped grenades and put them in the pockets of her white sweatpants.

By the time she was finished, Campbell was already back in the hallway and pulling her down the corridor toward a staircase.

As he forced her down the stairs two at a time toward One Deck, he spoke to her over his shoulder.

"They built an escape hatch into this place. It's down on One at the end of a side corridor. The hatch leads to a small tunnel that slowly slopes upward for about six miles until it opens to an exit on some small island. It's not much of a chance, but it's better than dying down here doing nothing."

Campbell got to the door on One Deck and slowly opened it. At the very least, he thought, the security team would be cautious and confused. For all they knew, he might have been on his way to kill Shelby Robertson or to do damage to Neptune.

When he looked into the hallway, he saw various civilians running back to their rooms per the orders of the loudspeakers located down the length of the hallway.

Campbell allowed himself a small smile. Big Brother was trying to clear the killing field so they would be easy prey.

As a group of civilians were running down the corridor in the direction they needed to go, Campbell waved Rachel behind him and then jogged behind the group, using them for cover.

When they got to the door that led to the short corridor with the escape hatch, he stopped. From his tour with the president, which now seemed like years ago, he remembered that the escape hatch was guarded by four commandos.

Campbell knew that in battle, hesitation or second-guessing often led to death. Running down the stairs he had formulated a quick plan and it was that or nothing.

He moved Rachel six feet to the side of the door, unslung the M-4 assault rifle, crouched down on one knee, opened the door, and saw two of the four commandos start to train their weapons at him. As they did, he let lose with four controlled bursts from his M-4. In the split second that he did, he thought he saw one man fall to the floor with the other three diving for cover.

As they scrambled to protect themselves, Campbell pulled the pin on the M67 fragmentation grenade and threw it the sixty feet or so to where the commandos were repositioning themselves.

The M67 had a killing radius of about fifty feet. After he threw it, he crawled over to where Rachel was to wait for the explosion. As soon as he heard it, he went back to the door and threw another M67 toward the guards.

Once that explosion stopped reverberating, he crawled over to the door with his M-4 and took a quick look down the hallway. He could hear the moaning of one man near the escape hatch, but other than that, there was no movement.

Campbell slowly stood with his weapon pointed at what was left of the guards and motioned Rachel to follow him.

As he got closer, he saw that three of the four guards were dead and had various limbs and body parts blown off by the force of the two fragmentation grenades. The fourth was barely alive as he lay on the floor in shock while trying to force his exposed intestines back into the hole blown through his stomach.

Campbell turned and looked at Rachel. "Keep your eyes on me. Don't look at anyone. Just focus on me and keep walking. Don't look down."

One second after Campbell admonished her not to, Rachel looked at the bloody massacre that had been four men. One second after she looked, she once again vomited all over the floor.

As her vomit mixed in with the blood and other body fluids oozing across the white-tiled floor of the hallway, Campbell pulled her violently toward the escape hatch. Once there, he positioned her behind a heavy metal desk that was part of the security station, and removed the hand grenades from her pockets.

With her behind cover, he grabbed one of the chairs next to the desk and walked back down the corridor toward the door they entered. When he was halfway down the hallway, he stopped, stood on the chair, knocked out a ceiling panel with the butt of his M-4, pulled the safety pin on an MK 3A2 concussion grenade, and threw it up into the ceiling.

The MK 3A2 had a blast radius of about twelve feet. Because of its very powerful shock wave it was more for use as a bunker buster than to kill the enemy with shrapnel.

As the grenade rattled around the ceiling, Campbell jumped off the chair and ran to shield Rachel with his body. "Cover your ears!" he yelled just before the grenade exploded.

With his ears now ringing from a blast that was much louder than the M67 fragmentation grenades, Campbell looked up from the desk. The desired effect he was looking for was mostly achieved. A large majority of the hallway was now blocked from the debris that rained down from the ceiling and above.

Campbell then turned his attention to the escape hatch. It looked very much like the door to a walk-in safe at a bank. It had a large wheel at the center that controlled six-inch diameter steel columns that slid from the door into steel receptacles. Campbell started to spin the wheel until he heard all of the columns retract and the door click open.

Once he had the heavy steel door open, he was looking at a small ten-foot-by-six-foot airlock with the same type of door in the far wall. A door he knew led directly to the tunnel . . . and a chance.

He ushered Rachel into the airlock, and then stood atop the security desk, knocked down another ceiling panel, threw the last of his concussion grenades into the ceiling, and then ran into the airlock, closing the door behind him. Even through the heavy blast door the sound of the explosion was quite loud. Loud or not, he just hoped it accomplished the mission. To prevent or slow down anyone from following them.

As Campbell did one terrifying thing after another, Rachel was even more disgusted by his barbaric ability to kill, but intrigued that he could remain so focused on the horrific mission at hand. Was this, she wondered, the life of those nameless, faceless souls we send to faraway lands to fight our battles while we take freedom and our rights for granted?

By the time that those thoughts crossed her mind, Campbell already had the second door open.

She gaped into a tunnel for which she could see no end. It appeared to be about four feet wide and six feet high and lit, about every twenty feet or so, by small, florescent lights.

"Let's go!" yelled Campbell. "No matter what happens, I don't want to be down in this evil place when it does."

CHAPTER SEVENTY

"Conn, Radio. Receiving an EAM."

Commander Rutten looked over at his XO. "Shit, George. If it's what I think it is, this is the last emergency action message I ever want to see."

"Conn, Sonar. I'm getting hull noises from the target. She's popping. Her depth is changing. She's rising."

"Skipper," said McNeil with a tone of desperation. "If the *South Dakota* is going to 1SQ, then we will have no choice."

Rutten looked angry when he responded to his XO. "If Donovan is bringing his boat into the proper alignment to launch his missiles, then yes, we will have no choice. I need to know if he is about to hover at one three zero feet, with less than three degrees of angle and a knot and a half of headway. If he does all that, then fine, we have no choice. If not, I'm waiting. That's a United States naval vessel. Those are our friends out there. I'll be goddamned if I'm going to kill U.S. sailors because their commander *might* be nuts. I need proof or a direct order."

As he was saying that, McNeil was reading the EAM that was just handed to him. Without saying a word, he slowly passed it to Rutten.

Rutten took ten seconds to read it. Toward the end of those ten seconds, his eyes started to water and the hand holding the EAM started to shake.

"George," said Rutten in a voice so low that McNeil had to step closer to hear it. "They want us to sink the *South Dakota*—now. No warning, no contact, no chance of surrender. They want us . . ." Rutten's voice broke a little before he got it back under control. ". . . they want us to execute our friends. Right this second."

"Yes, Skipper. I know."

Rutten walked away from his XO and away from his crew to stand in a far corner of the control room.

As McNeil looked at the back of his friend and commanding officer he knew what he was doing. He knew that he was praying. He knew that he was asking God to forgive him and he knew . . . he knew that when Rutten turned around he was going to follow the order.

In anticipation of that, McNeil grabbed the handset for internal communications.

Rutten then turned, walked over to McNeil, and took the handset. "Give me 1MC."

"Aye, aye, Skipper." McNeil was not surprised that Rutten wanted to address the entire crew.

Rutten cleared his throat before speaking. "Men, this is the captain. As some of you may know, of late, we have been shadowing the *South Dakota*. It is my sad duty to report that we have been ordered to engage her. At this point, I want to stress in the strongest possible terms that I, and I alone, will accept responsibility for this action. We have been told that the officers on board are no longer loyal to our nation and are preparing to launch their Tridents. No matter the reason, what happens next falls on my shoulders. Period. Man your battle stations."

Rutten gave the handset back to his XO. "Does the *South Dakota* know we are out here, George?"

McNeil shook his head. "No, sir, Skipper. We are still in his blind spot. We've done this drill a number of times. The Virginia-Class has the lowest acoustic signature in the water. Even our own boomers can't see us coming."

"Let's hope so, XO. Do we have a firing solution on the *South Dakota*?"

"Yes, Skipper. We've got her. We are on her six and locked in. She seems to be oblivious to us out here and is still rising to what may be 1SQ."

"Is the special MK-48 loaded?"

"Yes, Skipper. The nuclear-tipped torpedo is loaded and ready as well as three conventional torpedoes with their standard six hundred and fifty pounds of high explosive each. The crew of the *South Dakota* will never know what hit them. They won't suffer, sir."

Rutten took a deep breath and blew it out slowly. "No . . . but we will. Flood the tubes."

"Tubes flooded," said McNeil after a few moments.

"What's the tube number for the special?" asked Rutten.

"Three, sir."

"All right," said Rutten. "Fire one, three, two, and then four in that order. If Donovan picks up the screws in the water, I don't want his countermeasures to take out the special."

"Yes, sir."

"We will fire in ten-second intervals."

"Yes, sir."

Rutten looked at the crew stationed in the state-of-the-art touch-screen control room, and then gave the order. "Fire one . . . fire three . . . fire two. . . . fire four."

"All four fish away. Eight thousand yards to target. They are locked on and accelerating to fifty knots."

Rutten folded his hands together. "May God have mercy on their souls . . . and may He forgive me for what I have done."

Eight thousand yards away and at three hundred feet beneath the surface and rising, Gerry Donovan was in the final stages of bringing his boat to 1SQ. Donovan's mind was filling with a number of thoughts. President Robertson had just given him the order to launch and . . .

"Conn, Sonar!" screamed the young sailor. "Screws in the water. Seven thousand yards and closing fast."

Donovan's mind was racing. He knew if he could not get to 1SQ he could not launch the missiles. He knew he needed a stable platform to do that. He also now knew that he was under attack. Clearly, by his own navy. As such, he knew that if he ran and tried to save the boat, they would hunt him down and never let him get this close again to 1SQ. No 1SQ meant he would dishonor his president, himself, and his faith.

Donovan looked over at his XO. "Our mission is clear. Our Lord will protect us. We will not fail."

"Yes, sir," answered Olsen with less enthusiasm.

"Release countermeasures. Continue to 1SQ. Prepare to launch the missiles the second we can," ordered Donovan. "The Lord *will* protect us."

The countermeasures of the *South Dakota* diverted the first torpedo. As they did, the nuclear-tipped MK-48 slammed into the *South Dakota* at midship while traveling at approximately sixty knots.

As the disintegrated boat, crew, and unlaunched Trident missiles dispersed through the warm waters of the Atlantic, the third and fourth torpedoes impacted on the largest pieces of the *South Dakota* they could find.

CHAPTER SEVENTY-ONE

"They've launched," said General Mullen in an abnormally calm voice.

Eileen Dale looked down the table toward the chairman of the Joint Chiefs of Staff. For the last fifteen minutes, he had been on the phone with the deputy commander of StratCom—the unified combatant command responsible for the nation's land-based nuclear missiles. The unified command that had been led by General Mitchell until he disappeared into Neptune.

Just before Mullen made the call, she had briefly addressed the American people from a small television studio at CIA headquarters. She explained to them that President Robertson had taken ill and was no longer able to execute his responsibilities as president of the United States. She explained that under the powers granted by the Twenty-fifth Amendment, she had assumed the office of president. She explained that obviously the reports of her assassination as detailed by the media were wrong. She explained that the reason she had just ordered the national guard into the streets was because she was dealing with a national emergency. She signed off by saying she would be back on the air as soon as possible.

"Who are you speaking with, General Mullen?" asked Dale in an equally calm voice that surprised everyone in the room—including herself.

"Lt. General Dean Chilton out at Offutt Air Force Base outside of Omaha, Nebraska. He's the deputy commander. He's running the show since Mitchell went . . . AWOL."

"Thank you, General," said Dale. "Please put him on speaker."

Mullen pushed the button to activate the speaker. As soon as he did, the conference room at CIA headquarters filled with the sounds of multiple voices, shouted orders, and controlled panic.

"General Chilton. Are you there? This is Eileen Dale. Can you hear me?"

"Quiet!" screamed the three-star general to those in the command center with him at Offutt. "Yes, Madame President. I can hear you just fine."

"What can you tell me? Please be as succinct and as accurate as you can."

The background noise coming from the speaker dropped noticeably as Chilton spoke.

"Yes, ma'am. The two-man launch crew at F.E. Warren Air Force Base in Wyoming did fire their Minutemen. All fifty of them. As best we could in the time allowed, we had teams at or near the fifty missile silos. Through a combination of Stinger missiles and frankly any firepower we could bring to bear that was in the vicinity, we managed to destroy thirty-nine of the fifty as soon as they exited the silos."

"What of the other eleven, General?"

"Yes, Madame President. We are trying to knock them down with our own ballistic missile defense shield. We really only have one shot at this and that is to hit them in the boost phase. That is the portion of flight immediately after launch. We've got about a five-minute window."

Dale thought of the eleven missiles pushing their nuclear warheads through the atmosphere and the reactions they would provoke in Russia and China.

"You can't do anything to stop them after that boost phase?"

"Not really, President Dale. After boost phase comes midcourse followed by terminal. Since we are using our own homeland missile defense shield, midcourse is almost assuredly out of range, while terminal is well out of range."

"What are you doing—"

Before Dale could finish the question there was screaming and then what sounded like a cheer coming from the speaker.

"I'm sorry, President Dale," said Chilton when he came back on. "My people just told me we have shot down three so far."

"Thank God. How?"

"Yes, ma'am. We had one advantage in that we knew where the missiles would be launched from. Knowing that, in conjunction with the Missile Defense Agency, and per General Mullen's earlier orders to get everything in place, we had three airborne lasers carried by three air force 747s basically orbiting Warren Air Force Base. The three aircraft fire a chemical, oxygen iodine laser which almost instantly superheats the metal skin of the missile until it cracks and. . . . what . . . how many . . . Madame President . . . sorry . . . I've just been told that we have knocked down four more . . . clearly, I don't have many details but I'm hearing that our mobile kinetic energy interceptors are also bringing down the missiles."

"Thank yo—"

"One more, Madame President. We just shot down one more. That's eight so far."

Dale did not say anything. She just stared at the speakerphone knowing that anything she said or did now would be irrelevant. That she was a hindrance rather than a help. It was all up to the futuristic missile defense technology of the United States to shoot down the centerpiece of the nation's strategic deterrent forces.

For thirty seconds, she and everyone in the conference room listened. For forty-five . . . for sixty . . . for eighty.

"General Chilton. What has happened?"

There was now an eerie silence coming from the speaker.

"General," repeated Dale.

"Yes, ma'am. Sorry. It appears . . . that we missed three."

Eileen Dale sank in her chair from the weight of the information. For the first time since the closing days of World War II, a few million people were about to be killed beneath and around the immorality that was an atomic fireball.

"Do we know the targets of those warheads, General?"

Dale heard the question, but it took her a moment to realize that she had just asked it.

"We are tracking their course now. I'm told I'll have the targeting information in fifteen seconds."

As the speaker mechanically hissed, Dale listened to the cries of several people in the conference room now openly weeping.

"Madame President?"

Here it comes, thought Dale. The names of the condemned.

"Yes, General."

"Those warheads are going to impact Jakarta, Indonesia, Khartoum, Sudan, and . . . San Francisco. San Francisco will be the first to be hit, Madame President."

CHAPTER SEVENTY-TWO

Shelby Robertson and the rest of the leadership of the Christian Ambassadors were still gathered in the executive conference room of Neptune.

Together, they had just finished watching the second of the two televised addresses to the nation, and the world, by President Eileen Dale. If what she had said was true, then they had failed in their mission.

As Robertson waited for the White House to connect him to Dale, he looked across the table at General Mitchell and smiled.

"What do you think, Wayne?"

The general returned the smile. "Whatever has happened must be the Lord's will."

Robertson looked around the table at those who had been closest to him in the world. Included in the room were his wife, their three children, and their seven grandchildren.

"Of course, Wayne. That's the only explanation. I have no dou—"

"Mr. President," Kent Riley said. "Vice President Dale is on line one."

Robertson looked at Riley and shook his head. All fear, no faith, he thought.

"Hello, Eileen," started Robertson in a chipper voice.

"I'm so sorry—hello *President* Dale. Congratulations on your battlefield promotion."

Dale went straight to the point. "Shelby, you just killed upwards of twenty million people."

"If that's true, then we have failed the Lord."

"Shelby. You have to be clinically insane. You don't speak for God. You don't speak for Jesus Christ. You speak only for yourself and the lost souls that blindly follow your heresy. I am a Christian, Shelby. The majority of Americans are Christian. I am here to tell you that no one who truly believes in Christ would ever condone your blasphemous actions. In fact, I have no doubt that they would do everything in their power to defeat you and your twisted cause. You and your followers are not Christians, Shelby. You are criminals and now mass murderers. I intend to see every one of you tried and then executed for the monstrous act you just committed."

Robertson quietly chuckled to himself. "Oh please, Eileen. I think you know better than that."

"Shelby, your Ohio-Class submarine with its traitorous crew was sunk before it could fire its missiles. The officers of your attack submarine stationed outside of Neptune have just surrendered. We shot down all but three of your land-based missiles. I'm told that we can fire nuclear-tipped torpedoes into the wall protecting Neptune until we breach it. You only have one option. You only—"

"Eileen," said Robertson. "Please stop. You know that's not going to happen. Simply put, our weakness of resolve—of faith—has led to our diminished results. We must accept that as the reason for our failure. That, or we must understand, in all of His wisdom, the Lord has now chosen a different path for us to walk. Whatever the answer, it is time for us to find out. So, no need to threaten us with destruction. We are happy to attend to that task ourselves."

"Shelby!" screamed Dale. "President Robertson. You can't do that. This is not Jonestown. You have hundreds of women and children down there with you. Haven't you killed enough innocent people for one day? At least send them up before . . ."

As Eileen Dale pleaded, Shelby Robertson turned the key that opened a drawer hidden beneath him under the conference table. When the drawer was opened, it displayed a console with a receptacle for another key and beside it a red button the size of a half-dollar protected by a hinged plastic case locked in place on the console.

Robertson inserted the next key into the receptacle on the console and then turned it to the right. When he did, the red button under the plastic canopy started to flash off and on to signify that the ten, two-thousand-pound bombs imbedded inside strategic locations throughout Neptune were now armed.

Robertson then used a smaller third key to unlock the plastic canopy that protected the flashing red button. Once done, he flipped open the case and smiled.

As Eileen Dale amplified her tone and rhetoric, Robertson placed his right index finger on top of the flashing red button. With his left hand, he waved over his wife, his children, and his grandchildren. When they were gathered around him, he held out his free hand. First his wife grabbed it, then his children, with his grandchildren wrapped in hugs around their parents.

Robertson smiled contently as he looked at his grandchildren, his children, and finally his wife.

"See you all in Heaven," he said as he closed his eyes and pushed the button.

CHAPTER SEVENTY-THREE

Five hundred feet from the exit of the tunnel, Ian Campbell heard and felt a familiar sensation. Without looking back, he grabbed Rachel's hand and sprinted for the door.

The pressure in his ears was increasing with every second. As soon as he reached the end, he started to spin the wheel that would retract the bolts holding the steel door locked.

"Ian!" Rachel screamed above the terrifying noise accelerating toward them. "What's going on?"

Campbell ignored her as he continued to spin the wheel. The second he heard the *click,* he swung the door open, and dragged Rachel out of the tunnel and toward the right. As soon as he did, they both lost their footing in a very soft white sand of a beach.

Campbell stood up, pulled Rachel with him, and ran toward a stand of palm trees fifty yards farther to the right.

Just as they started, there was a tremendous whoosh that escaped from the tunnel followed by broken lights, cables, rocks, and assorted flying debris.

Campbell collapsed under the trees as Rachel fell down beside him. Still carrying the M-4, he took a quick look around. As far as he could tell, they were alone on a beach on the small Bahamian island he had been briefed about.

As he turned back to look at Rachel, he found her crying.

"Oh, Ian," she said as she touched his blood-soaked right pants leg. "Look what they've done to you."

Ian looked down at his thigh that had been on the receiving end of some shrapnel.

"It's okay, Rachel," he said as he pulled her into him. "I'm okay."

As he stroked her hair and softly whispered "sssshhhh," over and over again, he looked out toward the horizon and saw the ocean boiling and bubbling from the mushrooming explosion beneath.

Neptune was no more. Of that he was certain. The how and the why did not concern him. He was alive, Rachel was with him, and they would live to see at least one more day.

"We took care of our fanatics," said Campbell as he continued to stare at the ocean. "If they don't take care of theirs, then we have only postponed the inevitable."

DOUGLAS MACKINNON

Is the United States of America the nation our Founding Fathers intended it to be? Or has the government lost sight of our ideals? To some of the most powerful men and women in the country—including a former Chair-man of the Joint Chiefs of Staff and a former Director of the FBI—the answer is growing increasingly obvious, and so is the only possible solution: The time has come to revolt. Their daring plans will not only drive a govern-ment to its knees, they will change the course of history.

AMERICA'S LAST DAYS

ISBN 13: 978-0-8439-5802-7

PAUL CARSON

BETRAYAL

Frank Ryan knew his position as Chief Medical Officer at high-security Harmon Penitentiary was dangerous. After all, his predecessor had been murdered. But Frank never expected what happened to him the night he got that mysterious emergency call.

As he left his apartment he was
KIDNAPPED,
BEATEN,
DRUGGED,
and interrogated for six days.
Then, just as suddenly, released.

Now he can't find anyone who believes him, and his girlfriend has disappeared without a trace. His desperate search to find her—and some answers—lead Frank deeper and deeper into a sea of conspiracies, lies…and danger.

ISBN 13: 978-0-8439-6145-4

FIRST TO KILL

Nathan McBride was retired. The former Marine sniper and covert CIA operative had put the violence of his former life behind him.

But not anymore.

A deep-cover FBI agent has disappeared, along with one ton of powerful Semtex explosive, enough to unleash a disaster of international proportions. The U.S. government has no choice but to coax Nathan out of retirement. He's the only man with the skills necessary to get the job done.

On the one side is a ruthless adversary with a blood-chilling plan—and on the other are agents who will stop at nothing to see their own brand of justice done.

ANDREW PETERSON

Coming September 2008   ISBN 13: 978-0-8439-6144-7

HAGGAI CARMON

It seemed like a straightforward case of money-launder-ing. Dan Gordon had seen his share of those since leaving Mossad, the Israeli intelligence agency, to work for the U.S. Department of Justice. But in the Byzantine world of dirty money and international crime, nothing is ever what it seems.

Gordon's once-routine case has now become a desperate hunt across three continents for a devastating bio-terror weapon. Unless Gordon can uncover the truth in time, the population of the world will learn the horrors of…

THE RED SYNDROME

ISBN 13: 978-0-8439-6041-9

☐ **YES!**

Sign me up for the Leisure Thriller Book Club and send my
FREE BOOKS! If I choose to stay in the club, I will pay only
$8.50* each month, a savings of $7.48!

NAME: _____

ADDRESS: _____

TELEPHONE: _____

EMAIL: _____

☐ I want to pay by credit card.

☐ VISA   ☐ MasterCard.   ☐ DISCOVER

ACCOUNT #: _____

EXPIRATION DATE: _____

SIGNATURE: _____

Mail this page along with $2.00 shipping and handling to:
Leisure Thriller Book Club
PO Box 6640
Wayne, PA 19087
Or fax (must include credit card information) to:
610-995-9274
You can also sign up online at **www.dorchesterpub.com.**
*Plus $2.00 for shipping. Offer open to residents of the U.S. and Canada only. Canadian
residents please call 1-800-481-9191 for pricing information.
If under 18, a parent or guardian must sign. Terms, prices and conditions subject to
change. Subscription subject to acceptance. Dorchester Publishing reserves the right to
reject any order or cancel any subscription.